W9-BGN-829

Dear Reader:

The holiday season is special to all of us! It's a time to reflect on the past year, as well as to plan and hope for the future. It's also a time to spend with family and friends.

Your friends at Silhouette Books wanted to give you something special to celebrate, so we brought four of your favorite authors together in this one unique volume. Nora Roberts, Debbie Macomber, Maura Seger and Tracy Sinclair have each written a heartwarming Christmas story, believing there is no greater gift than love. Also, there's a personal message from each of them, and they share a favorite holiday recipe or craft.

We hope you enjoy these stories. They're written especially for you. All of us at Silhouette wish you the happiest of holidays.

The Editors
Silhouette Books

Silhouette Christmas Stories 1986

Nora Roberts
Debbie Macomber
Maura Seger
Tracy Sinclair

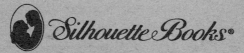

Silhouette Books®

Published by Silhouette Books New York
America's Publisher of Contemporary Romance

SILHOUETTE BOOKS
300 East 42nd St., New York, N.Y. 10017

Silhouette Christmas Stories 1986

All rights reserved. Except for use in any review, the
reproduction or utilization of this work in whole or in part
in any form by any electronic, mechanical or other means,
now known or hereafter invented, including xerography,
photocopying and recording, or in any information storage
or retrieval system, is forbidden without the permission of
the publisher, Silhouette Books, 300 E. 42nd St., New York,
N.Y. 10017

ISBN: 0-373-48251-5

Silhouette Christmas Stories 1986
Copyright © 1986 by Silhouette Books

Published Silhouette Books, 1986, 1988, 1992

All the characters in this book have no existence outside the
imagination of the author and have no relation whatsoever
to anyone bearing the same name or names. They are not
even distantly inspired by any individual known or unknown
to the author, and all incidents are pure invention.

The publisher acknowledges the copyright holders of the
individual works as follows:

HOME FOR CHRISTMAS
Copyright © 1986 by Nora Roberts
LET IT SNOW
Copyright © 1986 by Debbie Macomber
STARBRIGHT
Copyright © 1986 by Maura Seger
UNDER THE MISTLETOE
Copyright © 1986 by Tracy Sinclair

®: Trademark used under license and registered in the United
States Patent and Trademark Office, and in other countries.

Printed in the U.S.A.

CONTENTS

Home for Christmas

Nora Roberts

PLAIN OR PAINTED HOLIDAY COOKIES

Baking helps put me in the mood for the holidays. There's nothing like a little flour on your hands to start "Jingle Bells" ringing in your head. The tradition in my house goes this way: First put on an album of Christmas music. It isn't possible to work over a hot oven without the proper setting. Gather your ingredients:

¾ cup shortening	1 cup sugar
2 eggs	1 teaspoon vanilla extract
2½ cups flour	1 teaspoon baking powder
1 teaspoon salt	

optional: evaporated milk, food coloring, small paint-by-numbers type paintbrush, colored sugar or sprinkles

If you have kids, this is the time to step back and let them do some of the work. It makes it fun and the mess is almost worth it. Let one of them mix the shortening and sugar together. Let another one crack the eggs into the bowl. Then you can help by picking out the shells. Add the vanilla and mix thoroughly. Blend in the flour, the baking powder and the salt. Cover and chill for at least an hour.

Preheat your oven to 400°F. Now comes the time when the kids fight over who rolls out the dough. See that it's rolled about an ⅛ of an inch thick on a floured board. If you don't have cookie cutters in cute little Christmas shapes, you should. We generally stick to the tried and true angels, Santas and trees.

When you cut the cookies, make sure to dip the cutter into flour now and then or you'll end up with a jammed-up Santa. Place cookies on an ungreased cookie sheet. Now, you can either sprinkle the cookies with plain or colored sugar and be done with them, or if you're feeling adventurous you can use that little paintbrush you bought. Divide small amounts of evaported milk into several cups, along with a little food coloring in each. Then go ahead and paint. Remember, it doesn't matter if Santa's blue or the Christmas tree is red. And just add a little water if the mixture thickens.

Bake for six or seven minutes. Break off a couple of times to sing a round of "Deck the Halls." You'll feel better. You should have about four dozen cookies, but then, if you have children, forget it. When your husband comes home and asks what's for dinner, shove a cookie in his mouth. Merry Christmas!

Chapter One

So much can change in ten years. He was prepared for it. All during the flight from London and the long, winding drive north from Boston to Quiet Valley, New Hampshire, population 326—or it had been ten years before when Jason Law had last been there—he'd thought of how different things would be. A decade, even for a forgotten little town in New England was bound to bring changes. There would have been deaths and births. Houses and shops would have changed hands. Some of them might not be there at all.

Not for the first time since Jason had decided to visit his hometown did he feel foolish. After all, it was very likely he wouldn't even be recognized. He'd left a thin, defiant twenty-year-old in a scruffy pair of jeans. He was coming back a man who'd learned how to replace defiance with arrogance and succeed. His frame was still lean, but it fitted nicely into clothes tailored on Savile Row and Seventh Avenue. Ten years had changed him from a desperate boy determined to make his mark to an outwardly complacent man who had. What ten years hadn't changed, was what was inside. He was still looking for roots, for his place. That was why he was heading back to Quiet Valley.

The road still twisted and turned through the woods, up the mountains and down again, as it had when he'd headed in the opposite direction on a Greyhound. Snow covered the ground, smooth here, bumpy there where was heaped over rocks. In the sunlight trees shimmered with it. Had he missed it? He'd spent one winter in snow up to his waist in the Andes. He'd spent another sweltering in Africa. The years ran together, but oddly enough, Jason could remember every place he'd spent Christmas over the last ten years, though he'd never celebrated the holiday. The road narrowed and swept into a wide curve. He could see the mountains, covered with pines and dusted with white. Yes, he'd missed it.

Sun bounced off the mounds of snow. He adjusted his dark glasses and slowed down, then on impulse, stopped. When he stepped from the car his breath came in streams of smoke. His skin tingled with the cold but he didn't button his coat or reach in his pockets for his gloves. He needed to feel it. Breathing in the thin, icy air was like breathing in thousands of tiny needles. Jason walked the few feet to the top of the ridge and looked down on Quiet Valley.

He'd been born there, raised there. He'd learned of grief there—and he'd fallen in love. Even from the distance he could see her house—her parents' house, Jason reminded himself and felt the old, familiar surge of fury. She'd be living somewhere else now, with her husband, with her children.

When he discovered that his hands were balled into fists he carefully relaxed them. Channeling emotion was a skill he'd turned into an art over the past decade. If he could do it in his work, reporting on famine, war, and suffering, he could do it for himself. His feelings for Faith had been a boy's feelings. He was a man now, and she, like Quiet Valley, was only part of his childhood. He'd traveled more than five thousand miles just to prove it. Turning away, he got back in the car and started down the mountain.

From the distance, Quiet Valley had looked like a Currier and Ives painting, all white and snug between mountain and forest. As he drew closer, it became less idyllic and more approachable. The tired paint showed here and there on some of the outlying houses. Fences bowed under snow. He saw a few new houses in what had once been open fields. Change. He reminded himself he'd expected it.

Smoke puffed out of chimneys. Dogs and children raced in the snow. A check of his watch showed him it was half past three. School was out, and he'd been traveling for fifteen hours. The smart thing to do was to see if the Valley Inn was still in operation and get a room. A smile played around his mouth as he wondered if old Mr. Beantree still ran the place. He couldn't count the times Beantree had told him he'd never amount to anything but trouble. He had a Pulitzer and an Overseas Press Award to prove differently.

Houses were grouped closer together now, and he recognized them. The Bedford place, Tim Hawkin's house, the Widow Marchant's. He slowed again as he passed the widow's tidy blue clapboard. She hadn't changed the color, he noticed and felt foolishly pleased. And the old spruce in the front yard was already covered with bright-red ribbons. She'd been kind to him. Jason hadn't forgotten how she had fixed hot chocolate and listened to him for hours when he'd told her of the travels he wanted to make, the places he dreamed of seeing. She'd been in her seventies when he'd left, but of tough New England stock. He thought he might still find her in her kitchen patiently fueling the wood stove and listening to her Rachmaninoff.

The streets of the town were clear and tidy. New Englanders were a practical lot, and Jason thought, as sturdy as the bedrock they'd planted themselves on. The town had not changed as he'd anticipated. Railings Hardware still sat on the corner off Main and the post office still occupied a brick building no bigger than a garage. The same red garland was strung from lamppost to lamppost as it had been all through his youth during each holiday season. Children were building a snowman in front of the Litner place. But whose children? Jason wondered. He scanned the red mufflers and bright boots knowing any of them might be Faith's. The fury came back and he looked away.

The sign on the Valley Inn had been repainted, but nothing else about the three-story square stone building was different. The walkway had been scraped clean and smoke billowed out of both chimneys. He found himself driving beyond it. There was something else to do first, something he'd already known he would have to do. He could have turned at the corner, driven a block and seen the house where he grew up. But he didn't.

Near the end of Main would be a tidy white house, bigger than most of the others with two big bay windows and a wide front porch. Tom Monroe had brought his bride there. A reporter of Jason's caliber knew how to ferret out such information. Perhaps Faith had put up the lace curtains she'd always wanted at the windows. Tom would have bought her the pretty china tea sets she'd longed for. He'd have given her exactly what she'd wanted. Jason would have given her a suitcase and a motel room in countless cities. She'd made her choice.

After ten years he discovered it was no easier to accept. Still, he forced himself to be calm as he pulled up to the curb. Faith and he had been friends once, lovers briefly. He'd had other lovers since, and she had a husband. But he could still remember her as she'd looked at eighteen, lovely, soft, eager. She had wanted to go with him, but he wouldn't let her. She had promised to wait, but she hadn't. He took a deep breath as he climbed from the car.

The house was lovely. In the big bay window that faced the street was a Christmas tree, cluttered and green in the daylight. At night it would glitter like magic. He could be sure of it because Faith had always believed so strongly in magic.

Standing on the sidewalk he found himself dealing with fear. He'd covered wars and interviewed terrorists but he'd never felt the stomach-churning fear that he did now, standing on a narrow snow-brushed sidewalk facing a pristine white house with holly bushes by the door. He could turn around, he reminded himself. Drive back to the inn or simply out of town again.

There was no need to see her again. She was out of his life. Then he saw the lace curtains at the window and the old resentment stirred, every bit as strong as fear.

As he started down the walk a girl raced around the side of the house just ahead of a well-aimed snowball. She dived, rolled and evaded. In an instant, she was up again and hurling one of her own.

"Bull's-eye, Jimmy Harding!" With a whoop, she turned to run and barreled into Jason. "Sorry." With snow covering her from head to foot, she looked up and grinned. Jason felt the world spin backward.

She was the image of her mother. The sable hair peeked out of her cap and fell untidily to her shoulders. The small, triangular face was dominated by big blue eyes that seemed to hold jokes all of their own. But it was the smile, the one that said, isn't this fun? that caught him by the throat. Shaken, he stepped back while the girl dusted herself off and studied him.

"I've never seen you before."

He slipped his hands into his pockets. But I've seen you, he thought. "No. Do you live here?"

"Yeah, but the shop's around the side." A snowball landed with a plop at her feet. She lifted a brow in a sophisticated manner. "That's Jimmy," she said in the tone of a woman barely tolerating a suitor. "His aim's lousy. The shop's around the side," she repeated as she bent to ball more snow. "Just walk right in."

She raced off holding a ball in each hand. Jason figured Jimmy was in for a surprise.

Faith's daughter. He hadn't asked her name and nearly called her back. It didn't matter, he told himself. He'd only be in town a few days before he took the next assignment. Just passing through, he thought. Just cleaning the slate.

He backtracked to walk around the side of the house. Though he couldn't imagine what sort of shop Tom could have, he thought it might be best to see him first. He almost relished it.

The little workshop he'd half expected turned out to be a miniature of a Victorian cottage. The sleigh out in front held two life-size dolls dressed in top hats and bonnets, cloaks and top boots. Above the door was a fancy hand-painted sign that read Doll House. To the accompaniment of bells, Jason pushed the door open.

"I'll be right with you."

Hearing her voice again was like stepping back and finding no solid ground. But he'd deal with it, Jason told himself. He'd deal with it because he had to. Slipping off his glasses, he tucked them into his pocket and looked around.

Child-size furniture was set around the room in the manner of a cozy parlor. Dolls of every shape and size and style occupied chairs, stools, shelves and cabinets. In front of an elf-size fireplace where flames shimmered, sat a grandmother of a doll in lace cap and apron. The illusion was so strong Jason almost expected her to begin rocking.

"I'm sorry to keep you waiting." With a china doll in one hand and a bridal veil in the other, Faith walked through the doorway. "I was right in the middle of..."

The veil floated out of her hand as she stopped. It waltzed to the floor with no sound at all. Color rushed away from her face, making the deep-blue eyes nearly violet in contrast. In reaction, or defense, she gripped the doll to her breast. "Jason."

Chapter Two

Framed in the doorway with the thin winter light creeping through the tiny windows she was lovelier than his memory of her. He'd hoped it would be different. He'd hoped his fantasies of her would be exaggerated as so many fantasies are. But she was here, flesh and blood, and so beautiful she took his breath away. Perhaps because of it, his smile was cynioal and his voice cool.

"Hello, Faith."

She couldn't move, forward or back. He trapped her now as he had so many years before. He didn't know it then, she couldn't let him know it now. Emotion, locked and kept secret for so long struggled against will and was held back. "How are you?" she managed to ask, her hands like a vise around the doll.

"Fine." He walked toward her. God, how it pleased him to see the nerves jumping in her eyes. God, how it tormented him to learn she smelled the same. Soft, young, innocent. "You look wonderful." He said it carelessly, like a yawn.

"You were the last person I expected to see walk through the door." One she'd learned to stop looking for. Determined to control herself, Faith loosened her grip on the doll. "How long are you in town?"

"Just a few days. I had the urge."

She laughed and hoped it didn't sound hysterical. "You always did. We read a lot about you. You've been able to see all the places you always wanted to see."

"And more.".

She turned away, giving herself a moment to close her eyes and pull her emotions together. "They ran it on the front page when you won the Pulitzer. Mr. Beantree strutted around as though he'd been your mentor. 'Fine boy, Jason Law,' he said. 'Always knew he'd amount to something.'"

"I saw your daughter."

That was the biggest fear, the biggest hope, the dream she'd put to rest years ago. She bent casually to pick up the veil. "Clara?"

"Just outside. She was about to mow down some boy named Jimmy."

"Yes, that's Clara." The smile came quickly and just as stunningly as it had on the child. "She's a vicious competitor," she added and wanted to say like her father, but didn't dare.

There was so much to say, so much that couldn't be said. If he had had one wish at that moment it would have been to reach out and touch her. Just to touch her once and remember the way it had been.

"I see you have your lace curtains."

Regret washed over her. She'd have settled for bare windows, blank walls. "Yes, I have my lace curtains and you your adventures."

"And this place." He turned to look around again. "When did all this start?"

She could deal with it, she promised herself, this hatefully casual small talk. "I opened it nearly eight years ago now."

He picked a rag doll from a bassinet. "So you sell dolls. A hobby?"

Something else came into her eyes now. Strength. "No, it's my business. I sell them, repair them, even make them."

"Business?" He set the doll down and the smile he gave her had nothing to do with humor. "It's hard for me to picture Tom approving of his wife setting up a business."

"Is it?" It hurt, but she set the china doll on a counter and began to arrange the veil on its head. "You always were perceptive, Jason, but you've been away a long time." She looked over her shoulder and her eyes weren't nervous or even strong. They were simply cold. "A very long time. Tom and I were divorced eight years ago. The last time I heard he was living in Los Angeles. You see, he didn't care for small towns either. Or small-town girls."

He couldn't name the things that stirred in him so he pushed them aside. Bitterness was simpler. "Apparently you picked badly, Faith."

She laughed again but the veil crumpled in her hand. "Apparently I did."

"You didn't wait." It was out before he could stop it. He hated himself for it, and her.

"You were gone." She turned back slowly and folded her hands.

"I told you I'd come back. I told you I'd send for you as soon as I could."

"You never called, or wrote. For three months I—"

"Three months?" Furious, he grabbed her arms. "After everything we'd talked about, everything we'd hoped for, three months was all you could give me?"

She would have given him a lifetime, but there hadn't been a choice. Struggling to keep her voice calm, she looked into his eyes. They were the same— intense, impatient. "I didn't know where you were. You wouldn't even give me that." She pulled away from him because the need was as great as it had always been. "I was eighteen and you were gone."

"And Tom was here."

She set her jaw. "And Tom was here. It's been ten years, Jason, you never once wrote. Why now?"

"I've asked myself the same thing," he murmured and left her standing alone.

Her dreams had always been too fanciful. As a child Faith had envisioned white chargers and glass slippers. Reality was something to be faced daily in a family where money was scarce and pride was not but dreams weren't just for nighttime.

She'd fallen in love with Jason when she'd been eight and he ten and he'd bravely vanquished three boys who'd tossed her into the snow. It had taken three of them. Faith could still look back on that with a sense of satisfaction. But it had been Jason fiercely coming to her rescue and sending her opponents scattering that she remembered best. He'd been thin, and his coat had been too large and mended at the elbows. She remembered his eyes, deep, deep brown under brows drawn close in annoyance as he'd looked down at her. Snow had coated his pale-blond hair and reddened his face. She'd looked into his eyes and fallen in love. He'd muttered at her, hauled her up and scolded her for getting in trouble. Then he'd stalked off with his ungloved hands thrust into the pockets of his too-big coat.

Through childhood and into adolescence she'd never looked at another boy. Of course she'd pretended to from time to time hoping it might make Jason Law notice her.

Then when she'd been sixteen and her mother had sewn her a dress for the spring dance at the town hall, he'd noticed. So had several other boys, and Faith had flirted outrageously, with one goal in mind: Jason Law. Sulky and defiant he'd watched her dance with one boy after another. She'd made sure of it. Just as she'd made sure she looked directly at him before she'd stepped outside to take the air. He'd followed her, just as she'd hoped. She'd pretended to be sophisticated. He'd been rude. And he'd walked her home under a fat full moon.

There'd been other walks after that—spring, summer, fall, winter. They were in love as only the young can be, carelessly, heedlessly, innocently. She told him of her longings for a house and children, for lace curtains and china cups. He told her of his passion to travel, to see everything, and write it down. She knew he'd felt trapped in the small town, hampered by a father who gave him no love and little hope. He knew she dreamed of quiet rooms with flowers in crystal vases. But they were drawn together and tangled all the dreams into one.

Then one night in the summer when the air was sweet with wild grass they stopped being children and their love stopped being innocent.

"Mom, you're dreaming again."

"What?" Up to her elbows in soapy water, Faith turned. Her daughter stood at the doorway to the kitchen, snugly wrapped in a flannel gown that came up to her chin. With her hair freshly brushed and her face scrubbed clean, she looked like an angel. Faith knew better. "I guess I was. You've finished your homework?"

"Yeah. It's dumb having homework when school's nearly out."

"Don't remind me."

"You're grumpy," Clara declared and eyed the cookie jar. "You should go for one of your walks."

"Just one," Faith said, easily outguessing her daughter. "And don't forget to brush your teeth." She waited while Clara rooted through the jar. "Did you see a man this afternoon? A tall man with blond hair?"

"Uh-huh." Mouth full, Clara turned back to her mother. "He was walking up to the house. I sent him to the shop."

"Did he—say anything to you?"

"Not really. He looked at me kind of funny at first, like he'd seen me before. Do you know him?"

While her heart began a slow, dull thud, Faith dried her hands. "Yes. He used to live here a long time ago."

"Oh. Jimmy liked his car." She wondered if she could talk herself into another cookie.

"I think I will take that walk, Clara, but I want you in bed."

Recognizing the tone, she knew the cookie would have to wait. "Can I count the presents under the tree again?"

"You've counted them ten times."

"Maybe there's a new one."

Laughing, Faith gathered her up. "Not a chance." Then she grinned and carried Clara into the living room. "But it won't hurt to count them one more time."

The air was brittle when she stepped outside and it smelled of snow. There was no reason to lock the doors in a town where she knew everyone. Bundling her coat closer, she glanced back at the second-story window where her daughter slept. Clara was the reason why the house wasn't cold, why her life wasn't empty when both things could easily have been true.

She'd left the tree burning and the lights around the door sent out festive color. Four days until Christmas, she thought, and the wonder of it came home again. From where she stood, the town looked as pretty as a postcard with the strings of lights, the tree with its star in the town square, the street lamps burning. She could smell smoke from the chimneys and the bursting scent of pine.

Some might find it too settled, others would find it dull. But Faith had made it a home for herself and her daughter. She'd altered her life to suit her, and it fitted her well.

No regrets, she promised with one last glance at her daughter's window. No regrets at all.

The wind picked up a bit as she walked. There'd be snow for Christmas. She could feel it. She'd look forward to that, not back any longer.

"Still fond of walking?"

Chapter Three

Had she known he'd find her? Perhaps she had. Perhaps she'd needed him to. "Some things don't change," she said simply as Jason fell into step beside her.

"I've found that out in one afternoon." He thought of the town that had stayed so much the same. And of his feelings for the woman beside him. "Where's your daughter?"

"She's sleeping."

He was calmer than he'd been that afternoon, and determined to stay that way. "I didn't ask you if you had other children."

"No." He heard the wistfulness in her voice, just a sigh of it. "There's only Clara."

"How did you pick the name?"

She smiled. It was so like him to ask questions no one else would think of. "From the Nutcracker. I wanted her to be able to dream." As she had. Dropping her hands in her pockets she told herself they were simply two old friends walking through a quiet town. "Are you staying at the inn?"

"Yeah." Amused, Jason rubbed a hand over his chin. "Beantree took my bags up himself."

"Local boy makes good." She turned to look at him. It was easier somehow walking like this. Odd, she realized, she'd seen the boy when she'd looked at him the first time. Now she saw the man. His hair had darkened a bit but was still very blond. It was no longer unkempt, but cut in a carelessly attractive style that had it falling over his brow. His face was still thin, hollow at the cheeks in the way that had always fascinated her. And his mouth was still full, but there was a hardness around it that hadn't been there once. "You did make good, didn't you? You made everything you wanted happen."

"Most everything." When his eyes met hers she felt all the old longings come back. "What about you, Faith?"

She shook her head, watching the sky as she walked. "I never wanted as much as you, Jason."

"Are you happy?"

"If a person isn't, it's their own fault."

"That's too simple."

"I haven't seen the things you've seen. I haven't had to deal with what you've had to deal with. I am simple, Jason. That was the problem, wasn't it?"

"No." He turned her to face him and slid his hands up to her face. He wore no gloves, and his fingers warmed against her skin. "God, you haven't changed." As she stood very still he combed his fingers up through her hair, then down to where the tips brushed her shoulders. "I've thought about the way you look in the moonlight countless times. It was just like this."

"I've changed, Jason." But her voice was breathless. "So have you."

"Some things don't," he reminded her and gave into the need.

When his mouth touched hers, he knew that he'd come home. Everything he remembered, everything he thought he'd lost was his again. She was soft and smelled of springtime even when snow dusted the ground around them. Her mouth was willing, even as it had been the first time he'd tasted it. He couldn't explain, even to himself, that every other woman he'd held had been nothing but a shadow of his memory of her. Now she was real, wrapped in his arms and giving him everything he'd forgotten he could have.

Just once, she promised herself as she melted against him. Just once more. How could she have known her life had such a void in it? She'd tried to close the door on the part of her life that included Jason, though she'd known it wasn't possible. She'd tried to tell herself it was only youthful passion and girlish fancy but she'd known that was a lie. There'd been no other men, only memories of one, and wishes, half-forgotten dreams.

She was holding no memory now but Jason, as real and urgent as he'd always been. Everything about him was so familiar, the taste of his lips on hers, the feel of his hair as her fingers raked through it, the scent of man, rough and rugged that he'd always carried with him even as a boy. He murmured her name and drew her closer, as if the years were trying to separate them again.

She wrapped her arms around him, as willing, as eager, and as in love as she'd been the last time he'd held her. The wind whipped around their ankles, puffing up clouds of snow while the moonlight held them close.

But it wasn't yesterday, she reminded herself as she stepped back. It wasn't tomorrow. It was today, and today had to be faced. She wasn't a child any longer without responsibilities and a love so big it overshadowed anything else. She was a woman with a child to raise and a home to make. He was a gypsy. He'd never pretended to be anything else.

"It's over for us, Jason." But she held his hand a moment longer. "It's been over for a long time."

"No." He caught her before she could turn away. "It isn't. I told myself it was, and that I'd come back and prove it. You've been eating at me half my life, Faith. It's never going to be over."

"You left me." The tears she promised herself she wouldn't shed spilled over. "You broke my heart. It's barely had time to mend, Jason. You won't break it again."

"You know I had to leave. If you'd waited—"

"It doesn't matter now." With a shake of her head she backed away. She would never be able to explain to him why it hadn't been possible to wait. "It doesn't matter because in a few days you'll be gone again. I won't let you whirl in and out of my life and leave my emotions in chaos. We both made our choices, Jason."

"Damn it, I missed you."

She closed her eyes. When she opened them again they were dry. "I had to stop missing you. Please leave me alone, Jason. If I thought we could be friends—"

"We always were."

"Always is gone." Nonetheless she held out both hands and took his. "Oh, Jason, you were my best friend, but I can't welcome you home because you scare the hell out of me."

"Faith." He curled his fingers around hers. "We need more time, to talk."

Looking at him she let out a long breath. "You know where to find me, Jason. You always did."

"Let me walk you home."

"No." Calmer, she smiled. "Not this time."

From the window of his room, Jason could see most of Main Street. He could, if he chose, watch the flow of business in Porterfield's Five and Dime or the collection of people who walked through and loitered in the town's square. Too often he found the direction of his gaze wandering to the white house near the end of the street. Because he'd been restless, Jason had been up and at the window when Faith had walked outside with Clara to see her off to school with a group of other children. He'd seen her crouch down to adjust the collar of her daughter's coat. And he'd seen her stand, hatless, her back to him, as she'd watched the children drag themselves off for a day of books. She'd stood there a long time with the wind pulling and tugging at her hair, and he'd waited for her to turn, to look at the inn, to acknowledge somehow that she knew he was there. But she'd walked around the side of the house to her shop without looking back.

Now, hours later, he was at the window again, still restless. From the number of people he could see walk back to the Doll House, her business was thriving. She was working, busy, while he was standing unshaven at a window with his portable typewriter sitting silent on the desk beside him.

He'd planned to work on his novel for a few days— the novel he'd promised himself he'd write. It was just one more promise he'd never been able to keep because of the demands of travel and reporting. He'd expected to be able to work here, in the quiet, settled town of his youth away from the demands of journalism and the fast pace he'd set for himself. He'd expected a lot of things. What he hadn't expected was to find himself just as wildly in love with Faith as he'd been at twenty.

Jason turned away from the window and stared at his typewriter. The papers were there, notes bulging in manila envelopes, the half-finished manuscript pages. He could sit down and make himself work through the day into the night. He had the discipline for it. But in his life there was more than a book that was half finished. He was just coming to realize it.

By the time he'd shaved and dressed, it was past noon. He thought briefly about walking across the street to Mindy's to see if she still served the best homemade soup in town. But he didn't feel like chatty counter talk. Deliberately he turned south, away from Faith. He wouldn't make a fool of himself by chasing after her.

As he walked, he passed a half a dozen people he knew. He was greeted with thumps on the back, handshakes and avid curiosity. He'd strolled down the Left Bank, up Carnaby Street and along the narrow streets of Venice. After a decade of absence he found the walk down Main Street just as fascinating. There was a barber pole that swirled up and around and back into itself. A life-size cardboard Santa stood outside a dress shop gesturing passersby inside.

Spotting a display of poinsettias, Jason slipped into the store and bought the biggest one he could carry. The saleswoman had been in his graduating class and detained him for ten minutes before he could escape. He'd expected questions, but he hadn't guessed that he'd become the town celebrity. Amused, he made his way down the street as he had countless times before. When he reached the Widow Marchant's, he didn't bother with the front door. Following an old habit, he went around the back and knocked on the storm door. It still rattled. It was a small thing that pleased him enormously.

When the widow opened the door, and her little bird's eyes peered through the bright-red leaves of the flowers he found himself grinning like a ten-year-old.

"It's about time," she said as she let him in. "Wipe your feet."

"Yes, ma'am." Jason scrubbed his boots against the rough mat before he set down the poinsettia on her kitchen table.

No more than five feet tall, the widow stood with her hands on her hips. She was bent a bit with age and her face was a melody of lines and wrinkles. The bib apron she wore was covered with flour. Jason smelled cookies in the oven and heard the majestic sound of classical music from the living-room speakers. The widow nodded at the flowers.

"You always went for the big statement." When she turned to look him up and down, Jason found himself automatically standing tall. "Put on a few pounds I see, but more wouldn't hurt. Come, give me a kiss."

He bent to peck her cheek dutifully, then found himself gathering her close. She felt frail; he hadn't realized it by looking at her, but she still smelled of all the good things he remembered—soap and powder and warm sugar.

"You don't seem surprised to see me," he murmured as he straightened up.

"I knew you were here." She turned to fuss at the oven because her eyes had filled. "I knew before the ink dried where you signed the registration at the inn. Sit down and take off your coat. I have to get these cookies out."

He sat quietly while she worked and absorbed the feeling of home. It was here he'd always been able to come as a child and feel safe. While he watched, she began to heat chocolate in a dented little pan on the stove.

"How long you staying?"

"I don't know. I'm supposed to be in Hong Kong in a couple of weeks."

"Hong Kong." The widow pursed her lips as she arranged cookies on a plate. "You've been to all your places, Jason. Were they as exciting as you thought?"

"Some were." He stretched out his legs. He'd forgotten what it was to relax, body, soul and mind. "Some weren't."

"Now you've come home." She walked over to put the cookies on the table. "Why?"

He could be evasive with anyone else. He could even lie to himself. But with her there could only be the truth. "Faith."

"It always was." Back at the stove, she stirred the chocolate. He'd been a troubled boy, now he was a troubled man. "You heard she married Tom."

And with her, he didn't have to hide the bitterness. "Six months after I left I called. I'd landed a job with *Today's News*. They were sending me to a hole in the wall in Chicago, but it was something. I called Faith, but I got her mother. She was very kind, even sympathetic when she told me that Faith was married, had been married for three months and was going to have a baby. I hung up, I got drunk. In the morning I went to Chicago." He plucked a cookie from the plate and shrugged. "Life goes on, right?"

"It does, whether it tows us along with it or rolls right over us. And now that you know she's divorced?"

"We promised each other something. She married someone else."

She made a sound like steam escaping from a kettle. "You're a man now from the looks of you, not a bull-headed boy. Faith Kirkpatrick—"

"Faith Monroe," he reminded her.

"All right then." Patiently, she poured heated chocolate into mugs. After she set them on the table, she seated herself with a quiet wheeze. "Faith is a strong, beautiful woman inside and out. She's raising that little girl all alone and doing a good job of it. She's started a business and she's making it work. Alone. I know something about being alone."

"If she'd waited—"

"Well, she didn't. Whatever thoughts I have about her reasons I'm keeping to myself."

"Why did she divorce Tom?"

The old woman sat back, resting her elbows on the worn arms of her chair. "He left her and the baby when Clara was six months old."

His fingers tightened around the handle of the mug. "What do you mean, he left her?"

"You should know the meaning. You did so yourself." She picked up her chocolate and held it in both hands. "I mean he packed his bags and left. She had the house—and the bills. He cleaned out the bank account and headed west."

"But he has a daughter."

"He hasn't laid eyes on the girl since she was in diapers. Faith pulled herself out. She had the child to think of after all if not herself. Her parents stood behind her. They're good people. She took a loan and started the doll business. We're proud to have her here."

He stared out the window to where the boughs of an old sycamore spread, dripping with snow and ice. "So I left, she married Tom, then he left. Seems Faith has a habit of picking the wrong men."

"Think so?"

He'd forgotten how dry her voice could be and nearly smiled. "Clara looks like Faith."

"Hmm. She favors her mother." The widow smiled into her mug. "I've always been able to see her father in her. Your chocolate's getting cold, Jason."

Absently, he sipped. With the taste came floods of memories. "I hadn't expected to feel at home here again. It's funny. I don't think I felt at home when I lived here, but now..."

"You haven't been by your old place yet?"

"No."

"There's a nice couple in there now. They put a porch on the back."

It meant nothing to him. "It was never home." He set the chocolate down and took her hand. "This was. I never knew any mother but you."

Her hand, thin, dry as paper, gripped his. "Your father was a hard man, harder maybe because he lost your mother so young."

"I only felt relief when he died. I can't even be sorry for it. Maybe that's why I left when I did. With him gone, the house gone, it seemed the time was right."

"Maybe it was, for you. Maybe the time's right to come back again. You weren't a good boy, Jason. But you weren't so bad either. Give yourself some of that time you were always so desperate to beat ten years ago."

"And Faith?"

She sat back again. "As I recall, you never did much courting. Seems to me the girl chased after you with her eyes wide open. A man who's been all the places you been oughta know how to court a woman. Probably picked up some of those fancy languages."

He picked up a cookie and bit into it. "A phrase or two."

"Never knew a woman who wouldn't flutter a bit with some fancy language."

Leaning over he kissed both her hands. "I missed you."

"I knew you'd come back. At my age, you know how to wait. Go find your girl."

"I think I might." Rising, he slipped into his coat. "I'll come back and visit again."

"See that you do." She waited until he opened the door. "Jason—button your coat." She didn't pull out her handkerchief until she heard the door close behind him.

Chapter Four

The sun was high and bright when he stepped outside. Across the street a snowman was rapidly losing weight. He found the streets as he'd found them yesterday on his drive in—full of children fresh out of school. He felt the surge of freedom himself. As he headed north, he saw a girl break away from a group of children and come toward him. Even bundled in hat and scarf he recognized Clara.

"'Scuse me. Did you use to live here?"

"That's right." He wanted to tuck her hair into her cap but stopped himself.

"My mother said you did. Today in school, the teacher said you went away and got famous."

He couldn't stop the grin. "Well, I went away."

"And you won a prize. Like Marcie's brother won a trophy for bowling."

He thought of his Pulitzer and managed, barely, not to laugh. "Something like that."

To Clara he looked like a regular person, not someone who bounded around the world on adventures. Her eyes narrowed. "Did you really go to all those places like they said?"

"That depends on what they said." In tacit agreement they began to walk together. "I've been to some places."

"Like Tokyo? That's the capital of Japan, we learned that in school."

"Like Tokyo."

"Did you eat raw fish?"

"Now and again."

"That's really disgusting." But she seemed pleased all the same. She bent and scooped up snow without breaking rhythm. "Do they squish grapes with their feet in France?"

"I can't say I ever saw it for myself, but I've heard tell."

"I sure wouldn't drink it after that. Did you ever ride a camel?"

He watched her bullet the snowball into the base of a tree. "As a matter of fact, I did."

"What was it like?"

"Uncomfortable."

It was a description she readily accepted because she'd already figured it out for herself. "The teacher read one of your stories today. The one about this tomb they found in China. Did you see the statues?"

"Yes, I did."

"Was it like *Raiders*?"

"Like what?"

"You know, the movie with Indiana Jones."

It took him a minute, then he laughed. Without thinking he tipped her cap over her eyes. "I guess it was, a little."

"You write good."

"Thank you."

They were standing on the sidewalk in front of her house. Jason glanced up, surprised. He hadn't realized they'd come so far and found himself regretting he hadn't slowed his pace a bit. "We have to do this report on Africa." Clara wrinkled her nose. "It has to be five whole pages long. Miss Jenkins wants it in right after Christmas vacation."

"How long have you had the assignment?" It hadn't been that long since his school days.

Clara drew a circle in the snow at the edge of her lawn. "Couple of weeks."

No, he realized with some pleasure, it hadn't been so very long. "I guess you've started on it."

"Well, sort of." Then she turned that quick, beautiful smile on him. "You've been to Africa, haven't you?"

"A couple of times."

"I guess you know all kinds of things about climate and culture and stuff like that."

He grinned down at her. "Enough."

"Maybe you should stay for dinner tonight." Without giving him a chance to answer, she took his hand and led him around to the shop.

When they walked in, Faith was boxing a doll. Her hair was pinned up in the back and she wore a baggy sweatshirt over jeans. She was laughing at something her customer had said. "Lorna, you know you wouldn't have it any other way."

"Bah, humbug." The woman put a hand on her enormous stomach and sighed. "I really wanted this baby to make an appearance before Christmas."

"You still have four days."

"Hi, Mom!"

Faith turned to smile at her daughter. As she spotted Jason the spool of ribbon in her hand spun in a red stream to the floor. "Clara, you didn't wipe your feet," she managed to say, but kept her eyes on Jason.

"Jason! Jason Law." The woman rushed over and grabbed him by both arms. "It's Lorna—Lorna McBee."

He looked down into the pretty round face of his longtime neighbor. "Hello, Lorna." His gaze drifted down, then back up. "Congratulations."

With a hand on her stomach she laughed. "Thanks, but it's my third."

He thought of the scrawny, bad-tempered girl next door. "Three? You work fast."

"So does Bill. You remember Bill Easterday, don't you?"

"You married Bill?" He remembered a boy who had hung out in the town square looking for trouble. A few times Jason had helped him find it.

"I reformed him." When she smiled, he believed it. "He runs the bank." His expression had her giggling. "I'm serious, stop in sometime. Well, I've got to be moving along. This box has to go into a locked closet before my oldest girl sees it. Thanks, Faith, it's just lovely."

"I hope she likes it."

To keep her hands busy, Faith began to rewind the spool of ribbon. A puff of cold air came in, then was cut off as Lorna breezed out.

"Was that the bride doll?" Clara wanted to know.

"Yes, it was."

"Too fussy. Can I go over to Marcie's?"

"What about homework?"

"I don't have any except that dumb Africa report. He's going to help me." Jason met her smile with a lifted brow. "Aren't you?"

Jason would have dared any man within a hundred miles to resist that look. "Yes, I am."

"Clara, you can't—"

"It's okay 'cause I asked him to dinner." She beamed, almost sure her mother would be trapped by the good manners she was always talking about. "There's no school now for ten whole days so I can do the report after dinner, can't I?"

Jason decided it wouldn't hurt to apply a little pressure from his side. "I spent six weeks in Africa once. Clara might just get an A."

"She could use it," Faith muttered. They stood together, looking at her. Her heart already belonged to both of them. "I guess I'd better start dinner."

Clara was already racing across the yard next door before Faith pulled the door of the Doll House shut and turned the sign around to read Closed.

"I'm sorry if she was a nuisance, Jason. She has a habit of badgering people with questions."

"I like her," he said simply and watched Faith fumble with the latch.

"That's nice of you, but you don't have to feel obliged to help her with this report."

"I said I would. I keep my word, Faith." He touched a pin in her hair. "Sooner or later."

She had to look at him then. It was impossible not to. "You're welcome to dinner, of course." Her fingers worried the buttons of her coat as she spoke. "I was just going to fry chicken."

"I'll give you a hand."

"No, that's not—"

He cut her off when he closed his fingers over hers. "I never used to make you nervous."

With an effort, she steadied herself. "No, you didn't." He'd be gone again in a few days, she reminded herself. Out of her life. Maybe she should take whatever time she was given. "All right then, you can help."

He took her arm as they crossed the lawn. Though he felt her initial resistance, he ignored it. "I went to see Widow Marchant. I had cookies right from the oven."

Faith relaxed as she pushed open the door of her own kitchen. "She has every word you've ever written."

The kitchen was twice the size of the one he'd just left and there were signs of a child in the pictures hanging on the front of the refrigerator and a pair of fuzzy slippers kicked into a corner. Moving with habit, Faith switched on the burner under the kettle before she slipped out of her coat. She hung it on a peg by the door, then turned to take his. His hands closed over hers.

"You didn't tell me Tom left you."

She'd known it wouldn't take him long to hear it, or long to question. "It's not something I think about on a daily basis. Coffee?"

She draped his coat over a hook and turned to find him blocking her way. "What happened, Faith?"

"We made a mistake." She said it calmly, even coolly. It was a tone he'd never heard from her before.

"But there was Clara."

"Don't." Fury came into her eyes quickly and simmered there. "Leave it alone, Jason, I mean it. Clara's my business. My marriage and divorce are my business. You can't expect to come back now and have all the answers."

They stood a moment, facing each other in silence. When the kettle let out a whistle, she seemed to breathe again. "If you want to help, you can peel some potatoes. They're in the pantry over there."

She worked systematically, he thought angrily, as she poured oil to heat in a skillet and coated chicken. Her temper was nothing new to him. He'd felt the brunt of it before, sometimes deflecting it, sometimes meeting it head-on. He also knew how to soothe it. He began talking, almost to himself as first, about some of the places he'd been. When he told her about waking with a snake curled next to his head while he'd been camping in South America she laughed.

"I didn't find it too funny at the time. I was out of the tent in five seconds flat, buck naked. My photographer got a very interesting roll of pictures. I had to pay him fifty to get the negatives."

"I'm sure they were worth more. You didn't mention the snake in your series on San Salvador."

"No." Interested, he put down his paring knife. "You read it?"

She arranged chicken in the hot oil. "Of course. I've read all your stories."

He took the potatoes to the sink to wash them. "All of them?"

She smiled at the tone but kept her back to him. "Don't let your ego loose, Jason. It was always your biggest problem. I'd estimate that ninety percent of the people in Quiet Valley have read all your stories. You might say we all feel we have a stake in you." She adjusted the flame. "After all, no one else around here's had dinner at the White House."

"The soup was thin."

Chuckling, she put a pan of water on the stove and dumped in the potatoes. "I guess you just have to take the good with the bad—so to speak. I saw a picture of you a couple of years ago." She adjusted a pin in her hair and her voice was bland. "I think it was taken in New York, at some glitzy charity function. You had a half-naked woman on your arm."

He rocked back on his heels. "Did I?"

"Well, she wasn't actually half-naked," Faith temporized. "I suppose it just seemed that way because she had so much more hair than dress. Blond—very blond if my memory serves me. And let's say—top-heavy."

He ran his tongue around his teeth. "You meet a lot of interesting people in my business."

"Obviously." With the efficiency born of habit she turned chicken. Oil hissed. "I'm sure you find it very stimulating."

"Not as stimulating as this conversation."

"If you can't stand the heat," she murmured.

"Yeah. It's getting dark. Shouldn't Clara be home?"

"She's right next door. She knows to be home by five-thirty."

He went to the window anyway and glanced at the house next door. Faith studied his profile. It was stronger now, tougher. She supposed he was too, had had to be. How much was left of the boy she'd loved so desperately? Maybe it was something neither of them could be sure of.

"I thought of you a lot, Faith." Though his back was to her she could almost feel the words brush over her skin. "But especially at this time of year. I could usually block you out when I had work to do, deadlines to meet, but at Christmas you wouldn't let go. I remember every one we spent together, the way you'd drag me through the shops. Those few years with you made up for all the times as a kid I woke up to nothing."

The old sympathy welled up. "Your father couldn't face the holidays, Jason. He just couldn't handle it without your mother."

"I understand that better now. After losing you." He turned back. She wasn't looking at him now but bent industriously over the stove. "You've been spending Christmas alone too."

"No, I have Clara."

She tensed as he walked to her. "No one to fill the stockings with you, or share secrets about what's under the tree."

"I manage. You have to alter life to suit yourself."

"Yeah." He took her chin in his hand. "I'm beginning to believe it."

The door slammed open. Wet and beaming, Clara stood dripping on the mat. "We made angels in the snow."

Faith raised a brow. "So I see. Well, you've got fifteen minutes to get out of those wet things and set the table."

She struggled out of her coat. "Can I turn on the tree?"

"Go ahead."

"Come on." Clara held out a hand for Jason. "It's the best one on the block."

Emotions humming, Faith watched them walk out together.

Chapter Five

They were still humming when the meal was over. She knew her daughter was a friendly, sometimes outrageously open child, but Clara had taken to Jason like a long lost friend. She chattered away at him as though she'd known him for years.

It's so obvious, Faith thought as she watched Clara stack dishes. Neither of them noticed. What would she do if they did? She didn't believe in lies, yet she'd been forced to live one.

The other two paid little attention to her as they settled down with Clara's books. In the easy, flowing style he'd been born with, Jason began to tell her stories about Africa—the desert, the mountains, the thick green jungle that teemed with its own life and its own dangers.

As their heads bent together over a picture in Clara's book Faith felt a flood of panic. "I'm going to go next door," she said on impulse. "I have a lot of work backed up."

"Mm-hmm." With that, Jason dismissed her. A laugh bubbled in her throat until it ached. Grabbing her coat, Faith escaped.

They were more than toys to her. They were certainly more than a business. To Faith the dolls who filled her shop were the symbol of youth, of innocence, of believing in miracles. She'd wanted to open the shop soon after Clara had been born, but Tom had been adamantly set against it. Because she'd felt indebted, she'd let it pass, as she'd let so many other things pass. Then when she'd found herself alone, with a child to support, it had seemed the natural thing.

She worked long hours there, to ease the void that even the love for her daughter couldn't fill.

In her workroom behind the store were shelves filled with pieces and parts of dolls. There were china heads, plastic legs and torsos. In another section lay the ones she called the sick and injured. Dolls with broken arms or battered bodies were brought to her for repair. Though she enjoyed selling and found a great creative thrill in making her own dolls, nothing satisfied her quite so much as taking a broken toy that was loved and making it whole again. She turned on the light and her radio and set to work.

It soothed her. As time passed, her nerves drained away. With crochet hook and rubber bands, with glue and painstaking care she replaced broken limbs. With a bit of paint and patience she brought smiles back to faceless dolls. Some were given new clothes or a fresh hairstyle, while others only needed a needle and thread plied by clever fingers.

By the time she picked up a battered rag doll she was humming.

"Are you going to fix that?"

Startled, she nearly stabbed herself with the needle. Jason stood in the doorway, hands in pockets, watching her. "Yes, that's what I do. Where's Clara?"

"She nearly fell asleep in her book. I put her to bed."

She started to rise. "Oh, well I—"

"She's asleep, Faith, with some green ball of hair she called Bernardo."

Determined to relax, Faith sat down again. "Yes, that's her favorite. Clara isn't much on ordinary dolls."

"Not like her mother?" Interested, he began to prowl the workroom. "I always thought when a toy broke or wore out it got tossed away."

"Too often. I've always thought that showed a tremendous lack of appreciation for something that's given you pleasure."

He picked up a soft plastic head, bald and smooth that grinned at him. "Maybe you're right, but I don't see what can be done about that pile of rags in your hand."

"Quite a lot."

"Still believe in magic, Faith?"

She glanced up and for the first time her smile was completely open, her eyes warm. "Yes, of course I do. Especially at Christmastime."

Unable to help himself he reached down to run a hand over her cheek. "I said before that I'd missed you. I don't think I realized how much."

She felt the need shimmer and the longing plead inside her. Denying both, she concentrated on the doll. "I appreciate you helping Clara, Jason. I don't want to keep you."

"Does it bother you to have someone watch you work?"

"No." She began to replace stuffing. "Sometimes a concerned mother will stay here while I doctor a patient."

He leaned a hip against the counter. "I imagined a lot of things when I was coming back. I never imagined this."

"What?"

"That I'd be standing here watching you stuff life back into a rag. You may not have noticed, but it doesn't even have a face."

"It will. How did the report go?"

"She needs to do the final draft."

Faith glanced up from her work. Her eyes were wide with the joke. "Clara?"

"She had the same reaction." Then he smiled as he leaned back. The room smelled of her. He wondered if she knew. "She's a bright kid, Faith."

"Sometimes uncomfortably so."

"You're lucky."

"I know." With quick skillful movements, she pushed the stuffing into place.

"Kids love you no matter what, don't they?"

"No." She looked at him again. "You have to earn it." With needle and thread she began to secure the seams.

"You know, she was out on her feet, but she insisted on stopping at the tree to count the presents. She tells me she had this feeling there's going to be one more."

"I'm afraid she's doomed to disappointment. Her list looked like an army requisition. I had to draw the line." Putting down the thread, she picked up her paintbrush. "My parents already spoil her."

"They still live in town?"

"Mmm-hmm." She'd already gotten a sense of the doll's personality as she'd worked with it. Now, she began to paint it on. "They mumble about Florida from time to time, but I don't know if they'll ever go. It's Clara. They just adore her. You might go by and see them, Jason. You know my mother was always fond of you."

He examined a slinky red dress no bigger than his palm. "Your father wasn't."

She grinned at that. "He just didn't quite trust you." She sent him a quick, saucy smile. "What father would have?"

"He had good reason." As he walked toward her, he saw the doll she held. "I'll be damned." Charmed, he took it, holding it under the light. What had been a misshapen pile of rags was now a plump, sassy doll. Exaggerated lashes spiked out from wide eyes. Curls had been sewn back into place so that they fell teasingly over the brow. It was soft, friendly and pretty as a picture. Even a full grown man could recognize what would make a small girl smile.

She felt a ridiculous sense of accomplishment at seeing him smile at her work. "You approve?"

"I'm impressed. How much do you sell something like this for?"

"This one's not for sale." Faith set it in a large box at the back of the room. "There are about a dozen little girls in town whose families can't afford much of a Christmas. There are boys too, of course, but Jake over at the five-and-dime and I worked a deal a few years back. On Christmas Eve, a box is left on the doorstep. The girls get a doll, the boys a truck or a ball or whatever."

He should have known. It was so typical of her, so much what she was. "Santa lives."

She turned to smile at him. "He does in Quiet Valley."

It was the smile that did it. It was so open, so familiar. Jason closed the distance between them before either of them realized it.

"What about you? Do you get what you want for Christmas?"

"I have everything I need."

"Everything?" His hands cupped her face. "Aren't you the one who used to dream? Who always believed in wishes?"

"I've grown up. Jason, you should go now."

"I don't believe that. I don't believe you've stopped dreaming, Faith. Just being with you makes me start again."

"Jason." She pressed her hands to his chest, knowing she had to stop what could never be finished. "You know we can't always have what we want. You'll leave in a few days. You can walk away and go on to a hundred other things, a hundred other places."

"What does that have to do with right now? It's always right now, Faith." He drew his hands through her hair so that pins scattered. Rich warm sable tumbled over his fingers. He'd always loved the feel of it, the smell of it. "You're the only one," he murmured. "You've always been the only one."

She closed her eyes before he could draw her close. "You'll go. I have to stay here. Once before I stood and watched you walk away. I don't think I can bear it if I let you in again. Can't you understand?"

"I don't know. I know I understand I want you so much more now than I ever did. I'm not sure you can keep me out, Faith." But he backed away, for both of them. "Not for long anyway. You said before I didn't have a right to all the answers. Maybe that's true. But I need one."

It was a reprieve, it was space to think. She let out a long breath and nodded. "All right. But you promise that you'll go now if I answer?"

"I'll go. Did you love him?"

She couldn't lie. It wasn't in her. So her eyes were direct and pride kept her chin high. "I never loved anyone but you."

It came into his eyes—triumph, fury. He reached for her but she pulled away. "You said you'd go, Jason. I trusted your word."

She had him trapped. She had him aching. "You should've trusted it ten years ago." He swung from the workroom and into the frigid night.

Chapter Six

Quiet Valley bustled with Christmas energy. From a jerry-rigged loudspeaker on top of the hardware store roof carols rang out. An enterprising young man from a neighboring farm got a permit and gave buggy rides up and down Main Street. Kids, keyed up with lack of school and anticipation shouted and raced on every corner. The skies had clouded over, but the snow held off.

Jason sat at the counter in the diner and sipped coffee while he listened to town gossip. Word was the Hennessys' oldest had the chicken pox and would be scratching himself through the holidays. Carlotta's was selling Christmas trees at half price and the hardware store had a sale on ten-speeds.

Ten years before Jason would have found the conversations mundane. Now he sat content, sipping his coffee and listening. Maybe this was what had been missing from the novel he'd been trying to write for so long. He'd been around the world, but everything had always been so fast paced, so urgent. There had been times when his life as well as his story had been on the line. You didn't think about it when it was happening. You couldn't. But now, sitting in the warm diner with the scent of coffee and frying bacon he could look back.

He'd taken assignments, a great many of them dangerous, because he hadn't given a damn. He'd already lost the part of himself he'd valued. It was true that over the years he'd built something back, inch by gritty inch, but he'd never found the whole—because he'd left it here, where he'd grown up. Now he just had to figure out what the hell to do with it.

"Guess they serve almost anybody in here."

Jason glanced up idly then grinned. "Paul. Paul Tydings." His hand was gripped by two enormous ones.

"Damn it, Jas, you're as good-looking and skinny as ever."

Jason took a long look at his oldest friend. Paul's hair was thick and curly around a full, ruddy face offset now by a bushy moustache. His bull-like frame had assured him a starting place on the offensive line. Over the years, it had thickened into what was politely termed a successful build. "Well," Jason decided. "You're as good-looking."

With a roar of laughter, Paul slapped him on the back. "I never expected to see you back here."

"Nor I you. I thought you were in Boston."

"Was. Made myself some money, got married."

"No kidding? How long?"

"Seven years come spring. Five kids."

Jason choked on his coffee. "Five?"

"Three and a set of twins. Anyway, I brought my wife back for a visit six years back and she fell in love. Had a jewelry store in Manchester, so I opened one here too. I guess I've got you to thank for a lot of it."

"Me? Why?"

"You were always filling my head with ideas. Then you took off. It made me think I should try my hand at seeing a few places. In about a year I was working in this jewelry store in Boston and in walks the prettiest little thing I ever laid eyes on. I was so flustered I never imprinted her credit card. She came back the next day with the blank receipt and saved my job. Then she saved my life and married me. Never even would have met her if it hadn't been for you talking about all the places there were to see." Paul nodded as his coffee was served. "Guess you've seen Faith."

"Yeah, I've seen her."

"Throw a lot of business her way being as three of my kids are girls and all of 'em are brats." He grinned and added two packages of sugar to his coffee. "She's as pretty as she was when she was sixteen and dancing in the town hall. Settling in this time, Jason?"

With a half laugh he pushed his cooling coffee aside. "Maybe."

"Come by the house and meet the family, will you? We're just south of town, the two-story stone place."

"I saw it driving in."

"Then don't go out again without coming in. A man doesn't have many friends who go back to red wagons with him, Jason. You know—" he glanced at his watch "—seems to me Faith breaks for lunch about now. I've got to get back." With a last slap on the back, Paul left him at the counter.

Thoughtfully, Jason sipped at his coffee. He'd been away ten years, a long time by any standard, yet everyone in town he ran into saw him and Faith as a couple. It seemed it was easy to blink away a decade. Easy for everyone, he added, but for himself and Faith. Maybe he could brush away the years, the time lost, but how could he ignore her marriage and her child?

He still wanted her. That hadn't changed. He still hurt. That hadn't eased. But how did she feel? She'd told him the night before that she'd never loved another man. Did that mean she still loved him? Jason dropped a bill on the counter and rose. There was only one way to find out. He'd ask her.

The Doll House was crowded with children. Noisy children. When Jason walked in shouts and laughter bounced off the walls. Helium-filled balloons hugged the ceiling and cookie crumbs littered the floor. In the doorway of the workroom was a tall cardboard castle. Just in front of a shiny white curtain stood a puppet of Santa Claus and a green-suited elf. With a lot of chatter and exaggerated effort, they loaded a glittering golden sleigh with colorful boxes. Twice the elf fell on his face while lifting a box and sent the children into peals of laughter. After a great deal of confusion, all the presents were loaded. With a belly-bursting *Ho-ho-ho!* Santa climbed into the sleigh. Bells jingling, it rocked its way through the curtain.

To the clatter of applause, a series of puppets crossed the stage for bows. Jason saw Mrs. Claus, two elves and a reindeer with a telltale red nose before Santa took the stage with a ringing *Merry Christmas!* He didn't even realize he was leaning back against the door and grinning when Faith popped around the castle for a bow of her own.

But she saw him. Feeling foolish, she took another bow as the children clambered up. With the ease of a veteran kindergarten teacher, she maneuvered them toward the punch and cookies.

"Very impressive," Jason murmured in her ear. "I'm sorry I missed most of the show."

"It's not much." She combed her fingers through her hair. "I've been doing it for years now without much variation." She glanced over at the group of children. "It doesn't seem to matter."

"I'd say it does." He took her hand and brought it to his lips while a group of girls giggled. "Very much."

"Mrs. Monroe." A little boy with carrot-red hair and a face full of freckles tugged on her slacks. "When's Santa coming?"

Faith crouched down and smoothed at his hair. "You know, Bobby, I heard he was awfully busy this year."

His bottom lip poked out. "But he always comes."

"Well, I'm sure he'll find a way to get the presents here. I'm going to go in the back in a minute and see."

"But I have to talk to him."

The pout nearly did her in. "If he doesn't make it, you can give me a letter for him. I'll make sure he gets it."

"Problem?" Jason murmured when she straightened up again.

"Jake always plays Santa after the puppet show. We give out a few little things, it's nothing really, but the kids depend on it."

"Jake can't make it this year?"

"He caught the chicken pox from the Hennessy boy."

"I see." He hadn't celebrated Christmas in years, not since . . . since he'd left Faith. "I'll do it," he told her and surprised himself.

"You?"

Something in her expression made him determined to be the best St. Nick since the original. "Yeah, me. Where's the suit?"

"It's in the little room off the back, but—"

"I hope you remembered the pillows," he said before he sauntered away.

She didn't think he'd pull it off. In fact, five minutes after he walked away, Faith was sure he'd changed his mind altogether and continued out the back door. No one, including the group of kids with mouths full of cookies was more enchanted than she when Santa walked in the front door with a bag over his shoulder.

He had the chance for one booming *Merry Christmas* before he was surrounded. Too stunned to move, she watched the children bounce and jump and tug.

"Santa needs a chair." Jason sent her a long intense look that had her swallowing before her feet could move. Dashing into the back room, she brought out a high-backed chair and set it in the center of the room.

"Now you have to line up," she began, scooting children around. "Everyone gets a turn." Grabbing a bowl of candy canes, she set them on a table beside the chair. One by one, the children climbed up on Jason's knee. Faith needn't have worried. She'd had to school Jake to make the right responses, and most importantly, not to promise and risk disappointing. After the third child had climbed down, Faith relaxed. Jason was wonderful.

And having the time of his life. He'd done it just to help her out, perhaps even to impress her, but he got a great deal more. He'd never had a child sit on his lap and look at him with complete faith and love. He listened to their wishes, their confessions and complaints. Each one was allowed to reach in the sack he carried and pull out one gift.

He was hugged, kissed with sticky mouths and poked. One enterprising boy had a good grip on his beard before Jason managed to distract him. Happy, they began to file out of the shop with their parents or in groups.

"You were great." Faith turned her sign around after the last child had left to give herself a chance to catch her breath.

"Want to sit on my lap?"

Laughing, she walked to him. "I mean it, Jason, you were. I can't tell you how much I appreciate it."

"Then show me." He pulled her down onto his lap where she sank into pillows. She laughed again and kissed his nose.

"I've always been crazy about men in red suits. I wish Clara could have been here."

"Why wasn't she?"

With a little sigh, Faith let herself relax against him. "She's too old for all this now—so she tells me. She went shopping with Marcie."

"Nine's too old?"

She didn't speak for a minute, then moved her shoulders. "Kids grow up fast." She turned her head so she could look at him. "You made a lot of them happy today."

"I'd like to make you happy." Reaching up, he stroked her hair. "There was a time when I could."

"Do you ever wish we could go back?" Content, she let herself be cradled in his arms. "When we were teenagers, everything seemed so simple. Then you close your eyes for a minute and you're an adult. Oh, Jason, I wanted you to carry me away, to a castle, to a mountaintop. I was so full of romance."

He continued to stroke her hair as they sat, surrounded by dolls and the echo of children's laughter. "I didn't have enough of it, did I?"

"You had your feet on the ground, I had my head in the clouds."

"And now?"

"Now, I have a daughter to raise. It's terrifying sometimes to realize you're responsible for another life. Did you...?" She hesitated, knowing the ground was dangerous. "Did you ever want kids?"

"I haven't thought about it. Sometimes I have to go into places where it's tough enough being responsible for your own life."

She'd thought of that—had nightmares about it. "It still excites you."

He thought of some of the things he'd seen, the cruelty, the misery. "It stopped exciting me a long time ago. But I'm good at what I do."

"I suppose I always knew you would be. Jason."
She shifted again so that her eyes were level with his.
"I am glad you came back."

His fingers tightened when she rested her cheek
against his. "You had to wait until I was stuffed like
a walrus to tell me that."

With a laugh, she wrapped her arms around his
neck. "It seems to be the safest time."

"Don't bet your life on it." He pressed his lips to
hers and felt hers tremble. "What's so funny?"

Choking back the laugh, she drew away. "Oh
nothing, nothing at all. I've always dreamed of being
kissed by a man in a beard wearing a red hat and bells.
I've got to clean up this mess."

When she rose, he hauled himself up. "The timing
has to click sooner or later." She said nothing as she
gathered up bits of colored paper. Jason picked up his
sack and glanced inside. "There's one more box in
here."

"It's for Luke Hennessy. Chicken pox."

He looked at the box, then back at her. Her hair
curtained her face as she pulled a sticky candy cane
from the carpet. "Where does he live?"

Still holding the candy, she stood up. Some might
say he looked foolish, padded from chest to hips,
wrapped in red and with his face half concealed by a
curly white beard. Faith thought he'd never looked
more wonderful. She walked to him to pull the beard
down to his chin. Her arms went around him, her
mouth found his.

Her kiss was warm as it always was, full of hope and
simple goodness. Desire raced through him and set-

tled into sweet contentment. "Thank you." She kissed him again in friendship. "He lives on the corner of Elm and Sweetbriar."

He waited a moment until he was steady. "Can I get a cup of coffee when I get back?"

"Yeah." She adjusted his beard again. "I'll be next door."

Chapter Seven

He had to admit, it had given him a kick to walk through town. Kids flocked after him. Adults called out and waved. He was offered uncountable cookies. The biggest satisfaction had been the awe on the young Hennessy boy's face. That had topped the wide-eyed shock of his mother when she'd opened the door to S. Claus.

Jason took his time walking back, strolling through the square. It was strange, he discovered, how easy it was to take on the personality of a set of clothes. He felt . . . well, benevolent. If anyone he'd ever worked with had seen him now, they'd have fallen into the snow in a dead faint. Jason Law had a reputation for being impatient, brutally frank and quick-tempered. He hadn't won the Pulitzer for benevolence. Yet somehow, at the moment, he felt more satisfaction in the polyester beard and dime store bells than he did with all the awards he'd ever earned.

He was ho-hoing his way along when Clara stepped out of the five-and-dime. She and the little brunette at her side went off in peals of giggles.

"But you're—"

One narrow-eyed stare from Jason did the trick. Cutting herself off, Clara cleared her throat and offered her hand. "How do you do, Santa."

"I do very well, Clara."

"That's not Jake," Marcie informed Clara. She stepped closer to try to recognize the face behind the puffs of white.

Enjoying himself, Jason sent her a wink. "Hello, Marcie."

The brunette's eyes widened. "How'd he know my name?" she whispered to her friend.

Clara covered another giggle with her hand. "Santa knows everything, don't you, Santa?"

"I have my sources."

"There isn't any Santa really." But Marcie's grown-up sophistication was wavering.

Jason leaned over and flicked at the fluffy ball on top of her cap. "There is in Quiet Valley," he told her and nearly believed it himself. He saw Marcie stop looking beyond the beard and accept the magic. Deciding against pressing his luck, he continued on down the street.

It wasn't easy for a fat man in a red suit to slip into a door inconspicuously, but Jason had had some experience. Once he was in the back room of Faith's shop, he shed the Santa clothes. He wanted to do it again. As Jason slipped into his own slim slacks, he realized he hadn't had so much fun in years. Part of it had been the look in Faith's eyes, the way she'd warmed to him, if only briefly. Part had been the simple act of giving pleasure. How long had it been since he'd done something without an angle? On an assignment there was constant bargaining. You give me this, I'll give you that. He'd had to toughen himself against sympathy, against compassion to find the truth and report it. If his style had a hard edge, it was because he'd always gone for the story that demanded it. It had helped him forget. Now that he'd come home it was impossible not to remember.

What kind of man was he really? He wasn't sure anymore, but he knew there was one woman who could make or break him. Leaving the suit in the closet, he went to find her.

She had been waiting for him. She was ready to admit she'd been waiting for him for ten years. Throughout the rest of the afternoon, Faith had made her own decisions. She'd made a success of her life. Though the search hadn't always been easy, she'd found contentment. Confidence had come with the years and she knew she could go on alone. It was time to stop being afraid of what her life would be like when Jason left again and to accept the gift she'd been offered. He was here, now, and she loved him.

When he came into the house he found her curled in a chair by the tree, her cheek resting on the arm. She waited until he came to her. "Sometimes at night I sit like this. Clara's asleep upstairs and the house is quiet. I can think about little things, enormous things, just as I did as a child. The lights all blend together and the tree smells like heaven. You can go anywhere, sitting just like this."

He picked her up, felt her yield, then settled in the chair with her on his lap. "I remember sitting like this with you at Christmastime in your parents' house. Your father grumbled."

She snuggled close. There was no padding now, just the long lean body she knew so well. "My mother dragged him into the kitchen so we could be alone for a little while. She knew you didn't have a tree at home.''

''Or anything else.''

''I never asked where you live now, Jason, whether you found a place that makes you happy.''

''I move around a lot. I have a base in New York.''

''A base?''

''An apartment.''

''It doesn't sound like a home,'' she murmured. ''Do you put a tree in the window at Christmas?''

''I guess I have once or twice, when I've been around.''

It broke her heart, but she said nothing. ''My mother always said you had wanderlust. Some people are born with it.''

''I had to prove myself, Faith.''

''To whom?''

''To myself.'' He rested his cheek on top of her head. ''Damn it, to you.''

She breathed in the scent of pine while the lights danced on the tree. They'd sat like this before, so long ago. The memories were nearly as sweet as the reality. ''I never needed you to prove anything to me, Jason.''

''Maybe that's one of the reasons I had to. You were too good for me.''

''That's ridiculous.'' She would have shifted, but he held her still.

''You were, and still are.'' He too stared at the tree. The tinsel shimmered in the lights like the magic he'd always wanted to give her. ''Maybe that's why I had to leave when I did—maybe it's why I came back. You're all the good things, Faith. Just being with you brings out the best parts of me. God knows, there aren't many."

"You were always too hard on yourself. I don't like it." This time she did shift so that her hands were on his shoulders and her eyes were directly on his. "I fell in love with you. There were reasons for it. You were kind though you pretended not to be. You wanted to be considered tough and a troublemaker because you felt safer that way."

He smiled and ran a finger down her cheek. "I was a troublemaker."

"Maybe I liked that too. You didn't just accept things, you weren't afraid to question."

"I nearly got kicked out of school twice because I questioned."

The old anger stirred. Had no one understood him but herself? Had no one else been able to see what had been racing and straining inside him? "You were smarter than anyone else. You've proved that if you needed to."

"You spent a lot of time defending me, didn't you?"

"I believed in you. I loved you."

He reached for her face in an old gesture that melted her heart. "And now?"

She had too much to say and not enough ways to say it. "Do you remember that night in June, after my Senior Prom? We drove out of town. The moon was full and the air was so sweet with summer."

"You wore a blue dress that made your eyes look like sapphires. You were so beautiful I was afraid to touch you."

"So I seduced you."

She looked so pleased with herself he laughed. "You did not."

"I certainly did. You would never have made love with me." She touched her lips to his. "Do I have to seduce you again?"

"Faith—"

"Clara's having dinner next door at Marcie's. She's going to spend the night. Come to bed with me, Jason."

Her quiet voice raced along his skin. The touch of her hand to his cheek seared like fire. But tangled with his need for her was a love that had never grown old. "You know I want you, Faith, but we're not children now."

"We're not children." She turned her face to press her lips into his palm. "And I want you. No promises, no questions. Love me the way you did on that one beautiful night we had together." Rising, she held out her hand. "I want something for the next ten years."

With their hands linked they walked up the stairs. He pushed away all thought of the other man she'd chosen, of the other life she'd lived. He, too, would block out ten years of loss and take what was offered.

Night came early in the winter so the light was dim. In silence she lit candles so that the room glowed gold and shifted with shadows. When she turned back to him she was smiling, with all the confidence and knowledge of a woman in her eyes. Saying nothing, she came to him, lifted her mouth and offered everything.

Her fingers were steady as she reached for the buttons of his shirt. His trembled as he reached for hers. Murmuring, she waited for the brush of his hands against her skin, then sighed from the sheer glory of it. They undressed each other slowly, not tentatively, but with the quiet understanding that every moment, every instant would be treasured.

When he saw her, as slim, as lovely, as unexplainably innocent as she'd been the first time, his head spun with needs, with doubts, with desires. But she stepped to him, pressed her body against his and dissolved all choices. She was stronger than she'd been. He could feel it, not in muscle but in spirit. Perhaps she had changed, but the longings that were racing through him were the same as they'd been in the boy on the brink of manhood. As heedlessly as the children they'd once been, they tumbled onto the bed.

They didn't relive the experience. It was as fresh, as wildly thrilling as the first time. But they were man and woman now, more demanding, hungrier. She drew him closer, running her hands over him with an urgency just discovered, with a turbulence just released. She'd waited so long, so very long and wouldn't wait a moment longer.

But he took her hand and brought it to his lips. He quieted her tumbling breath with his mouth.

"I hardly knew what to do with you the first time." Gently he nuzzled at her throat until she moaned in frenzied anticipation. Raising his head, he smiled at her. "Now I do."

Then he took her places she'd never been. Higher, still higher he drew her, then just as suddenly plunged her deep where the air was thick and dark. Trapped in the whirlwind, she clung. She'd wanted to give, but he left her helpless. Tender, soft, easy, his fingers caressed until her body shuddered. He drank in her sigh with lips abruptly urgent, ruthlessly demanding, then patiently soothed her again. Sensations rocketed inside her, leaving no room for thought, for reason or even for memories.

When they came together it was everything for both of them. Time didn't slip back but trapped them and held them close in the here and now.

He kept his arms tightly around her and they were quiet. With her eyes closed, she absorbed the unity. She loved, and for the moment there was nothing else. For him both ecstasy and contentment were troubled with questions. She was so warm, so free with her emotions. She loved him. He needed no words to know it and never had. But the loyalty he'd always understood as an intrinsic part of her had been broken. How could he rest without knowing why?

"I have to know why we lost ten years, Faith." When she said nothing, he turned her head toward him. Her eyes glistened in the shifting light but the tears didn't fall. "Now more than ever I have to know."

"No questions, Jason. Not tonight."

"I've waited long enough. We've waited long enough."

On a long breath, she sat up. Bringing her knees to her chest, she wrapped her arms around them. Her hair cascaded down her back. He couldn't resist taking a handful. She'd been his once, completely. No one else had ever touched her as he had. He knew he had to accept her marriage, and that her child belonged to another man, but he needed to understand first why she had turned to someone else so soon after he'd gone away.

"Give me something, Faith. Anything."

"We loved each other, Jason, but we wanted different things." She turned her head to look at him. "We still want different things." She took his hand and brought it to her cheek. "If you had let me I would have gone anywhere with you. I would have left my home, my family and never looked back. You needed to go alone."

"I didn't have anything for you," he began. She stopped him with a look.

"You never gave me a choice."

He reached for her once more. "If I gave you one now?"

She closed her eyes and let her forehead rest on his. "Now I have a child, and she has a home I can't take away from her. What I want doesn't come first." She drew back far enough to look at him. "What you want can't come first. Before somehow I never thought you'd really go. This time I know you will. Let's just take what we have, give each other this one Christmas. Please."

She closed her mouth over his and stopped all questions.

Chapter Eight

Christmas Eve was magic. Faith had always believed it. When she awoke with Jason beside her, it was more than magic. For a while, she simply lay there, watching him sleep. She'd imagined it before, as a girl, as a woman, but now she didn't need the dreams. He was here beside her, warm, quiet, and outside an early morning snow was falling. Careful not to wake him, Faith slipped out of bed.

When he rolled over, he smelled her—the springtime scent her hair had left on the pillowcase. For a few minutes, he lay still and let it seep into his system. Content, he lay back and looked at the room he hadn't been able to see in the dark.

The walls were papered, ivory, with little sprigs of violets. At the windows were fussy priscillas. There was an antique rosewood bureau cluttered with colored bottles and boxes. On a vanity was an old-fashioned silver-handled brush and comb. He watched the snow fall and smelled the potpourri on the stand beside the bed. The room was so like her—charming, fresh, and very, very feminine. A man could relax there even knowing he might find stockings draped over a chair or a blouse mixed with his shirts. He could relax there. And he wasn't letting her go again.

He smelled the coffee before he was halfway down the stairs. She had Christmas music on the stereo and bacon frying. He hadn't known it would feel so good just to walk into a kitchen and find your woman cooking for you.

"So you're up." She was wrapped from head to foot in a bright flannel robe. Desire dragged quietly at his stomach muscles. "There's coffee."

"I could smell it." He went to her. "I could smell you the moment I woke."

She rested her head on his shoulder, trying not to think that this was the way it might have been—if only. "You look as though you could have slept for hours. It's a good thing you didn't or the bacon would be cold."

"If you'd stayed in bed a few more minutes, we might have—"

"Mom! Mom! It's snowing!" Clara burst through the door and danced around the kitchen. "We're going to go caroling tonight in the hay wagon and there's snow all over the place." She stopped in front of Jason and grinned. "Hi."

"Hi yourself."

"Mom and I are going to build a snowman. She says Christmas snowmen are the best. You can help."

She hadn't known just what reaction Clara would have to finding Jason at the breakfast table. With a shake of her head, Faith began to beat eggs. She should have known Clara would be willing to accept anyone she'd decided to like. "You have to have some breakfast."

Clara fingered the plastic Santa on her lapel, tugging on the string so that the nose lit up. It never failed to please her. "I had cereal at Marcie's."

"Did you thank her mother for having you?"

"Yeah." She stopped a minute. "I think I did. Anyway we're going to build two of them and have a wedding and everything. Marcie wanted the wedding," she added to Jason.

"Clara would prefer a war."

"I figured we could have that after. Maybe I should have some hot chocolate first." She eyed the cookie jar and calculated her chances. Slim at best.

"I'll fix it. And you can have a cookie after the snowman," Faith told her without bothering to turn. "Hang your things by the door."

Scrambling out of her coat, she chattered at Jason. "You're not going back to Africa, are you? I don't think Africa would be much fun at Christmas. Marcie's mother said you'd probably be going to some other neat place."

"I'm supposed to go to Hong Kong in a few weeks." He glanced at Faith. She didn't turn. "But I'll be around for Christmas."

"Do you have a tree in your room?"

"No."

She gave him a wide-eyed look. "Well, where do you put your presents? It's not Christmas without a tree, is it, Mom?"

Faith thought of the years Jason had grown up without one. She remembered how hard he'd tried to pretend it didn't matter. "A tree's only so that we can show other people it's Christmas."

Unconvinced, Clara plopped into a chair. "Well, maybe."

"She used to say the same thing to me," Jason told Clara. "In any case, I don't think Mr. Beantree would like it if I left pine needles all over the floor."

"We've got a tree, so you can have dinner with us," Clara declared. "Mom makes this big turkey and Grandma and Grandpa come over. Grandma brings pies and we eat till we're sick."

"Sounds great." Amused, he looked over as Faith scooped eggs onto a plate. "I had Christmas dinner with your grandparents a couple of times."

"Yeah?" Interested, Clara studied him. "I guess I heard somewhere that you used to be Mom's boyfriend. How come you didn't get married?"

"Here's your hot chocolate, Clara." Faith set it down. "You'd better hurry, Marcie's waiting."

"Are you coming out?"

"Soon." Grateful that her daughter was easily distracted, she set the platter of bacon and eggs on the table. Ignoring the half-amused lift of brow from Jason, she took her seat.

"We need carrots and scarves and stuff."

"I'll take care of it."

With a grin Clara gulped down chocolate. "And hats?"

"And hats."

A snowball hit the kitchen window. Clara was up like a shot. "There she is. Gotta go. Come soon, Mom, you make the best."

"Soon as I'm dressed. Don't forget your top button."

Clara hesitated at the back door. "I've got a little plastic tree in my room. You can have it if you want."

Moved, he only stared at her. Just like her mother, he thought, and fell in love a second time. "Thanks."

"'Sokay. Bye."

"She's quite a kid," Jason commented as the door slammed behind her.

"I like her."

"I'll give her a hand with the snowman."

"You don't have to, Jason."

"I want to, then I've got some things to take care of." He checked his watch. It was only Christmas Eve for so long. When a man was being offered a second chance, it wasn't wise to waste time. "Can I get an invitation for tonight?"

Faith smiled but simply pushed the food around on her plate. "You've never needed one."

"Don't cook, I'll bring something."

"It's okay, I—"

"Don't cook," he repeated, rising. He bent to kiss her, then lingered over it. "I'll be back."

He took his coat from the hook where it had hung beside Clara's. When he was gone, Faith looked down at the toast she'd crumbled in her hand. Hong Kong. At least this time she knew where he was going.

The snow people in the side yard grinned at him as he struggled past. Boxes balanced, Jason knocked on the back door with the toe of his boot. The snow hadn't let up a whit.

"Jason." Speechless, Faith stepped back as he teetered inside.

"Where's Clara?"

"Clara?" Still staring, she pushed back her hair. "She's upstairs getting ready for the hayride."

"Good. Take the top box."

"Jason, what in the world have you got here?"

"Just take the top box unless you want pizza all over the floor."

"All right, but..." As the enormous box in his arms shifted, she laughed. "Jason, what have you done?"

"Wait a minute."

Holding the pizza, she watched him drag the box into the living room. "Jason, what is that thing?"

"It's a present." He started to set it under the tree then discovered there wasn't enough room. With a bit of rearranging, he managed to lean the box against the wall beside the tree. He was grinning when he turned to her. If he'd ever felt better in his life, he couldn't remember it. "Merry Christmas."

"Same to you. Jason, what is that box?"

"Damn, it's cold out there." Though he rubbed his hands together now, he hadn't even noticed the biting wind. "Got any coffee?"

"Jason."

"It's for Clara." He discovered that feeling a bit foolish didn't dim the warmth.

"You didn't have to get her a present," Faith began, but her curiosity got the better of her. "What is it?"

"This?" Jason patted the six-foot box. "Oh, it's nothing."

"If you don't tell me you don't get any coffee." She smiled. "And I keep the pizza."

"Spoilsport. It's a toboggan." He took Faith's arm to lead her out of the room. "She happened to mention when we were building the snowman that some kid had this toboggan and it went down Red Hill like a spitfire."

"Spitfire," Faith murmured.

"And snow like this is just made for going down Red Hill like a spitfire, so..."

"Sucker," Faith accused and kissed him hard.

"Put that pizza down and call me that again."

She laughed and kept it between them.

"Wow!"

Faith raised a brow at the noise from the living room. "I think she saw the box."

At full speed, Clara barreled into the kitchen. "Did you see? I knew there'd be one more, I just knew. It's as tall as you are," she told Jason. "Did you see?" She grabbed his hand to drag him back. "It has my name on it."

"Imagine that." Jason picked her up and kissed both cheeks. "Merry Christmas."

"I can't wait." She threw her arms around his neck and squeezed. "I just can't wait."

Watching them, Faith felt her emotions tangle and knot until her bones ached with it. What should she do? What could she do? When Jason turned with Clara, the lights from the tree fell like wishes over their faces.

"Faith?" He didn't need words to recognize distress, pain, turmoil. "What is it?"

Her hands were digging into the cardboard of the box. "Nothing. I'm going to dish out this pizza before it's cold."

"Pizza?" Delighted, Clara bounced down. "Can I have two pieces? It's Christmas."

"Monkey," Faith scolded gently, tousling her hair. "Set the table."

"What is it, Faith?" Jason took her arm before she could follow her daughter into the kitchen. "Something's wrong."

"No." She had to control herself. She'd managed everything for so long. "You overwhelmed me." With a smile she touched his face. "It's happened before. Come on, let's eat."

Because she seemed to need to keep her thoughts to herself, he let it go and followed her into the kitchen where Clara was already peeking into the cardboard box. He'd never seen a child plow through food with such unrestrained glee. He'd never known Christmas Eve could be special simply because there was someone beside him.

Clara swallowed the last of her second piece. "Maybe if I opened one present tonight there'd be less confusion in the morning."

Faith seemed to consider. "I like confusion," she decided and Jason realized the conversation was an old tradition.

"Maybe if I opened just one present tonight, I could get right to sleep. Then you wouldn't have to wait so long to creep around and fill the stockings."

"Hmm." Faith pushed aside her empty plate and enjoyed the wine Jason had brought. "I like creeping around late at night."

"If I opened—"

"Not a chance."

"If I—"

"Nope."

"But Christmas is just hours and hours away."

"Awful, isn't it?" Faith smiled at her. "And you're going caroling in ten minutes, so you'd better get your coat."

Clara walked over to tug on her boots. "Maybe when I get back, there'll be just one present that you'll figure isn't really important enough to wait until morning."

"All the presents under the tree are absolutely vital." Faith rose to help her on with her coat. "And so are the following instructions. Stay with the group. Keep your mittens on; I want you to keep all your fingers. Don't lose your hat. Remember that Mr. and Mrs. Easterday are in charge."

"Mom." Clara shifted her feet and sighed. "You treat me like a baby."

"You are my baby." Faith gave her a smacking kiss. "So there."

"Jeez, I'll be ten years old in February. That's practically tomorrow."

"And you'll still be my baby in February. Have a good time."

Clara sighed, long-suffering and misunderstood. "Okay."

"Okay," Faith mimicked. "Say good-night."

Clara peeked around her mother. "Are you going to stay until I get back?"

"Yeah."

Satisfied, she grinned and pulled open the door. "Bye."

"Monster," Faith declared and began to stack plates.

"She's terrific." Standing, Jason helped clear the clutter. "Little for her age, I guess. I didn't realize she was almost ten. It's hard to—" He stopped as Faith clattered dishes in the sink. "She'll be ten in February."

"Umm. I can't believe it myself. Sometimes it seems like yesterday, and then again..." She trailed off, abruptly breathless. With studied care, she began to fill the sink with soapy water. "I'll just be a minute here if you'd like to take your wine into the living room."

"In February." Jason took her arm. When he turned her, he saw the blood drain from her face. His fingers tightened, bruising without either of them noticing. "Ten years in February. We made love that June. God, I don't know how many times that night. I never touched you again, we never had the chance to be alone like that again before I left, just a few weeks later. You must have married Tom in September."

Her throat was dry as bone. She couldn't even swallow, but stared at him.

"She's mine," he whispered and it vibrated through the room. "Clara's mine."

She opened her mouth to speak, but there seemed to be nothing she could say. Lips trembling, eyes drenched, she nodded.

"God!" He had her by both arms, nearly lifting her off her feet before he backed her into the counter. The fury in his eyes would have made her cringe if she hadn't been willing to accept it. "How could you? Damn you, she's ours and you never told me. You married another man and had our baby. Did you lie to him too? Did you make him think she was his so you could have your cozy house and lace curtains?"

"Jason, please—"

"I had a right." He thrust her away before he could give into the violence that pushed him on. "I had a right to her. Ten years. You stole that from me."

"No! No it wasn't like that. Jason, please! You have to listen!"

"The hell with you." He said it calmly, so calmly she stepped back as though she'd been slapped. The anger she could argue with, even reason with. Quiet rage left her helpless.

"Please, let me try to explain."

"There's nothing you can say that could make up for it. Nothing." He yanked his coat from the wall and stormed out.

"You're a damn fool, Jason Law." The Widow Marchant sat in her kitchen rocker and scowled.

"She lied to me. She's been lying for years."

"Hogwash." She fiddled with the tinsel on the little tree on the stand by the window. Cheerful strains from the Nutcracker floated in from the living room.

"She did what she had to do, nothing more, nothing less."

He prowled around the room. He still wasn't sure why he'd come there instead of heading for Clancy's Bar. He'd walked in the snow for an hour, maybe more, then found himself standing on the widow's doorstep. "You knew, didn't you? You knew I was Clara's father."

"I had my ideas." The rocker squeaked gently as she moved. "She had the look of you."

That brought a peculiar thrill, one he didn't know what to do with. "She's the image of Faith."

"True enough if you don't look hard. The eyebrows are you, and the mouth. The sweet Lord knows the temperament is. Jason, if you'd known you were to be a father ten years back, what would you have done?"

"I'd have come back for her." He turned, dragging a hand through his hair. "I'd have panicked," he said more calmly. "But I'd have come back."

"I always thought so. But it—well, it's Faith's story to tell. You'd best go on back and hear it."

"It doesn't matter."

"Can't stand a martyr," she muttered.

He started to snap, then sighed instead. "It hurts. It really hurts."

"That's life for you," she said not unsympathetically. "Want to lose them both again?"

"No. God, no. But I don't know how much I can forgive."

The old woman raised both brows. "Fair enough. Give Faith the same courtesy."

Before he could speak again, the kitchen door burst open. In the doorway stood Faith, covered with snow, face washed with tears. Ignoring the wet she brought in with her, she ran to Jason. "Clara," she managed to stammer.

When he took her arms he felt the shudders. Terror flowed from her into him. "What's happened?"

"She's missing."

Chapter Nine

"They're going to find her." Jason held her arm as they both stumbled through the snow to her car. "They probably have already."

"One of the kids said he thought she and Marcie went behind this farmhouse to look at the horses in the barn. But when they went back, they weren't there. It's dark." Faith fumbled with her keys.

"Let me drive."

She gave him no argument as she climbed in the passenger side. "Lorna and Bill called the sheriff from the farmhouse. Half the town's out there looking for them. But there's so much snow, and they're just little girls. Jason—"

He took her face in his hands, firmly. "We're going to find them."

"Yes." She wiped away tears with the heels of her hands. "Let's hurry."

He couldn't risk more than thirty miles an hour. They crept down the snow-covered road, searching the landscape for any sign. The hills and fields lay pristine and undisturbed. To Faith they looked unrelenting. But while fear still overwhelmed her, she'd conquered the tears.

Ten miles out of town the fields were lit up like noonday. Groups of cars crisscrossed the road and men and women tramped through the snow calling. Jason had barely stopped when Faith was out and running toward the sheriff.

"We haven't found them yet, Faith, but we will. They won't have gone far."

"You've searched the barn and the outbuildings?"

The sheriff nodded at Jason. "Every inch."

"How about in the other direction?"

"I'm going to send some men that way."

"We'll go now."

The snow was blinding as he weaved through the other cars. He slackened his speed even more and started to pray. He'd been on a search party once in the Rockies. He hadn't forgotten what a few hours in the wind and snow could do.

"I should have made her wear another sweater." Faith gripped her hands together in her lap as she strained to see out the window. In her hurry she'd forgotten her gloves but didn't notice her numb fingers. "She hates it so when I fuss and I didn't want to spoil the evening for her. Christmas is so special for Clara. She's been so excited." Her voice broke as a ripple of fear became a wave. "I should have made her wear another sweater. She'll be— *Stop!*"

The car fishtailed as he hit the brakes. It took every ounce of control for him to deal with the swerve. Faith pushed open the door and stumbled out. "Over there, it's—"

"It's a dog." He had her by the arms before she could run across the empty field. "It's a dog, Faith."

"Oh, God." Beyond control, she collapsed against him. "She's just a little girl. Where could she be? Oh,

Jason, where is she? I should have gone with her. If I'd been there she—"

"Stop it!"

"She's cold and she must be frightened."

"And she needs you." He gave her a quick shake. "She needs you."

Struggling for control, she pressed a hand to her mouth. "Yes. Yes, I'm all right. Let's go. Let's go a little further."

"You wait in the car. I'm going to walk across this field for a bit and see if I spot something."

"I'll go with you."

"I can move faster alone. I'll only be a few minutes." He started to urge her toward the car when a flash of red caught his eye. "Over there."

He gripped her arm as he tried to see through the snow. Just at the edge of the field, he saw it again.

"It's Clara." Faith was already struggling away. "She has a red coat." Snow kicked up around her as she ran. It fell cold and wet to mix with the tears that blinded her vision. With all the breath she had she called out. Arms spread wide, she caught both girls to her. "Oh God, Clara, I've been so scared. Here, here now, you're frozen, both of you. We'll get to the car. Everything's going to be fine. Everything's all right now."

"Is my mom mad?" Shivering, Marcie wept against her shoulder.

"No, no, she's just worried. Everyone is."

"Up you go." Jason hauled Clara up in his arms. For one brief minute he gave himself the luxury of nuzzling his daughter. Looking back, he saw Faith gathering up Marcie. "Can you manage?"

She smiled, holding the still weeping girl close. "No problem."

"Then let's go home."

"We didn't mean to get lost." Clara's tears ran down his collar.

"Of course you didn't."

"We just went to look at the horses and we got all turned around. We couldn't find anybody. I wasn't scared." Her breath hitched as she pressed against him. "Just Marcie."

His child. He felt his own vision blur as he wrapped his arms tighter around her. "You're both safe now."

"Mom was crying."

"She's okay too." He stopped at the car. "Can you handle them both on your lap in the front? They'll be warmer."

"Absolutely." After Faith had settled in with Marcie, Jason handed her Clara. For one long moment, their gazes held over her head.

"We couldn't find the lights of the house with all the snow," Clara murmured as she held onto her mother. "Then we couldn't find the road for the longest time. It was so cold. I didn't lose my hat."

"I know, baby. Here, get your wet mittens off. You, too, Marcie. Jason has the heater turned all the way up. You'll be cooked before you know it." She ran kisses over two cold faces and fought the need to break down. "What Christmas carols did you sing?"

"Jingle Bells," Marcie said with a sniffle.

"Ah, one of my favorites."

"And Joy to the World," Clara put in. The heater was pumping warm air over her hands and face. "You like that one better."

"So I do but I can't remember just how it starts. How does it start, Marcie?" She smiled at Clara and snuggled her closer.

In a thin, piping voice still wavery with tears Marcie started to sing. She was nearly through the first verse when they came to the rest of the search party.

"It's my dad!" Bouncing on Faith's lap, Marcie started to wave. "He doesn't look mad."

With a half laugh, Faith kissed the top of her head. "Merry Christmas, Marcie."

"Merry Christmas, Mrs. Monroe. See you tomorrow, Clara." Marcie barely had time to open the door before she was scooped up.

"What a night." There were waves and cheers as the car weaved through the crowd.

"It's Christmas Eve," Clara reminded her mother. The world was safe and warm again. "Maybe I should open that one big present tonight."

"Not a chance," Jason told her and tugged at her hair.

Faith turned Clara in her arms and squeezed tight.

"Don't cry, Mom."

"I have to, for just a minute." True to her word, her eyes were dry when they arrived home. An exhausted Clara dozed on Jason's shoulder as he carried her inside. "I'll take her up, Jason."

"We'll take her up."

She let her arms fall back to her sides and nodded.

They pulled off boots and socks and sweaters and wrapped Clara in warm flannel. She murmured a bit and tried to stay awake but the adventures of the evening took their toll. "It's Christmas Eve," she mumbled. "I'm going to get up real early in the morning."

"As early as you like," Faith told her as she pressed a kiss to her cheek.

"Can I have cookies for breakfast?"

"Half a dozen," Faith agreed recklessly. She smiled and was asleep before Faith pulled the blankets around her.

"I was afraid..." She let her hand linger on her daughter's cheek. "I was afraid I'd never see her like this again. Safe, warm. Jason, I don't know how to thank you for just being there. If I'd been alone—" She broke off and shook her head.

"I think we should go downstairs, Faith."

The tone made her press her lips together. She'd be ready, she promised herself, to handle the accusations, the bitterness, the resentment. "I think I'd like a drink," she said as they walked downstairs. "Some brandy. It looks like the fire's gone out."

"I'll take care of it. You get the brandy. There are some things I have to say."

"All right." She left him to go to the little cabinet in the dining room. When she came back, the fire was just catching. He straightened from it and took a snifter.

"Do you want to sit down?"

"No, I can't." She sipped, but it would have taken more than brandy to steady her nerves. "Whatever you have to say, Jason, you should say it."

Chapter Ten

She stood looking at him, her back straight, her eyes burning with emotion, her hands clasping the snifter tightly. Part of him wanted to go to her, gather her close and just hold on. He'd found a child and nearly lost her in the same night. Did anything else matter? But inside was a void that had to be filled. Questions, demands, accusations had to be answered. There had to be an accounting before there could be understanding, and understanding before there could be forgiveness. But where did he start?

He walked to the tree. There was a star on top that shed silver light over all the other colors. "I'm not sure I know what to say. It isn't every day a man turns around and finds himself with a half-grown daughter. I feel cheated out of watching her learn to walk, hearing her talk, Faith. Nothing you can do or say can ever give that back to me, can it?"

"No."

He turned to see her holding the brandy at waist level. Her face was very pale and calm. Whatever emotions she was feeling she managed to restrain. Yes, this was a different Faith than the one he'd left. The girl would never have been able to exert the self-control the woman did. "No excuses, Faith?"

"I guess I thought I had them, then tonight when I thought I'd lost her..." Her voice trailed off and she shook her head. "No excuses, Jason."

"She thinks Tom's her father."

"No!" Her eyes weren't calm now but brilliant. "Do you think I'd let her believe her father had deserted her, that he didn't care enough even to write? What she knows is basically the truth. I never lied to her."

"What is the truth?"

She took a steadying breath. When she looked at him her face was still pale but her voice was calm again. "That I loved her father, and he loved me, but he had to go away before he even knew about her and he wasn't able to come back."

"He would have."

Something rushed into her eyes but she turned away. "I told her that too."

"Why?" The fury came back and he fought against it. "I have to know why you did what you did. I lost all those years."

"You?" Her temper was less easily controlled than her grief. Years of holding back bubbled inside her and burst out. "*You* lost?" she repeated as she whirled around. "You were gone and I was eighteen years old, pregnant and alone."

Guilt flared. He hadn't expected it. "I wouldn't have left if you'd told me."

"I didn't know." She put the brandy down and pushed back her hair with both hands. "It was just a week after you'd gone that I found out I was carrying our baby. I was thrilled." With a laugh, she wrapped her arms around her chest. For a moment she looked heartbreakingly young and innocent. "I was so happy. I waited every day, every night for you to call so I could tell you." Her eyes sobered. The smile faded. "But you never called, Jason."

"I needed time to set things up—a steady job, a place I could ask you to live in."

"You never understood it didn't matter where I lived, as long as it was with you." She shook her head before he could speak. "It doesn't matter now. That part's over. A week passed, then two, then a month. I got ill, just tension, morning sickness, but I began to realize you weren't going to call. You weren't coming back. I was angry for a while, acknowledging you just hadn't wanted me enough. Small-town girl."

"That's not true. That was never true."

She studied him a moment, almost dispassionately. The lights of the tree fell over his dark-blond hair, glimmered in the deep, deep eyes that had always held their own secrets. Restlessness. "Wasn't it?" she murmured. "It was certainly true that you wanted out. I was part of Quiet Valley and you wanted out."

"I wanted you with me."

"But not enough to let me go with you." She shook her head when he started to speak. "Not enough to let me come to you until you'd proved the things you needed to prove. I didn't always understand that, Jason, but I began to when you came back."

"You weren't ever going to tell me about Clara, were you?"

She heard the bitterness again and closed her eyes against it. "I don't know. I honestly don't."

He drank, hoping it would warm the ice in his veins. "Tell me the rest."

"I wanted the baby, but I was scared, too scared even to tell my mother."

She picked up the brandy again but merely warmed her hands with it. "I should have of course, but I wasn't thinking clearly."

"Why did you marry Tom?" But even as he asked, he realized the old jealousies were fading. He only wanted to understand.

"Tom would come by almost every night. We'd talk. He didn't seem to mind me talking about you and God knows I needed to. Then one night we were sitting on the porch and I just broke down. I was three months pregnant and my body was changing. That morning I hadn't been able to snap my jeans." With a shaky laugh, she ran a hand over her face. "It sounds so silly, but I hadn't been able to snap my jeans and it was terrifying. It made me realize there was no going back. Everything just poured out while we sat there. He said he'd marry me. Of course I said no, but he began to reason it all out. You weren't coming back and I was pregnant. He loved me and wanted to marry me. The baby would have a name, a home, a family. It sounded so right the way he said it and I wanted the baby to be safe. I wanted to be safe."

She drank now because her throat ached. "It was wrong, right from the beginning. He knew I didn't love him, but he just wanted me, or thought he did. The first few months he tried, we both really tried. But after Clara came, he couldn't handle it. I could see every time he looked at her he thought of you. There was nothing I could do to change the fact that she was yours." She paused and found it easier to say it all. "There was nothing I would have done to change that. As long as I had her, I had part of you. Tom knew it, no matter how much I tried to be what he wanted. He started drinking, picking fights, staying out. It was as though he wanted me to ask for a divorce."

"But you didn't."

"I didn't because I . . . well, I felt I owed him. Then one day I came home from taking Clara out and he was gone. Divorce papers came in the mail, and that was that."

"Why didn't you ever try to contact me, Faith, through one of the magazines or newspapers?"

"And say what? Jason, remember me? By the way, you have a daughter back here in Quiet Valley. Drop in some time."

"One word—one word from you and I'd have left everything and come back. I never stopped loving you."

She closed her eyes. "I watched you walk away from me. I watched you get on the bus and leave me without a trace. I stood there for hours, half believing you'd get off at the next stop and come back. I was the one who had to stay behind, Jason."

"I called. Damn it, Faith, it only took me six months to get something started."

She smiled. "And when you called I was seven months pregnant. My mother didn't tell me for a long time, not until after Tom had left. She said you made her promise."

"I needed my pride."

"I know."

That she didn't question. He saw the way she smiled as she said it, as if she'd always understood. "You must have been terrified."

Her smile softened. "There were moments."

"You must have hated me."

"Never. How could I? You went away but you left me with the most beautiful thing in my life. Maybe you were right, maybe I was. Maybe we were both wrong, but there was Clara. Every time I looked at her, I could remember how much I loved you."

"How do you feel now?"

"Shaky." She laughed a little, then folded her hands, determined to do what was right. "Clara should be told. I'd prefer doing it myself."

The idea made him reach for the brandy again. "How do you think she'll take it?"

"She's learned to get along without a father. It doesn't mean she hasn't needed one." She sat up straight and raised her chin. "You have a right, of course, to see her whenever you like, but I won't have her bounced around. I also realize you can't be here for her all the time because of your work, but don't think you can just pop into her life and out again. You'll have to make an effort, to keep in touch with her Jason."

So this was another fear she'd lived with, he realized. Maybe he deserved it. "You don't trust me, do you?"

"Clara's too important." She let out a little sigh. "So are you."

"If I told you I fell for her before I knew, would it make a difference?"

She thought of the toboggan, of the way he'd looked when Clara had thrown her arms around his neck. "She needs all the love she can get. We all do. She's so much like you, I—" She broke off when her eyes filled. "Damn, I don't want to do this." Impatient, she brushed tears away. "I'll tell her tomorrow, Jason. On Christmas. You and I can work out the arrangements. I know you're leaving soon, but if you could stay a few more days, give her some time, it would make it easier for all of us."

He rubbed at the tension at the back of his neck. "You never asked me for much of anything, did you?"

She smiled. "I asked you for everything. We were both too young to realize it."

"You always believed in magic, Faith." He pulled a box out of his pocket. "It's nearly midnight. Open it now."

"Jason." She pushed her hands through her hair. How could he think of presents now? "I don't think this is the time."

"It's ten years past time."

When he thrust the box at her she found herself gripping it with both hands. "I don't have anything to give you."

He touched her face, almost hesitantly. "You've just given me a daughter."

Relief poured through her. Instead of bitterness, she heard gratitude. Love, never dimmed, shimmered in her eyes. "Jason—"

"Please, open it."

She pulled off the glossy red paper and revealed the black velvet box beneath. With fingers not quite steady she opened it. The ring was a teardrop, frozen in place, glorious with the reflected lights from the tree.

"Paul told me it was the best he had."

"You bought this before you knew—"

"Yeah, before I knew I was going to ask the mother of my child to marry me. We'll be legal, the three of us." He took her hand and waited. "How about a second chance? I won't let you down, Faith."

"You never did." Close to tears again, she reached out her hand to his cheek. "It wasn't you, it wasn't me, it was life. Oh, Jason, I want this. Understand, all I've ever really wanted was to be married to you, have a family with you."

"Then let me put the ring on."

"Jason, it's not just me. If it were I'd leave with you this instant. We'd go to Hong Kong, Siberia, Peking. Anywhere. But it's not just me; I have to stay."

"It's not just you," he repeated. He took the ring and tossed the box aside. "And *I* have to stay. Do you think I'd leave you again? Do you think I could leave what's upstairs or the chance to have more that I can watch grow up? I'm not going anywhere."

"But you said—Hong Kong."

"I quit." When he grinned he felt the pressure of years melt away. "Today. That was one of the things I took care of this afternoon. I'm going to write a book." He took her by the shoulders. "I'm out of a job, I'm living in a room at the inn and asking you to marry me."

The breath backed up in her lungs. Her heart was pounding. Yes, she'd always believed in magic. It was standing in front of her. "Ten years ago, I thought I loved you as much as it was possible to love. You were a boy. In the last few days I've learned that loving a man is something quite different." She paused and saw the ring in his hand explode with the joyful lights on the tree. "If you'd asked me ten years ago I'd have said yes."

"Faith—"

With a laugh, she threw her arms around his neck. "You're going to get the same answer now. Oh, I love you, Jason, more than ever."

"We've got years to make up for."

"Yes." She met his mouth with equal hunger, equal hope. "We will. The three of us."

"The three of us." He let his forehead rest against hers. "I want more."

"We've more than enough time to give Clara a baby brother or sister for next Christmas." Her lips sought his again. "We've got more than enough time for everything."

They both heard the bells peal out from the town hall. Midnight.

"Merry Christmas, Faith."

She felt the ring slide onto her finger. All wishes were granted. "Welcome home, Jason."

* * * * *

A Note from Nora Roberts

When the idea of writing a Christmas story was first suggested, I was excited. I'm a sucker for all of the seasonal trimmings and I become unabashedly sentimental. A carol remembered since childhood can make me sniffle. The movie *It's A Wonderful Life* still makes me cry. Buckets. So I very much wanted to write a Christmas story, something sentimental and happy-ever-after, because the holidays are the time for wishes coming true. The only problem was to come up with the idea.

As it happened, I was just working out my Christmas story when I saw a commercial on TV, a coffee commercial, I think, where a woman was making a doll, and a man—lover, husband, stranger, I'm not sure—watched her. I saw my own heroine and hero sharing something that simple and the rest fell into place.

I hope you enjoy *Home for Christmas,* and can share the spirit in which it was written. My wish is for all of you to experience the goodwill, excitement and wide-eyed wonder that make Christmas the most special time of year.

Happy Holidays,

Nora Roberts

Let it Snow

Debbie Macomber

For Joyce Beaman
Fellow author, fortune cookie collector
and above all, dear friend.

ROYAL ICING

1 lb powdered sugar
3 egg whites
½ teaspoon cream of tartar
½ teaspoon vanilla

Beat until very stiff and color with paste or gel, then fill frosting bags. Decorate using size 7 icing tips.

Chapter One

"Ladies and gentlemen, this is your captain speaking."

Shelly Griffin's fingers compressed around the armrest until her neatly manicured nails threatened to cut into the fabric of the airplane seat. Flying had never thrilled her, and she avoided planes whenever possible. It had taken her the better part of a month to convince herself that she'd be perfectly safe. She told herself that the Boeing 727 would take off without incident from San Francisco and land unscathed ninety minutes later in Seattle. Flying, after all, was said to be relatively riskless. But if it wasn't Christmas, if she wasn't so homesick and if she'd had more than four days off, she would have done anything to get home for the holidays—except fly.

"Seattle reports heavy snow and limited visibility," the captain continued. "We've been rerouted to Portland International until the Seattle runways can be cleared."

A low groan filled the plane.

Shelly relaxed. Snow. She could handle snow. She wasn't overjoyed with the prospect of having to land twice, but she was so close to home now that she would have willingly suffered anything to see a welcoming smile light up her father's eyes.

In an effort to divert her thoughts away from impending tragedy, Shelly studied the passengers around her. A grandmotherly type slept sedately in the seat beside her. The man sitting across the aisle was such a classic businessman that he was intriguing. Almost from the moment they'd left San Francisco, he'd been working out of his briefcase. He hadn't so much as cracked a smile during the entire flight. The captain's announcement had produced little more than a disgruntled flicker in his staid exterior.

Shelly had seen enough men like him in her job as a reporter in the federal court to catalog him quickly. Polished. Professional. Impeccable. Handsome, too, Shelly supposed, if she was interested, which she wasn't. She preferred her men a little less intense. She managed to suppress a tight laugh. Men! What men? In the ten months she'd been living in the City by the Bay, she hadn't exactly developed a following. A few interesting prospects now and again but nothing serious.

As the Boeing 727 slowly made its descent, Shelly's fingers gripped the armrest with renewed tension. Her gaze skimmed the emergency exits as she reviewed affirmations on the safety of flying. She mumbled them under her breath as the plane angled sharply to the right, aligning its giant bulk with the narrow runway ahead.

Keeping her eyes centered on the seat in front of her, Shelly held her breath until she felt the wheels gently bounce against the runway in a flawless landing. A burst of noise accompanied the aircraft as it slowed to a crawl.

The oxygen rushed from Shelly's lungs in a heart-felt sigh of relief. Somehow the landings were so much worse than the takeoffs. As the tension eased from her rigid body, she looked around to discover the businessman slanting his idle gaze over her. His dark eyes contained a look of surprise. He seemed amazed that anyone could be afraid of flying, and he was utterly indifferent to her apprehension. The blood mounted briefly in her pale features, and Shelly decided she definitely didn't like this cheerless executive.

The elderly woman sitting next to her placed a hand on Shelly's forearm. "Are you all right, dear?"

"Of course." Relief throbbed in her voice. Now that they were on the ground, she could feign the compo-sure that seemed to come so easily to the other pas-sengers.

"I hope we aren't delayed long. My daughter's tak-ing off work to meet my flight."

"My dad's forty minutes from the airport," Shelly murmured, hoping that he'd called the airline to check if her flight was on time. She hated the thought of him anxiously waiting for her.

The other woman craned her neck to peek out the small side window. "It doesn't seem to be snowing much here. Just a few flakes floating down like lazy goose feathers."

Shelly grinned at the verbal picture. "Let's hope it stays that way."

She remained seated while several of the other pas-sengers got up and left the plane. The businessman was among those who quickly vacated their seats. From what the captain had said, they wouldn't be in

Portland long, and Shelly didn't want to take a chance of missing the flight.

After checking her watch every ten minutes for forty minutes, Shelly was convinced that they'd never leave Oregon. The blizzard had hit the area, and whirling snow buffeted the quiet plane with growing intensity. Her anxieties mounted with equal force.

"This is the captain speaking." His faint Southern drawl filled the plane. "Unfortunately, Seattle reports that visibility hasn't improved. They're asking that we remain here in Portland for another half hour, possibly longer."

Frustration and disappointment erupted from the passengers seated on the plane, and they all began speaking at once.

"This is the captain again," the pilot added, his low drawl riddled with wry humor. "I'd like to remind those of you who are upset by our situation that it's far better to be on the ground wishing you were in the sky than to be in the sky *praying* you were on the ground."

Shelly added a silent amen to that! As it was, she was beginning to feel claustrophobic trapped inside the plane. Unsnapping her seat belt, she stood, reached for her purse and headed down the narrow aisle toward the front of the plane.

"Do I have time to make a phone call?"

"Sure," the flight attendant answered with a cordial smile. "Don't be long, though. The conditions in Seattle could change quickly."

"I won't," Shelly promised and made her way into the airport terminal.

It wasn't until she was sorting through her purse for change that she noted the unsympathetic businessman from her flight had the phone booth adjacent to hers.

"This is Slade Garner again," he announced with the faintest trace of impatience creeping into his voice. "My plane's still in Portland."

A pause followed while Shelly dumped the contents of her coin purse into her hand and scowled. She didn't have change for the phone.

"Yes, yes, I understand the snow's a problem on your end as well," he continued smoothly. "I doubt that I'll make it in this afternoon. Perhaps we should arrange the meeting for first thing tomorrow morning. Nine o'clock?" Another pause. "Of course I realize it's the day before Christmas."

Rummaging in her purse for a quarter, Shelly managed to dredge up a token for the cable car, a dried peach pit and a lost button.

Pressing her lips tightly together, she mused what a coldhearted tycoon this businessman had to be to insist upon a meeting so close to Christmas. Instantly she felt guilty because her thoughts were so judgmental. Of course he'd want to keep his appointment. He certainly hadn't taken this flight for his health. Her second regret was that she had intentionally eavesdropped on his conversation, looking for excuses to justify her dislike of him. Such behavior was hardly in keeping with the Christmas spirit.

Pasting on a pleasant smile, Shelly stepped forward when Slade Garner replaced the receiver. Abruptly he turned around.

"Excuse me." His gaze refused to meet hers, and for a second Shelly didn't think that he'd heard her.

"Yes?" His expression was bored, frustrated.

"Have you got change for a dollar?" She unfolded a crisp one-dollar bill, anticipating the exchange.

Slade uninterestedly checked the contents of his pocket, glaring down at the few coins in his palm. "Sorry." Dispassionately he tucked them back in his pocket and turned away from her.

Shelly was ready to approach someone else when Slade turned back to her. His dark brows drew together in a frown as something about her registered in his preoccupied thoughts. "You were on the Seattle flight?"

"Yes."

"Here." He handed her a quarter.

The corners of Shelly's mouth curved up in surprise. "Thanks." She was convinced that he hadn't heard her as he briskly walked away. Shelly didn't know what difference it made that they'd shared the same plane. Without analyzing his generosity any further, she dropped the coin in the slot.

After connecting with the operator, Shelly shifted her weight from one foot to the other while the phone rang, waiting for her father to answer.

"Dad."

"Merry Christmas, Shortcake."

Her father had bestowed this affectionate title on Shelly when she was a young teen and her friends had sprouted around her. To her dismay Shelly had remained a deplorable five foot until she was seventeen. Then within six months she had grown five inches. Her height and other attributes of puberty had been hormonal afterthoughts.

"I'm in Portland."

"I know. When I phoned Sea-Tac, the lady at the reservation desk told me you'd been forced to land there. How are you doing?"

"Fine." She fibbed about her dread of flying. "I'm sorry about the delay."

"That's not your fault."

"But I hate wasting precious hours sitting here when I could be with you."

"Don't worry about it. We'll have plenty of time together."

"Have you decorated the tree yet?" Since her mother's death three years before, Shelly and her father had made a ritual of placing the homemade ornaments on the tree together.

"I haven't even bought one. I thought we'd do that first thing in the morning."

Shelly closed her eyes, savoring the warmth of love and security that the sound of her father's voice always gave her. "I've got a fantastic surprise for you."

"What's that?" her father prompted.

"It wouldn't be a surprise if I told you, would it?"

Her father chuckled and Shelly could visualize him rubbing his finger over his upper lip the way he did when something amused him.

"I've missed you, Dad."

"I know. I've missed you, too."

"Take care."

"I will." She was about to hang up. "Dad," she added hastily, her thoughts churning as her gaze focused on a huge wall advertisement for a rental car agency. "Listen, don't go the the airport until I phone."

"But—"

"By the time you arrive, I'll have collected my things and be waiting outside for you. That way you won't have to park."

"I don't mind, Shortcake."

"I know, but it'll work better this way."

"If you insist."

"I do." Her brothers claimed that their father was partial to his only daughter. It was a long-standing family joke that she was the only one capable of swaying him once he'd made a decision. "I do insist."

They said their goodbyes, and after Shelly disconnected the line, she checked for the quarter that had slipped into the change slot. Feeling light-hearted and relieved, she flipped it in the air with a flick of her thumb and caught it with a dexterity that surprised her. Instead of heading down the concourse toward the plane, she ventured in the opposite direction, taking the escalators to the lower level and the rental car agencies.

To her surprise Shelly found that she wasn't the only one with alternate transportation in mind. The businessman who had loaned her the quarter was talking with a young man at the first agency. Shelly walked past him to the second counter.

"How much would it cost to rent a car here and drop it off in Seattle?" she asked brightly.

The tall, college-aged woman hardly looked up from the computer screen. "Sorry, we don't have any cars available."

"None?" Shelly found that hard to believe.

"Lots of people have had the same idea as you," the clerk explained. "A plane hasn't landed in Seattle in hours. No one wants to sit around the airport waiting. Especially at Christmas."

"Thanks, anyway." Shelly scooted down to the third agency and repeated her question.

"Yes, we do," the clerk said with a wide grin. "We only have one car available at the moment." She named a sum that caused Shelly to swallow heavily. But already the idea had gained momentum in her mind. Every minute the plane remained on the ground robbed her of precious time with her father. And from what he'd told her, the snow was coming down fast and furiously. It could be hours before the plane was able to take off. She freely admitted that another landing at another airport in the middle of the worst snowstorm of the year wasn't her idea of a good time. As it was, her Christmas bonus was burning a hole in her purse. It was a good cause. Surely there was some unwritten rule that stated every favorite daughter should spend Christmas with her father.

"If she doesn't take the car, I will." Slade Garner spoke from beside Shelly. A wide, confident smile spread across his handsome features.

"I want it," she cried. His aura of self-assurance bordered on arrogance.

"I have to get to Seattle."

"So do I!" she informed him primly. In case he mentioned that he'd loaned her the quarter, she pulled it from her jacket pocket and handed it to him.

"I've got an important meeting."

"As a matter of fact, so do I." Turning back to the counter, Shelly picked up a pen and prepared to fill in the rental form.

"How much?" Slade asked. His features tightened with unrelenting resolve that negated his manly appeal.

"I beg your pardon?"

"How much do you want for the car?" His hand slipped into the pocket of his suit coat, apparently prepared to pay her price.

Squaring her shoulders with angry frustration, Shelly exchanged looks with the clerk. "Get your own car."

"There's only one car available. This one."

"And I've got it," she told him with a deceptively calm smile. The more she saw of this man, the more aggravating he became.

His jaw tightened. "I don't think you understand," he said and breathed out with sharp impatience. "My meeting's extremely important."

"So is mine. I'm—"

"You could share the car," the clerk suggested, causing both Shelly and Slade to divert their shocked gazes to the impromptu peacemaker.

Shelly hesitated.

Slade's brows arched. "I'll pay the full fee for the car," he offered.

"You mention money one more time and the deal's off," she shot back hotly.

"Don't be unreasonable."

"I'm not being unreasonable. You are."

Slade rubbed a hand along the back of his neck and forcefully expelled his breath. "Have we or have we not got a deal?"

"I'm not going to Seattle."

He gave her a sharp look of reproach. "I just heard you say Seattle."

"I'm headed for Maple Valley. That's in south King County."

"Fine. I'll drop you off and deliver the car to the rental place myself."

That would save her one hassle. Still, she hesitated. Two minutes together and they were already arguing. Shelly wondered how they'd possibly manage three hours cooped up in the close confines of a car.

"Listen," he argued, his voice tinged with exasperation. "If I make it into Seattle this afternoon, I might be able to get this meeting over with early. That way I can be back in San Francisco for Christmas."

Quickly he'd discerned the weakest link in her chain of defenses and had aimed there. Christmas and home were important to her.

"All right," she mumbled. "But I'll pay my share of the fee."

"Whatever you want, lady."

For the first time since she'd seen him, Slade Garner smiled.

Chapter Two

"What about your luggage?" Slade asked as they strolled down the concourse toward the plane.

"I only have one bag. It's above my seat." Honey-brown hair curled around her neck, and she absently lifted a strand and looped it over her ear. A farm girl's wardrobe didn't fit in with the formal business attire she needed in San Francisco so Shelly had left most of her clothes with her father. Now she realized that having packed light was a blessing in disguise. At least there wouldn't be the hassle of trying to get her suitcase back.

Shelly's spirits buoyed up; she was heading home and she wasn't flying!

"Good. I only have a garment bag with me."

Shelly hesitated. "I have another bag filled with presents."

Slade's gaze briefly scanned hers. "That shouldn't be any problem."

When he sees the monstrosity, he might change his mind, Shelly mused good-naturedly. In addition to a variety of odd-sized gifts, she had brought her father several long loaves of sourdough bread. The huge package was awkward, and Shelly had required the flight attendant's assistance to place it in the compartment above her seat. Normally Shelly would have checked a bundle that size with the airline. But with the long loaves of bread sticking out like doughy antennas, that had been impossible.

The plane was nearly empty when they boarded, confirming her suspicion that the delay was going to be far longer than originally anticipated. Checking her watch, she discovered that it was nearly noon. The other passengers had probably gone to get something to eat.

Standing on the cushioned seat beside hers, Shelly opened the storage compartment.

"Do you need help?" Slade asked. A dark gray garment bag was folded neatly over his forearm.

"Here." Shelly handed him her one small bag. She heard him mumble something about appreciating a woman who packed light and smiled to herself.

Straining to stretch as far as she could to get a good grip on her package, she heard Slade grumble.

"Look at what some idiot put up there."

"Pardon?"

"That bag. Good grief, people should know better than to try to force a tuba case up there."

"That's mine and it isn't a tuba case." Extracting the bag containing the bread, she handed it down to him.

Slade looked at it as if something were about to leap out and bite him. "Good heavens, what is this?"

What is it! Bread had to be the most recognizable item in the world. And to have it shaped in long, thin loaves wasn't that unusual, either!

"A suitcase for a snake," she replied sarcastically.

The beginnings of a grin touched his usually impassive features as he gently moved in front of her. "Let me get that thing down before you fall."

Shelly climbed down from the cushioned seat. "Suitcase for a snake, huh?" Unexpectedly Slade Garner smiled, and the effect on Shelly was dazzling. She had the feeling that this man didn't often take the time to laugh and enjoy life. Only minutes before she'd classified him as cheerless and intense. But when he smiled, the carefully guarded facade cracked and she was given a rare glimpse of the intriguing man inside. And he fascinated her.

By the time they'd cleared their tickets with the airline, the courtesy car from the rental agency had arrived to deliver them to their rented vehicle.

"I put everything in my name," Slade said on a serious note. The snow continued to fall, creating a picturesque view.

"That's fine." He'd taken the small suitcase from her, leaving her to cope with the huge sack filled with Christmas goodies.

"It means I'll be doing all the driving."

One glance at the snowstorm and Shelly was grateful.

"Well?" He looked as though he expected an argument.

"Do you have a driver's license?"

Again a grin cracked the tight line of his mouth, touching his eyes. "Yes."

"Then there shouldn't be any problem."

He paused, looking down on her. "Are you always so witty?"

Shelly chuckled, experiencing a rush of pleasure at her ability to make him smile. "Only when I try to be. Come on, Garner, loosen up. It's Christmas."

"I've got a meeting to attend. Just because it happens to fall close to a holiday doesn't make a whit's difference."

"Yeah, but just think, once you're through, you can hurry home and spend the holidays with your family."

"Right." The jagged edge of his clipped reply was revealing, causing Shelly to wonder if he had a family.

As they deposited their luggage in the trunk of the rented Camaro, Shelly had the opportunity to study Slade. The proud, withdrawn look revealed little of his thoughts; there was an air of independence about him. Even with a minimum of contact, she realized that he must possess a keen and agile mind. He was a man of contrasts—pensive yet decisive, cultured while maintaining a highly organized facade.

Standing in the fallen snow, the young man at the rental agency handed Slade a map of the city and pointed him in the direction of the nearest freeway entrance ramp.

After studying the map thoroughly, Slade handed it to Shelly. "Are you ready?"

"Forward, James," she teased, climbing into the passenger seat and rubbing her bare hands together to generate some warmth. When she'd left San Francisco that morning, she hadn't dressed for snow.

With a turn of the key, Slade started the engine and adjusted the heater. "You'll be warm in a minute."

Shelly nodded, burying her hands in her jacket pockets. "You know, if it gets much colder, we might get snow before we reach Seattle."

"Very funny," he muttered dryly, snapping his seat belt into place. Hands gripping the wheel, Slade hesitated. "Do you want to find a phone and call your husband?"

"I'm visiting my dad," she corrected. "I'm not married. And no. If I told him what we're doing, he'd only worry."

Slade shifted gears and they pulled onto the road.

"Do you want to contact . . . your wife?"

"I'm not married."

"Oh." Shelly prayed that the small expression wouldn't reveal her satisfaction at the information. It wasn't often that she found herself so fascinated by a man. The crazy part was that she wasn't entirely sure she liked him, but he attracted her.

"I'm engaged," he added.

"Oh." She swallowed convulsively. So much for that. "When's the wedding?"

The windshield wipers hummed ominously. "In approximately two years."

Shelly nearly choked in an effort to hide her shock.

"Both Margaret and I have professional and financial goals we hope to accomplish before we marry." He drove with his back stiff, his expression sullen. "Margaret feels we should save fifty thousand dollars before we think about marriage and I agree. We both have strong feelings about having a firm financial foundation."

"I can't imagine waiting two years to marry the man I loved."

"But then you're entirely different from Margaret."

As far as Shelly was concerned, that was the nicest thing anyone had said to her all day. "We do agree on one thing, though. I feel a marriage should last forever." But for Shelly love had to be more spontaneous and far less calculated. "My parents had a marvelous marriage," she said, filling the silence. "I only hope that, when I marry, my own will be as happy." She went on to elaborate how her parents had met one Christmas and were married two months later on Valentine's Day. Their marriage, Shelly told him complacently, had been blessed with love and happiness for nearly twenty-seven years before her mother's unexpected death. It took great restraint not to mention that her parents had barely had twenty dollars between them when they'd taken their vows. At the time her father had been a student of veterinary medicine with only two years of schooling behind him. They'd managed without a huge bank balance.

From the tight lines around his mouth and nose, Shelly could tell that Slade found the whole story trite.

"Is your sweet tale of romance supposed to touch my heart?"

Furious, Shelly straightened and looked out the side window at the snow-covered trees that lined the side of Interstate 5. "No. I was just trying to find out if you had one."

"Karate mouth strikes again," he mumbled.

"Karate mouth?" Shelly was too stunned at Slade's unexpected display of wit to do anything more than repeat his statement.

"You have the quickest comeback of anyone I know." Admiration flashed unchecked in his gaze before he turned his attention back to the freeway.

Shelly was more interested in learning about Margaret so she tried to keep the conversation away from herself. "I imagine you're anxious to get back to spend Christmas with Margaret." She regretted her earlier judgmental attitude toward Slade. He had good reason for wanting this meeting over.

"Margaret's visiting an aunt in Arizona during the holidays. She left a couple of days ago."

"So you won't be together." The more she heard of Margaret, the more curious Shelly became about a woman who would agree to wait two years for marriage. "Did she give you your Christmas gift before she left?" The type of gift one gave was always telling.

Slade hesitated. "Margaret and I agreed to forgo giving gifts this year."

Shelly had barely managed to control her tongue when he had spouted off about his long engagement, but this was too much. "Not exchange gifts? That's terrible."

"We have financial goals," Slade growled irritably. "Wasting money on trivialities simply deters us from our two-year plan. Christmas gifts aren't going to advance our desires."

At the moment Shelly sincerely doubted that good ol' Margaret and Slade had "desires."

"I bet Margaret's just saying she doesn't want a gift," Shelly offered. "She's probably secretly hoping you'll break down and buy her something. It doesn't have to be something big. Any woman appreciates roses."

Her companion gave an expressive shrug. "I thought flowers would be a nice touch myself, but Margaret claims they make her sneeze. Besides, roses at Christmas are terribly expensive. A waste of money, really."

"Naturally," Shelly muttered under her breath. She was beginning to get a clearer picture of this stuffy fellow and his ever-so-practical fiancée.

"Did you say something?" A hint of challenge echoed in his cool tones.

"Not really." Leaning forward, she fiddled with the radio dial, trying to find a station that was playing music. "What's Margaret do, by the way?"

"She's a systems analyst."

Shelly arched both eyebrows in mute comment. This was the type of occupation that she expected from a nuts-and-bolts person like Margaret. "What about children?"

"What about them?"

Shelly realized that she was prying, but she couldn't help herself. "Are you planning a family?"

"Of course. We're hoping that Margaret can schedule a leave of absence in eight years."

"You'll be near forty!" The exclamation burst from her lips before Shelly could hold it back.

"Forty-one, actually. Do you disapprove of that, too?"

Shelly swallowed uncomfortably and paid an inordinate amount of attention to the radio, not understanding why she couldn't get any music. "I apologize, I didn't mean to sound so judgmental. It's just that—"

"It's just that you've never been goal oriented."

"But I have," she argued. "I've always wanted to be a court reporter. It's a fascinating job."

"I imagine that you're good at anything you put your mind to."

The unexpected compliment caught her completely off guard. "What a nice thing to say."

"If you put your mind to it, you might figure out why you can't get the radio working."

Her gaze flickered automatically from Slade to the dial. Before she could comment, he reached over and twisted a knob. "It's a bit difficult to pick up the transmission waves when the radio isn't turned on."

"Right." She'd been too preoccupied with asking about Margaret to notice. Color flooded into her cheeks at her own stupidity. Slade flustered her and that hadn't happened in a long time. She had the feeling that, in a battle of words, he would parry her barbs as expertly as a professional swordsman.

Soft, soothing music filled the car. Warm and snug, Shelly leaned back against the headrest and cushioned seat and hummed along, gazing at the flakes of falling snow.

"With the snow and all it really feels like Christmas," she murmured, fearing more questions would destroy the tranquil mood.

"It's caused nothing but problems."

"I suppose, but it's so lovely."

"Of course it's lovely. You're sitting in a warm chauffeur-driven car with the radio playing."

"Grumble, grumble, grumble," she tossed back lightly. "Bah, humbug!"

"Bah, humbug," he echoed, and to her astonishment Slade laughed. The sound of it was rich and full and caused Shelly to laugh with him. When the radio played a Bing Crosby Christmas favorite, Shelly sang along. Soon Slade's deep baritone joined her clear soprano in sweet harmony. The lyrics spoke of dreaming, and Shelly's mind conjured up her own longings. She was comfortable with this man when she'd expected to find a dozen reasons to dislike him. Instead, she discovered that she was attracted to someone who was engaged to another woman. A man who was intensely loyal. This was the usual way her life ran. She was attracted to Slade, but she didn't know where this feeling would lead. She wasn't entirely sure that her insights about him were on base. As uncharitable as it sounded, she may have formed these feelings simply because she considered him too good for someone like Margaret.

Disgusted with herself, Shelly closed her eyes and rested her head against the window. The only sounds were the soft melodies playing on the radio and the discordant swish of the windshield wipers. Occasionally a gust of wind would cause the car to veer slightly.

A gentle hand on her shoulder shook her. "Shelly."

With a start she bolted upright. "What's wrong?"

Slade had pulled over to the shoulder of the freeway. The snow was so thick that Shelly couldn't see two feet in front of her.

"I don't think we can go any further," Slade announced.

Chapter Three

"We can't stay here," Shelly cried, looking at their precarious position beside the road. Snow whirled in every direction. The ferocity of the storm shocked her, whipping and howling around them. She found it little short of amazing that Slade had been able to steer the car at all. While she'd slept, the storm had worsened drastically.

"Do you have any other suggestions?" he said and breathed out sharply.

He was angry, but his irritation wasn't directed at her. Wearily she lifted the hair from her smooth brow. "No, I guess I don't."

Silence seeped around them as Slade turned off the car's engine. Gone was the soothing sound of Christmas music, the hum of the engine and the rhythmic swish of the windshield wipers. Together they sat waiting for the fury to lessen so that they could start up again. Staring out at the surrounding area between bursts of wind and snow, Shelly guessed that they weren't far from Castle Rock and Mount St. Helens.

After ten minutes of uneasiness, she decided to be the first to break the gloom. "Are you hungry?" She stared at the passive, unyielding face beside her.

"No."

"I am."

"Have some of that bread." He cocked his head toward the back seat where she'd stuck the huge loaves of sourdough bread.

"I couldn't eat Dad's bread. He'd never forgive me."

"He'd never forgive you if you starved to death, either."

Glancing down at her pudgy thighs, Shelly sadly shook her head. "There's hardly any chance of that."

"What makes you say that? You're not fat. In fact, I'd say you were just about perfect."

"Me? Perfect?" A burst of embarrassed laughter slid from her throat. Reaching for her purse, she removed her wallet.

"What are you doing?"

"I'm going to pay you for saying that."

Slade chuckled. "What makes you think you're overweight?"

"You mean aside from the fat all over my body?"

"I'm serious."

She shrugged. "I don't know. I just feel chubby. Since leaving home, I don't get enough exercise. I couldn't very well bring Sampson with me."

"Sampson?"

"My horse. I used to ride him every day."

"If you've gained any weight, it's in all the right places."

His gaze fell to her lips, and Shelly's senses churned in quivering awareness. He stared into her dark eyes and blinked as if not believing what he saw. For her part, Shelly studied him with open curiosity. His eyes were smoky dark, his face blunt and sensual. His brow was creased as though he was giving the moment grave consideration. Thick eyebrows arched heavily over his eyes.

Abruptly he pulled his gaze away and leaned forward to start the engine. The accumulated snow on the windshield was brushed aside with a flip of the wiper switch. "Isn't that a McDonald's up ahead?"

Shelly squinted to catch a glimpse of the world-famous golden arches. "Hey, I think it is."

"The exit can't be far."

"Do you think we can make it?"

"I think we'd better," he mumbled.

Shelly understood. The car had become their private cocoon, unexpectedly intimate and highly sensual. Under normal circumstances they wouldn't have given each other more than a passing glance. What was happening wasn't magic but something far more exhilarating.

With the wipers beating furiously against the window, Slade inched the car to the exit, which proved to be less than a half mile away.

Slowly they crawled down the side road that paralleled the freeway. With some difficulty Slade was able to find a place to park in the restaurant's lot. Shelly sighed with relief. This was the worst storm she could remember. Wrapping her coat securely around her, she reached for her purse.

"You ready?" she blurted out, opening the car door.

"Anytime."

Hurriedly Slade joined her and tightly grasped her elbow as they stepped together toward the front entrance of the fast-food restaurant. Pausing just inside the door to stamp the snow from their shoes, they glanced up to note that several other travelers were stranded there as well.

They ordered hamburgers and coffee and sat down by the window.

"How long do you think we'll be here?" Shelly asked, not really expecting an answer. She needed reassurance more than anything. This Christmas holiday hadn't started out on the right foot. But of one thing she was confident—the plane hadn't left Portland yet.

"Your guess is as good as mine."

"I'd say two hours, then," she murmured, taking a bite of her Big Mac.

"Why two hours?"

"I don't know. It sounds reasonable. If it's longer than that, I might start to panic. But, if worse comes to worst, I can think of less desirable places to spend Christmas. At least we won't starve."

Slade muttered something unintelligible under his breath and continued eating. When he finished, he excused himself and returned to the car for his briefcase.

Shelly bought two more cups of coffee and propped her feet on the seat opposite her. Taking the latest issue of *Mad Magazine* from her purse, she was absorbed in it by the time he returned. Her gaze dared him to comment on her reading material. Her reading *Mad Magazine* was a long-standing joke between

Shelly and her father. He expected it of her and read each issue himself so that he could tease her about the contents. Since moving, she'd fallen behind by several months and wanted to be prepared when she saw her dad again. She didn't expect Slade to understand her tastes.

He rejoined her and gave her little more than a conciliatory glance before reclaiming his seat and briskly opening the *Wall Street Journal.*

Their reading choices said a lot about each other, Shelly realized. Rarely had she seen two people less alike. A lump grew in her throat. She liked Slade. He was the type of man she'd willingly give up *Mad Magazine* for.

An hour later a contented Shelly set the December issue aside and reached in her purse for the romance novel that she kept tucked away. It wasn't often that she was so at ease with a man. She didn't feel the overwhelming urge to keep a conversation going or fill the silence with chatter. They were comfortable together.

Without a word she went to the counter and bought a large order of fries and placed them in the middle of the table. Now and then, her eyes never leaving the printed page, she blindly reached for a fry. Once her groping hand bumped another, and her startled gaze collided with Slade's.

''Sorry,'' he muttered.

''Don't be. They're for us both.''

''They get to be addictive, don't they?''

''Sort of like reading the *Wall Street Journal*?''

''I wondered if you'd comment on that.''

Shelly laughed. "I was expecting you to mention my choice."

"*Mad Magazine* is something I'd expect from you." He said it in such a way that Shelly couldn't possibly be offended.

"At least we agree on one thing."

He raised his thick brows in question.

"The French fries."

"Right." Lifting one from the package, he held it out for her.

Shelly leaned toward him and captured the fry in her mouth. The gesture was oddly intimate, and her smile faded as her gaze clashed with Slade's. It was happening again. That heart-pounding, room-fading-away, shallow-breathing syndrome. Obviously this... feeling... had something to do with the weather. Maybe she could blame it on the season of love and goodwill toward all mankind. Shelly, unfortunately, seemed to be overly infected with benevolence this Christmas. Experiencing the sensations she was, heaven only knows what would happen if she spied mistletoe.

Slade raked his hand through his well-groomed hair, mussing it. Quickly he diverted his gaze out the window. "It looks like it might be letting up a little."

"Yes, it does," she agreed without so much as looking out the window. The French fries seemed to demand her full attention.

"I suppose we should think about heading out."

"I suppose." A glance at her watch confirmed that it was well into the afternoon. "I'm sorry about your appointment."

Slade looked at her blankly for a moment. "Oh, that. I knew when I left that there was little likelihood that I'd be able to make it today. That's why I made arrangements to meet tomorrow morning."

"It's been an enjoyable break."

"Very," he agreed.

"Do you think we'll have any more problems?"

"We could, but there are enough businesses along the way that we don't need to worry about getting stranded."

"In other words, we could hit every fast-food spot between here and Seattle."

Slade responded with a soft chuckle. "Right."

"Well, in that case, bring on the French fries."

By the time they were back on the freeway, Shelly noted that the storm had indeed abated. But the radio issued a weather update that called for more snow. Slade groaned.

"You could always spend Christmas with me and Dad." Shelly broached the subject carefully. "We'd like to have you. Honest."

Slade tossed her a disbelieving glare. "You don't mean that?"

"Of course I do."

"But I'm a stranger."

"I've shared French fries with you. It's been a long time since I've been that intimate with a man. In fact, it would be best if you didn't mention it to my dad. He might be inclined to reach for his shotgun."

It took a minute for Slade to understand the implication. "A shotgun wedding?"

"I am getting on in years. Dad would like to see me married off and producing grandchildren. My brothers have been lax in that department." For the moment she'd forgotten about Margaret. When she remembered, Shelly felt her spirits rush out of her with all the force of a deflating balloon. "Don't worry," she was quick to add. "All you need to do is tell Dad about your fiancée and he'll let you off the hook." Somehow she managed to keep her voice cheerful.

"It's a good thing I didn't take a bite of your hamburger."

"Are you kidding? That would have put me directly into your last will and testament."

"I was afraid of that," he said, laughing good-naturedly.

Once again Shelly was reminded of how rich and deep the sound of Slade's laughter was. It had the most overwhelming effect on her. She discovered that, when he laughed, nothing could keep her spirits down.

Their progress was hampered by the swirling snow until their forward movement became little more than a crawl. Shelly didn't mind. They chatted, joked and sang along with the radio. She discovered that she enjoyed Slade's wit. Although a bit dry, under that gruff, serious exterior lay an interesting man with a warm but subtle sense of humor. Given any other set of circumstances, Shelly would have liked to get to know Slade Garner better.

"What'd you buy your dad for Christmas?"

The question came so unexpectedly that it took Shelly a moment to realize that he was speaking to her.

"Are you concerned that I wrapped up soup to go with the bread?"

Slade scowled, momentarily puzzled. "Ah, to go with the sourdough bread. No, I was just curious."

"First, I got him a box of his favorite chocolate-covered cherries."

"I should have known it'd be food."

"That's not all," she countered a bit testily. "We exchange the usual father-daughter gifts. You know. Things like stirrup irons, bridles and horse blankets. That's what Dad got me last Christmas."

Slade cleared his throat. "Just the usual items every father buys his daughter. What about this year?"

"Since I'm not around Sampson, I imagine he'll resort to the old standbys, like towels and sheets for my apartment." She was half hoping that, at the mention of her place in San Francisco, Slade would turn the conversation in that direction. He didn't, and she was hard-pressed to hide her disappointment.

"What about you?"

"Me?" His gaze flickered momentarily from the road.

"What did you buy your family?"

Slade gave her an uncomfortable look. "Well, actually, I didn't. It seemed simpler this year just to send them money."

"I see." Shelly knew that that was perfectly acceptable in some cases, but it sounded so cold and uncaring for a son to resort to a gift of money. Undoubtedly, once he and Margaret were married, they'd shop together for something more appropriate.

"I wish now that I hadn't. I think my parents would have enjoyed fresh sourdough bread and chocolate-covered cherries." He hesitated for an instant. "I'm not as confident about the stirrups and horse blankets, however."

As they neared Tacoma, Shelly was surprised at how heavy the traffic had gotten. The closer they came to Maple Valley, the more anxious she became.

"My exit isn't far," she told him, growing impatient. "Good grief, one would expect people to stay off the roads in weather like this."

"Exactly," Slade echoed her thoughts.

It wasn't until she heard the soft timbre of his chuckle that she realized he was teasing her. "You know what I mean."

He didn't answer as he edged the car ahead. Already the night was pitch-dark. Snow continued to fall with astonishing regularity. Shelly wondered when it would stop. She was concerned about Slade driving alone from Maple Valley to Seattle.

"Maybe it would be better if we found a place to stop and phoned my dad."

"Why?"

"That way he could come and pick me up and you wouldn't—"

"I agreed to deliver you to Maple Creek, and I intend to do exactly that."

"Maple Valley," she corrected.

"Wherever. A deal is a deal. Right?"

A rush of pleasure assaulted her vulnerable heart. Slade wasn't any more eager to put an end to their adventure than she was.

"It's the next exit," she informed him, giving him the directions to the ten-acre spread that lay on the outskirts of town. Taking out a pen and paper, she drew a detailed map for Slade so that he wouldn't get lost on the return trip to the freeway. Under the cover of night, there was little to distinguish one road from another, and he could easily become confused.

Sitting upright, Shelly excitedly pointed to her left. "Turn here."

Apparently in preparation for his departure to the airport, her father had shoveled the snow from the long driveway.

The headlights cut into the night, revealing the long, sprawling ranch house that had been Shelly's childhood home. A tall figure appeared at the window and almost immediately the front door burst open.

Slade had barely put the car into Park when Shelly threw open the door.

"Shortcake."

"Dad." Disregarding the snow and wind, she flew into his arms.

"You little... Why didn't you tell me you were coming by car?"

"We rented it." Remembering Slade, she looped an arm around her father's waist. "Dad, I'd like you to meet Slade Garner."

Don Griffin stepped forward and extended his

hand. "So you're Shelly's surprise. Welcome to our home. I'd say it was about time my daughter brought a young man home for her father to meet."

Chapter Four

Slade extended his hand to Shelly's father and grinned. "I believe you've got me confused with sourdough bread."

"Sourdough bread?"

"Dad, Slade and I met this morning on the plane." Self-conscious, Shelly's cheeks brightened in a pink flush.

"When it looked like the flight wasn't going to make it to Seattle, we rented the car," Slade explained further.

A curious glint darkened Don Griffin's deep blue eyes as he glanced briefly from his daughter to her friend and ran a hand through is thick thatch of dark hair. "It's a good thing you did. The last time I phoned the airport, I learned your plane still hadn't left Portland."

"Slade has an important meeting first thing tomorrow." Her eyes were telling Slade that she was ready to make the break. She could say goodbye and wish him every happiness. Their time together had been too short for any regrets.

"There's no need for us to stand out here in the cold discussing your itinerary," Don inserted and motioned toward the warm lights of the house.

Slade hesitated. "I should be getting into Seattle."

"Come in for a drink first," Don invited.

"Shelly?" Slade sought her approval. The unasked question in his eyes pinned her gaze.

"I wish you would." *Fool,* her mind cried out. It would be better to sever the relationship quickly, sharply and without delay before he had the opportunity to touch her tender heart. Her mind shouted fool, but her heart refused to listen.

"For that matter," Don continued, seemingly oblivious to the undercurrents between Slade and Shelly, "stay for dinner."

"I couldn't. Really." He made a show of glancing at his wristwatch.

"We insist," Shelly added. "After hauling this bread from here to kingdom come, the least I can offer you is a share of it."

To her astonishment Slade grinned, his dark eyes crinkling at the edges. The smile was both spontaneous and personal—a reminder of the joke between them. "All right," he agreed.

"That settles it, then." Don grinned and moved to the rear of the car while Slade extracted Shelly's suitcase and the huge sack.

"What's all this?"

"Presents."

"For me?"

"Well, who else would I be bringing gifts for?"

"A man. It's time you started thinking about a husband."

"Dad!" If her cheeks had been bright pink previously, now the color deepened into fire-engine red. In order to minimize further embarrassment, Shelly returned to the car and rescued the long loaves of sour-dough bread. Her father managed the huge "tuba case" full of gifts while Slade carried the one small carry-on bag.

The house contained all the warmth and welcome of home. Shelly paused in the open doorway, her gaze skimming over the crackling fireplace and the large array of family photos that decorated the mantel above the hearth. Ol' Dan, their seventeen-year-old Labrador, slept on the braided rug and did little more than raise his head when Don and Slade entered the house. But on seeing Shelly, the elderly dog slowly came to his feet and with some difficulty ambled to her side, tail wagging. Shelly set the bread aside and fell to her knees.

"How's my loyal, mangy mutt?" she asked, affectionately ruffling his ears and hugging him. "You keeping Dad company these days?"

"Yeah, but he's doing a poor job of it," Don complained loudly. "Ol' Dan still can't play a decent game of chess."

"Do you play?" Slade's gaze scanned the living room for a board.

"Forty years or more. What about you?"

"Now and again."

"Could I interest you in a match?"

Slade was already unbuttoning his overcoat. "I'd enjoy that, sir."

"Call me Don, everyone does."

"Right, Don."

Within a minute the chessboard was out and set up on a tray while the two men sat opposite each other on matching ottomans.

Seeing that the contest could last a long while, Shelly checked the prime rib roasting in the oven and added large potatoes, wrapping each in aluminum foil. The refrigerator contained a fresh green salad and Shelly's favorite cherry pie from the local bakery. There were also some carrots in the vegetable drawer; Shelly snatched a couple and put them in her pocket.

Grabbing her Levi jacket with its thick wool padding from the peg on the back porch and slipping into her cowboy boots, Shelly made her way out to the barn.

The scent of hay and horses greeted her, and Shelly paused, taking in the rich, earthy odors. "Howdy, Sampson." She spoke to her favorite horse first.

The sleek, black horse whinnied a welcome as Shelly approached the stall and accepted the proffered carrot without pause.

"Have you missed me, boy?"

Pokey, an Appaloosa mare, stuck her head out of her stall, seeking her treat. Laughing, Shelly pulled another carrot from her pocket. Midnight, her father's horse and Sampson's sire, stamped his foot, and Shelly made her way down to his stall.

After stroking his sleek neck, Shelly took out the grooming brushes and returned to Sampson. "I suppose Dad's letting you get fat and lazy now that I'm not around to work you." She glided the brush down the muscled flank in familiar fashion. "All right, I'll admit it. Living in San Francisco has made me fat and lazy as well. I haven't gained any weight, but I feel flabby. I suppose I could take up jogging, but it's foggy and rainy and—"

"Shelly?"

Slade stood just inside the barn, looking a bit uneasy. "Do you always carry on conversations with your horse?"

"Sure. I've talked out many a frustration with Sampson. Isn't that right, boy?"

Slade gave a startled blink when the horse answered with a loud snort and a toss of his head, as if agreeing with her.

"Come in and meet my favorite male," Shelly invited, opening the gate to the stall.

Hands buried deep in his pockets, Slade shook his head. "No, thanks."

"You don't like horses?"

"Not exactly."

Having lived all her life around animals, Shelly had trouble accepting his reticence. "Why not?"

"The last time I was this close to a horse was when I was ten and at summer camp."

"Sampson won't bite you."

"It's not his mouth I'm worried about."

"He's harmless."

"So is flying."

Surprised, Shelly dropped her hand from Sampson's hindquarters.

Slade strolled over to the stall, a grin curving up the edges of his mouth. "From the look on your face when we landed, one would assume that your will alone was holding up the plane."

"It was!"

Slade chuckled and tentatively reached out to rub Sampson's ebony forehead.

Shelly continued to groom the horse. "Is your chess match over already?"

"I should have warned your father. I was on the university chess team."

Now it was Shelly's turn to look amused. She paused, her hand in midstroke. "Did you wound Dad's ego?"

"I might have, but he's regrouping now. I came out to meet the horse you spoke of so fondly. I wanted to have a look before I headed for Seattle."

"Sampson's honored to make your acquaintance."

I am, too, her heart echoed.

Slade took a step in retreat. "I guess I'll get back to the house. No doubt your dad's got the board set for a rematch."

"Be gentle with him," Shelly called out, trying to hide a saucy grin. Her father wasn't an amateur when it came to the game. He'd been a member of the local chess club for several years, and briefly Shelly wondered at his strategy. Donald Griffin seldom lost at any game.

An hour later Shelly stamped the snow from her boots and entered the house through the back door, which led into the kitchen. Shedding the thick coat, she hung it on the peg and went to check the roast and baked potatoes. Both were done to perfection, and she turned off the oven.

Seeing that her father and Slade were absorbed in their game, Shelly moved behind her father and slipped her arms around his neck, resting her chin on the top of his head.

"Dinner's ready," she murmured, not wanting to break his concentration.

"In a minute," Don grumbled.

Slade moved the bishop, leaving his hand on the piece for a couple of seconds. Seemingly pleased, he released the piece and relaxed. As though sensing her gaze on him, he lifted his eyes. Incredibly dark eyes locked with hers as they stared at each other for long, uninterrupted moments. Shelly felt her heart lurch as she basked in the warmth of his look. She wanted to hold on to this moment, forget San Francisco, Margaret, the snowstorm. It became paramount that she capture this magic with both hands and hold on to it forever.

"It's your move." Don's words cut into the stillness.

"Pardon?" Abruptly Slade dropped his eyes to the chessboard.

"It's your move," her father repeated.

"Of course." Slade studied the board and moved a pawn.

Don scowled. "I hadn't counted on your doing that."

"Hey, you two, didn't you hear me? Dinner's ready." Shelly was shocked at how normal and unaffected her voice sounded.

Slade got to his feet. "Shall we consider it a draw, then?"

"I guess we better, but I demand a rematch someday."

Shelly's throat constricted. There wouldn't be another day for her or Slade. They were two strangers who had briefly touched each other's lives. Ships passing in the night and all the other clichés she had never expected would happen to her. But somehow Shelly had the feeling that she would never be the same again. Surely she wouldn't be so swift to judge another man. Slade had taught her that, and she would always be grateful.

The three chatted easily during dinner, and Shelly learned things about Slade that she hadn't thought to ask. He was a salesman, as she'd suspected. He specialized in intricate software programs for computers and was meeting with a Seattle-based company, hoping to establish the first steps of a possible distribution agreement. It was little wonder that he'd considered this appointment so important. It was. And although he didn't mention it, Shelly was acutely aware that if this meeting was successful, Slade would be that much closer to achieving his financial and professional goals—and that much closer to marrying dull, dutiful Margaret.

Shelly was clearing the dishes from the table when Slade set his napkin aside and rose. "I don't remember when I've enjoyed a meal more, especially the sourdough bread."

"A man gets the feel of a kitchen sooner or later," Don said with a crusty chuckle. "It took me a whole year to learn how to turn on the oven."

"That's the truth," Shelly added, sharing a tender look with her father. "He thought it was easier to use the microwave. The problem was he couldn't quite get the hang of that, either. Everything came out the texture of beef jerky."

"We survived," Don grumbled, affectionately looping an arm around Shelly's shoulder. The first eighteen months after her mother's death had been the most difficult for the family, but life goes on, and almost against their wills they'd adjusted.

Slade paused in the living room to stare out the window. "I can't ever remember it snowing this much in the Pacific Northwest."

"Rarely," Don agreed. "It's been three winters since we've had any snow at all. I'll admit this is a pleasant surprise."

"How long will it be before the snowplows are out?"

"Snowplow, you mean?" Don repeated with a gruff laugh. "King County is lucky if they have more than a handful. There isn't that much call for them." He walked to the picture window and held back the draperies with one hand. "You know, it might not be a bad idea if you stayed the night and left first thing in the morning."

Slade hesitated. "I don't know. If I miss this meeting, it'll mean having to wait over the Christmas holiday."

"You'll have a better chance of making it safely to Seattle in the morning. The condition of the roads tonight could be treacherous."

Slade slowly expelled his breath. "I have the distinct feeling you may be right. Without any streetlights Lord knows where I'd end up."

"I believe you'd be wise to delay your drive. Besides, that will give us time for another game of chess."

Slade's gaze swiveled to Shelly and softened. "Right," he concurred.

The two men were up until well past midnight, engrossed in one chess match after another. After watching a few of the games, Shelly decided to say good-night and go to bed.

She lay in her bed in the darkened room, dreading the approach of morning. In some ways it would have been easier if Slade had left immediately after dropping her off. And in other ways it was far better that he'd stayed.

Shelly fell asleep with the insidious hands of the clock ticking away the minutes to six o'clock when Slade would be leaving. There was nothing she could do to hold back time.

Without even being aware that she'd fallen asleep, Shelly was startled into wakefulness by the discordant drone of the alarm.

Tossing aside the covers, she automatically reached for her thick housecoat, which she'd left at her father's. Pausing only long enough to run a comb through her hair and brush her teeth, she rushed into the living room.

Slade was already dressed and holding a cup of coffee in his hands. "I guess it's time to say goodbye."

Chapter Five

Shelly ran a hand over her weary eyes and blinked. "You're right," she murmured, forcing a smile. "The time has come."

"Shelly—"

"Listen—"

Abruptly they each broke off whatever it was that they had planned to say.

"You first," Slade said and gestured toward her with his open hand.

Dropping her gaze, she shrugged one shoulder. "It's nothing really. I just wanted to wish you and Margaret every happiness."

His gaze softened and Shelly wondered if he knew what it had cost her to murmur those few words. She did wish Slade Garner happiness, but she was convinced that he wouldn't find it with a cold fish like Margaret. Forcefully she tossed her gaze across the room. For all her good intentions, she was doing it again—prejudging another. And she hadn't even met good ol' Margaret.

His eyes delved into hers. "Thank you."

"You wanted to say something," she prompted softly.

Slade hesitated. "Be happy, Shelly."

A knot formed in her throat as she nodded. He was telling her goodbye, really goodbye. He wouldn't see her again because it would be too dangerous for them both. Their lives were already plotted, their courses set. And whatever it was that they'd shared so briefly, it wasn't meant to be anything more than a passing fancy.

The front door opened and Don entered, brushing the snow from his pant legs. A burst of frigid air accompanied him and Shelly shivered.

"As far as I can see you shouldn't have a problem. We've got maybe seven to ten inches of snow, but there're plenty of tire tracks on the road. Just follow those."

Unable to listen anymore, Shelly moved into the kitchen and poured herself a cup of hot black coffee. Clasping the mug with both hands, she braced her hip against the counter and closed her eyes. Whatever was being said between Slade and her father had no meaning. She was safer in the kitchen where she wouldn't be forced to watch him walk out the door. The only sound that registered in her mind was the clicking noise of the front door opening and closing.

Slade had left. He was gone from the house. Gone from her life. Gone forever. Shelly refused to mope. He'd touched her and she should be glad. For a time she'd begun to wonder if there was something physically wrong with her because she couldn't respond to a man. Slade hadn't so much as kissed her, and she'd experienced a closeness to him that she hadn't felt with all the men she'd dated in San Francisco. Without even realizing it, Slade had granted her the priceless gift of expectancy. If he was capable of stirring her restless heart, then so would another.

Humming softly, Shelly set a skillet on the burner and laid thick slices of bacon across it. This was the day before Christmas, and it promised to be full. She couldn't be sad or filled with regrets when she was surrounded by everything she held dear.

The door opened again and Don called cheerfully. "Well, he's off."

"Good."

"He's an interesting man. I wouldn't mind having someone like him for a son-in-law." Her father entered the kitchen and reached for the coffeepot.

"He's engaged."

Don snickered and there was a hint of censure in his voice when he spoke. "That figures. The good men usually are snatched up early."

"We're about as different as any two people can be."

"That's not always bad, you know. Couples often complement each other that way. Your mother was the shy one, whereas I was far more outgoing. Our lives would have been havoc if we'd both had the same personalities."

Silently Shelly agreed, but to admit as much verbally would reveal more than she wished. "I suppose," she murmured softly and turned over the sizzling slices of bacon.

Shelly was sliding the eggs easily from the hot grease onto plates when there was a loud pounding on the front door.

Shelly's gaze clashed with that of her father's.

"Slade," they said simultaneously.

Her father rushed to answer the door, and a breathless Slade stumbled into the house. Shelly turned off the stove and hurried after him.

"Are you all right?" The tone of her voice was laced with concern. Her heart pounding, she checked him for any signs of injury.

"I'm fine. I'm just out of breath. That was quite a hike."

"How far'd you get?" Don wanted to know.

"A mile at the most. I was gathering speed to make it to the top of an incline when the wheels skidded on a patch of ice. The car, unfortunately, is in a ditch."

"What about the meeting?" Now that she'd determined that he was unscathed, Shelly's first concern was the appointment that Slade considered so important to him and his company.

"I don't know."

"Dad and I could take you into town," Shelly offered.

"No. If I couldn't make it, you won't be able to, either."

"But this meeting is vital."

"It's not important enough to risk your getting hurt."

"My truck has been acting up so I took it in for servicing," Don murmured thoughtfully. "But there's always the tractor."

"Dad! You'll be lucky if the old engine so much as coughs. You haven't used that antique in years." As far as Shelly knew, it was collecting dust in the back of the barn.

"It's worth a try," her father argued, looking to Slade. "At least we can pull your car out of the ditch."

"I'll contact the county road department and find out how long it'll be before the plows come this way," Shelly inserted. She didn't hold much hope for the tractor, but if she could convince the county how important it was that they clear the roads near their place, Slade might be able to make the meeting.

Two hours later, Shelly, dressed in dark cords and a thick cable-knit sweater the color of winter wheat, paced the living room carpet. Every few minutes she paused to glance out the large living room window for signs of either her father or Slade. Through some miracle they'd managed to fire up the tractor, but how much they could accomplish with the old machine was pure conjecture. If they were able to rescue Slade's car out of the ditch, then there was always the possibility of towing the car up the incline.

The sound of a car pulling into the driveway captured her attention, and Shelly rushed onto the front porch as Slade was easing the Camaro to a stop. He climbed out of the vehicle.

"I called the county. The road crew will try to make it out this way before nightfall," Shelly told him, rubbing her palms together to ward off the chill of the air. "I'm sorry, Slade, it's the best they could do."

"Don't worry." His gaze caressed her. "It's not your fault."

"But I can't help feeling that it is," she said, following him into the house. "I was the one who insisted you bring me here."

"Shelly." His hand cupped her shoulder. "Stop blaming yourself. I'll contact Bauer. He'll understand. It's possible he didn't make it to the office, either."

Granting him the privacy he needed to make his phone call, Shelly donned her coat and walked to the end of the driveway to see if she could locate her father. Only a couple of minutes passed before she saw him. Proudly he steered the tractor, his back and head held regally so that he resembled a benevolent king surveying all he owned.

Laughing, Shelly waved.

Don pulled to a stop alongside her. "What's so funny?"

"I can't believe you, sitting on top of a 1948 Harvester like you owned the world."

"Don't be silly, serf," Don teased.

"We've got a bit of a problem, you know." She realized that she shouldn't feel guilty about Slade, but she did.

"If you mean Slade, we talked about this unexpected delay. It might not be as bad as it looks. To his way of thinking, it's best not to appear overeager with this business anyway. A delay may be just the thing to get the other company thinking."

It would be just like Slade to say something like that, Shelly thought. "Maybe."

"At any rate, it won't do him any good to stew about it now. He's stuck with us until the snowplows clear the roads. No one's going to make it to the freeway unless they have a four-wheel drive. It's impossible out there.''

"But, Dad, I feel terrible.''

"Don't. If Slade doesn't seem overly concerned, then you shouldn't. Besides, I've got a job for you two.''

Shelly didn't like the sound of that. "What?''

"We aren't going to be able to go out and buy a Christmas tree.''

Shelly hadn't thought of that. "We'll survive without one.'' But Christmas wouldn't be the same.

"There's no need to. Not when we've got a good ten acres of fir and pine. I want Slade and you to go out and chop one down like we used to do in the good old days.''

It didn't take much to realize her father's game. He was looking for excuses to get Slade and her together.

"What's this, an extra Christmas present?'' she teased. From all the comments that Don had made about Slade, Shelly knew that her father thought highly of him.

"Nonsense. Being out in the cold would only irritate my rheumatism.''

"What rheumatism?''

"The one in my old bones.''

Shelly hesitated. "What did Slade have to say about this?''

"He's agreeable.''

"He is?''

"Think about it, Shortcake. Slade is stuck here. He wants to make the best of the situation.''

It wasn't until they were back at the house and Slade had changed into her father's woolen clothes and heavy boots that Shelly believed he'd fallen so easily in with her father's scheme.

"You don't have to do this, you know," she told him on the way to the barn.

"Did you think I was going to let you traipse into the woods alone?"

"I could."

"No doubt, but there isn't any reason why you should when I'm here."

She brought out the old sled from a storage room in the rear of the barn, wiping away the thin layer of dust with her gloves.

Slade located a saw, and Shelly eyed him warily.

"What's wrong now?"

"The saw."

"What's the matter with it?" He tested the sharpness by carefully running his thumb over the jagged teeth and raised questioning eyes to her.

"Nothing. If we use that rusty old thing, we shouldn't have any trouble bringing home a good-sized rhododendron."

"I wasn't planning to mow down a California redwood."

"But I want something a bit larger than a poinsettia."

Slade paused and followed her outside the barn. "Are you always this difficult to get along with?"

Jerking the sled along behind her in the snow, Shelly shouted, "There's nothing wrong with me. It's you."

"Right," he growled.

Shelly realized that she was acting like a shrew, but her behavior was a defense mechanism against the attraction she felt for Slade. If he was irritated with her, it would be easier to hold back her feelings for him.

"If my presence is such an annoyance to you, I can walk into town."

"Don't be silly."

"She shouts at me about cutting down rhododendrons and I'm silly." He appeared to be speaking to the sky.

Plowing through the snow, Shelly refused to look back. Determined, she started up a small incline toward the woods. "I just want you to know I can do this on my own."

His hand on her shoulder halted her progress, paralyzing her. "Shelly, listen to me, would you?"

She hesitated, her gaze falling on the long line of trees ahead. "What now?"

"I like the prospect of finding a Christmas tree with you, but if you find my company so unpleasant, I'll go back to the house."

"That's not it," she murmured, feeling ridiculously like an adolescent. "I have fun with you."

"Then why are we arguing?"

Against her will she smiled. "I don't know," she admitted.

"Friends?" Slade offered her his gloved hand.

Shelly clasped it in her own. She nodded wordlessly at him.

"Now that we've got that out of the way, just how large of a tree were you thinking of?"

"Big."

"Obviously. But remember it's got to fit inside the house so that sixty-foot fir straight ahead is out."

"But the top six feet isn't," she teased.

Chuckling, Slade draped his arm across her shoulder. "Yes, it is."

They were still within sight of the house. "I don't want to cut down something obvious."

"How do you mean?"

"In years to come I don't want to look out the back window and see a hole in the landscape."

"Don't be ridiculous. You've got a whole forest back here."

"I want to go a bit deeper into the woods."

"Listen, Shortcake, I'm not Lewis and Clark."

Shelly paused. He'd used her father's affectionate term for her. "What'd you call me?"

"Shortcake. It fits."

"How's that?"

His gaze roamed over her, his eyes narrowing as he studied her full mouth. It took everything within Shelly not to moisten her lips. A tingling sensation attacked her stomach, and she lowered her gaze. The hesitation lasted no longer than a heartbeat.

His breath hissed through his teeth before he asked, "How about this tree?" His fingers gripped the top of a small fir that reached his waist.

Shelly couldn't keep from laughing. "It should be illegal to cut down anything that small."

"Do you have a better suggestion?"

"Yes."

"What?"

"That tree over there." She marched ahead, pointing out a seven-foot pine.

"You're being ridiculous. We wouldn't be able to get that one through the front door."

"Of course we'd need to trim it."

"Like in half," he mocked.

Shelly refused to be dissuaded. "Don't be a spoilsport."

"Forget it. This tree would be a nice compromise." He motioned toward another small tree that was only slightly bigger than the first one he'd chosen.

Without hesitating, Shelly reached down and packed a thick ball of snow. "I'm not willing to compromise my beliefs."

He turned to her, exasperation written all over his tight features. Shelly let him have it with the snowball. The accuracy of her toss astonished her, and she cried out with a mixture of surprise and delight when the snowball slammed against his chest, spraying snow in his face.

His reaction was so speedy that Shelly had no time to run. "Slade, I'm sorry," she said, taking a giant step backward. "I don't know what came over me. I didn't mean to hit you. Actually, I was aiming at that bush behind you. Honest."

For every step she retreated, he advanced, packing a snowball between his gloved hands.

"Slade, you wouldn't." She implored him with open arms.

"Yes, I would."

"No," she cried and turned, running for all she was worth. He overtook her almost immediately, grabbing her shoulder. Shelly stumbled and they both went crashing to the snow-covered ground.

Slade's thick torso pressed her deeper into the snow. "Are you all right?" he asked urgently, fear and concern evident in the tone of his voice as he tenderly pushed the hair from her face.

"Yes," she murmured, breathless. But her lack of air couldn't be attributed to the fall. Having Slade this close, his warm breath fanning her face, was responsible for that. Her breasts felt the urgent pressure of his chest, and even through the thick coats Shelly could feel the pounding rhythm of his heart echoing hers.

"Shelly." He ground out her name like a man driven to the brink of insanity. Slowly he slanted his mouth over hers, claiming her lips in a kiss that rocked the very core of her being. Their lips caressed while their tongues mated until they were both panting and nearly breathless.

Her arms locked around his neck, and she arched against him desperately, wanting to give him more and more.

"Shelly." His hands closed around her wrists, jerking them free of his nape. He sat up with his back to her. All she could see was the uneven rise and fall of his shoulders.

"Don't worry," she breathed out in a voice so weak that it trembled. "I won't tell Margaret."

Chapter Six

"That shouldn't have happened." Slade spoke at last.

"I suppose you want an apology," Shelly responded, standing and brushing the snow from her pants. In spite of her efforts to appear normal, her hands trembled and her pulse continued to hammer away madly. From the beginning she'd known that Slade's kiss would have this effect upon her, and she cursed her traitorous heart.

He swiveled, shocked that she would suggest such a thing. "I should be the one to apologize to you."

"Why? Because you kissed me?"

"I'm engaged."

"I know." Her voice rose several decibels. "What's in a kiss, anyway? It wasn't any big deal. Right?" *Liar,* her heart accused, continuing to beat erratically. It'd been the sweetest, most wonderful kiss of her life. One that would haunt her for a lifetime.

"It won't happen again," Slade said without looking at her. He held his body stiffly away from her. His facade slipped tightly into place, locking his expression right before her eyes. Shelly was reminded of the man she'd first seen on the plane—that polished, impeccable businessman who looked upon the world with undisguised indifference.

"As I said, it wasn't any big deal."

"Right," he answered. The light treatment that she gave his kiss didn't appear to please him. Standing, he stalked in the direction of the trees and stopped at the one he'd offered as a compromise earlier. Without soliciting her opinion, he began sawing away at its narrow base.

Within minutes the tree toppled, crashing to the ground and stirring up the snow. Shelly walked over, prepared to help him load the small fir onto the sled, but he wouldn't let her.

"I'll do it," he muttered gruffly.

Offended, she folded her arms and stepped back, feeling awkward and callow. She'd feel better if they could discuss the kiss openly and honestly.

"I knew it was going to happen." She'd been wanting him to kiss her all day.

"What?" he barked, heading in the direction of the house, tugging the sled and Christmas tree behind him.

"The kiss," she called after him. "And if I was honest, I'd also admit that I wanted it to happen. I was even hoping it would."

"If you don't mind, I'd rather not talk about it."

Slade was making her angrier every time he opened his mouth. "I said *if* I was being honest, but since neither of us is, then apparently you're right to suggest we drop the issue entirely."

Slade ignored her, taking giant steps so that she was forced into a clumsy jog behind him. The north wind whipped her scarf across her mouth, and Shelly tucked it more securely around her neck. She turned and took several steps backward so that the bitter wind buffeted her back instead of her face.

Unexpectedly her boot hit a small, protruding rock, and Shelly momentarily lost her balance. Flinging her arms out in an effort to catch herself, she went tumbling down the hill, somersaulting head over feet until she lay sprawled, spread-eagled, at the base of the slope.

Slade blistered the wind with expletives as he raced after her, falling to his knees at her side, his eyes clouded with emotion. "Do you have to make a game out of everything?"

She'd nearly killed herself, and he accused her of acrobatics in the snow. She struggled to give him a sassy comeback, but the wind had been knocked from her lungs and she discovered that she couldn't speak.

"Are you all right?" Slade looked concerned for the first time.

"I don't know," she whispered tightly. Getting the appropriate amount of oxygen to her lungs seemed to require all her energy.

"Don't move."

"I couldn't if I wanted to."

"Where does it hurt?"

"Where doesn't it would be a more fitting question." Belying her previous answer, she levered herself up with one elbow and wiggled her legs. "I do this now and then so I can appreciate how good it feels to breathe," she muttered sarcastically.

"I said don't move," Slade barked. "You could've seriously injured something."

"I did," she cried, "my pride." Slowly coming to her feet, she mockingly bowed before him and said, "Stay tuned for my next trick when I'll single-handedly leap tall buildings and alter the course of the mighty Columbia River."

"You're not funny."

"I was desperately trying to be."

"Here." He tucked a hand under her elbow. "Let me help you back to the house."

"This may come as a shock to you, but I'm perfectly capable of walking on my own."

"Nothing you do anymore could shock me."

"That sounds amazingly like a challenge."

Slade's indifference almost melted away as he stared down at her with warm, vulnerable eyes. "Trust me, it isn't." He claimed her hand, lacing his fingers with hers. "Come on, your father's probably getting worried."

Shelly sincerely doubted it. What Slade was really saying was that things would be safer for them back at the house. Temptation could more easily be kept at bay with someone else present.

He placed his hand at the base of her neck, and they continued their short sojourn across the snowy landscape.

The house looked amazingly still and dark as they approached. A whisper of smoke drifted into the clear sky from the chimney as though the fire had been allowed to die. Shelly had expected to hear Andy Williams crooning from the stereo and perhaps smell the lingering scent of freshly popped popcorn.

Instead, they were greeted by an empty, almost eerie silence.

While Slade leaned the tree against the side of the house, Shelly ventured inside. A note propped against the sugar bowl in the middle of the kitchen table commanded her attention. She walked into the room and picked it up.

Sick horse at the Adler's. Call if you need me.

> Love,
> Dad.

She swallowed tightly, clenching the paper in her hand as the back door shut.

"Dad's out on a call," she announced without turning around. "Would you like a cup of coffee? The pot's full, although it doesn't look too fresh. Dad must have put it on before he left. He knew how cold we'd be when we got back." She realized she was chattering and immediately stopped. Not waiting for his response, she reached for two mugs.

"Coffee sounds fine." Slade's voice was heavy with dread. The same dread that Shelly felt pressing against her heart. Her father was the buffer they needed and he was gone.

Shelly heard Slade drag out a kitchen chair, and she placed the mug in front of him. Her thick lashes fanned downward as she avoided his gaze.

Reluctantly she pulled out the chair opposite his and joined him at the table. "I suppose we should put up the tree."

Slade paused. "We might."

From all the enthusiasm he displayed, they could have been discussing income taxes. Shelly's heart ached. She was embarrassed at having made the suggestion. No doubt good ol' Margaret had hers flocked and decorated without ever involving Slade.

Her hands compressed around the mug, burning the sensitive skin of her palms.

"Well?" he prompted.

"I think I'll wait until Dad's back. We—every year since Mom died, we've done it together. It's a fun time." The walls of the kitchen seemed to be closing in on them. With every breath Shelly drew, she became more aware of the man sitting across from her. They'd tried to pretend, but the kiss had changed everything. The taste of him lingered on her lips, and unconsciously she ran her tongue over them, wanting to recapture that sensation before it disappeared forever.

Slade's eyes followed her movement, and he abruptly stood, marching across the kitchen to place his half-full mug in the sink.

"I'll tend the fire," he offered, hastily leaving the room.

"Thank you."

After emptying her own mug in the sink, Shelly joined him, standing in the archway between the kitchen and living room.

Slade placed a small log in the red coals, and instantly flames sizzled over the dry bark. Soon the fire crackled and hissed at the fresh supply of wood with ardent, hungry flames.

"I wonder what's happening with the road crew," Slade said.

"They could be here any time."

Together they moved toward the phone, each intent on collecting the needed information. In their eagerness they collided. Shelly felt the full impact of the unexpected contact with Slade. Her breath caught someplace between her lungs and her throat but not from any pain.

"Shelly." His arms went around her faster than a shooting star. "Did I hurt you?"

One hand was trapped against his broad chest while the other hung loosely at her side. "I'm fine," she managed, her voice as unsteady as his. Still, he didn't release her.

Savoring his nearness and warmth, Shelly closed her eyes and pressed her head to his chest, listening to the beat of his heart beneath her ear.

Slade went utterly still until his arms tightened around her, and he groaned her name.

Nothing that felt this wonderful and good could be wrong. Shelly knew that in her heart, but her head buzzed with a nagging warning. Even though her eyes were closed, she could see flashing red lights. Slade had held and kissed her only once and had instantly regretted it. He'd even refused to talk about it, closing himself off from her.

Yet the arguments melted away like snow in a spring thaw when she was in his arms. His lips moved to her hair, and he breathed in deeply as though to capture her scent.

"Shelly," he pleaded, his voice husky with emotion. "Tell me to stop."

The words wouldn't form. She knew that she should break away and save them both the agony of guilt. But she couldn't.

"I want you to hold me," she whispered. "Just hold me."

Automatically his arms anchored her against him, and his lips nuzzled her ear, shooting tingles of pleasure down her spine. From her ear he found her cheek, her hair. For an eternity he hesitated.

The phone jingled and they broke apart with a suddenness that rocked Shelly. Slade's hand on her shoulder steadied her. Brushing the hair from her face, she drew in a steadying breath.

"Hello." Her voice was barely above a whisper when she answered.

"Shelly? Are you all right? You don't sound like yourself."

"Oh, hi, Dad." She glanced up guiltily at Slade. His returning look was heavy with consternation. He brushed a hand through his own hair and walked to the picture window. "We got the tree."

"That's good." Don Griffin paused. "Are you sure everything's fine?"

"Of course I'm sure," she answered, somewhat defensively. "How are things with the Adlers?"

"Not good. I may be here a while. I'm sorry to be away from you, but Slade's there to keep you company."

"How . . . long will you be?"

"A couple of hours, three at the most. You and Slade will be all right, won't you?"

"Oh, sure."

But her father didn't sound any more convinced than Shelly felt.

Five minutes later Shelly replaced the receiver. The air in the room seemed to vibrate with Slade's presence. He turned around and held her gaze. "I've got to get to Seattle."

What he was really saying was that he had to get away from her. "I know," she told him in a tortured whisper. "But how?"

"How'd your dad get to that sick horse?"

"The Adler's neighbor, Ted Wilkens, has a four-wheel drive. I suppose he came for Dad."

"Would it be possible for him to take me into Seattle?"

Shelly hadn't thought of that. "I'm not sure. I don't think he'd mind. I'll call."

"It's Christmas Eve." Slade sounded hesitant.

"They're that kind of people," she said, reaching for the phone. Slade paced the small area in front of her while she talked to Connie Wilkens.

"Well?" Slade studied her expectantly as she hung up the phone.

"Ted's out helping someone else, but Connie thinks he'll be back before dark. She suggested that we head their way, and by the time we arrive, Ted should be home."

"You're sure he won't mind?"

"Positive. Ted and Connie are always helping others."

"Good people—like you and your dad," Slade murmured softly.

Shelly laced her fingers together in front of her. "Yes. We're neighbors, although they're a good four miles from here. And friends." She scooted down in front of Ol' Dan and petted him in long, soothing strokes. "I told Connie that we'd start out soon."

Slade's brow furrowed as her words sank in. "But how? The tractor?"

"I couldn't run that thing if my life depended on it."

"Me, either. Shelly, we can't trek that distance on foot."

"I wasn't thinking of walking."

"What other way is there?"

A smile grew on her soft features until it touched her eyes, which sparkled with mischief. "We can always take the horses."

Chapter Seven

"You have to be kidding!" Slade gave her a look of pure disbelief.

"No," Shelly insisted, swallowing a laugh. "It's the only possible way I know to get there. We can go up through the woods where the snow isn't as deep."

Rubbing a hand over his eyes, Slade stalked to the far side of the room, made an abrupt about-face and returned to his former position. "I don't know. You seem to view life as one big adventure after another. I'm not used to..."

"Pokey's as gentle as a lamb," she murmured coaxingly.

"Pokey?"

"Unless you'd rather ride Midnight."

"Good grief, no. Pokey sounds more my speed."

Doing her best to hold back a devilish grin, Shelly led the way into the kitchen.

"What are you doing now?"

"Making us a thermos of hot chocolate."

"Why?"

"I thought we'd stop and have a picnic along the way."

"You're doing it again," he murmured, but she noticed that an indulgent half smile lurked just behind his intense dark eyes. Slade was a man who

needed a little fun in his life, and Shelly was determined to provide it for him. If she was only to touch
his life briefly, then she wanted to bring laughter and
sunshine with her. Margaret would have him forever.
But these few hours were hers, and she was determined to make the most of them.

"It'll be fun," she declared enthusiastically.

"No doubt Custer said the same thing to his men,"
Slade grumbled, following her out to the barn.

"Cynic," Shelly teased, holding open the barn
door.

Reluctantly he followed her inside.

"How do you feel about a lazy stroll in the snow,
Pokey?" she asked as she approached the Appaloosa's stall, petting the horse's nose. "I know Sampson's ready anytime."

"Don't let her kid you, Pokey," Slade added from
behind Shelly. "Good grief, now you've got me doing
it."

"Doing what?"

"Talking to the animals."

"They often show human characteristics," Shelly
defended both their actions. "It's only natural to express one's feelings to 'almost' humans."

"In which case we're in trouble. Pokey is going to
have a lot to say about how I feel when I climb on her
back."

"You'll be fine."

"Sure, but will Pokey?"

"You both will. Now stop worrying."

When Shelly brought out the riding tack, Slade
walked around the small barn, hands buried deep in

his pockets. He did what he could to help Shelly saddle the two horses. Mostly he moved around her awkwardly, looking doubtful and ambivalent.

When she'd finished, she led the horses out of the barn. Holding on to the reins, she motioned for Slade to mount first. "Will you need any help?" she asked. Slade looked so different from the staid executive she'd met in Portland that she had trouble remembering that this was the same man. The one facing her now was clearly out of his element and nothing like the unflappable man on the airplane.

"I don't think so," he said, reaching for the saddle and trying to follow Shelly's directions. Without much difficulty he swung his bulk onto Pokey's back. The horse barely stirred.

Looking pleased with himself, Slade smiled down at Shelly. "I suppose you told her to be gentle with me."

"I did," she teased in return. Double-checking the cinch, she asked, "Do you need me to adjust the stirrups or anything?"

"No." Slade shifted his weight slightly and accepted the reins she handed him. "I'm ready anytime you are."

Shelly mounted with an ease that spoke of years in the saddle. "It's going to be a rough ride until we get under the cover of the trees. Follow me."

"Anywhere."

Shelly was sure that she'd misunderstood him. "What did you say?" she asked, twisting around.

"Nothing." But he was grinning, and Shelly found him so devastatingly appealing that it demanded all her willpower to turn around and lead the way.

She took the path that led them through the woods. Gusts of swift wind blew the snow from the trees. The swirling flakes were nearly as bad as the storm had been. Even Pokey protested at having to be outside.

"Shelly," Slade said, edging the Appaloosa to Sampson's side. "This may not have been the most brilliant idea. Maybe we should head back."

"Nonsense."

"I don't want you catching cold on my account."

"I'm as snug as a bug in a rug."

"Liar," he purred softly.

"I want you to have something to remember me by." She realized she must sound like some lovesick romantic. He would be gone soon, and she must realize that she probably would never see him again.

"Like what? Frostbite?"

Shelly laughed. The musical sound of it was carried by the wind and seemed to echo in the trees around them. "How can you complain? This is wonderful. Riding along like this makes me want to sing."

Slade grumbled something unintelligible under his breath.

"What are you complaining about now?"

"Who says I'm complaining?"

Shelly grinned, her head bobbing slightly with the gentle sway of Sampson's gait. "I'm beginning to know you."

"All right, if you insist upon knowing. I happen to be humming. My enthusiasm for this venture doesn't compel me to burst into song. But I'm doing the best I can."

Holding this contented feeling to her breast, Shelly tried not to think about what would happen when they reached the Wilkens's. She was prepared to smile at him and bid him farewell. Freely she would send him out of her life. But it had been easier before she'd been in his arms and experienced the gentle persuasiveness of his kiss. So very much easier.

Together, their horses side by side, they ambled along, not speaking but singing Christmas songs one after the other until they were breathless and giddy. Their voices blended magically in two-part harmony. More than once they shared a lingering gaze. But Shelly felt her high spirits evaporating as they neared the landmark that pointed out the first half of their short journey.

"My backside is ready for a break," Slade announced unexpectedly.

"You aren't nearly as anxious to scoff at my picnic idea now, are you?" Shelly returned.

"Not when I'm discovering on what part of their anatomy cowboys get calluses." A grin slashed his sensuous mouth.

They paused in a small clearing, looping the horses' reins around the trunk of a nearby fir tree.

While Shelly took the hot chocolate and cookies from her saddlebags, Slade exercised his stiff legs, walking around as though he were on a pair of stilts.

"We'll have to share a cup," she announced, holding out the plastic top of the thermos to Slade. She stood between the two horses, munching on a large oatmeal cookie.

Slade lifted the cup to his lips and hesitated as their eyes met. He paused, slowly lowering the cup without breaking eye contact.

Shelly's breath came in shallow gasps. "Is something wrong?" she asked with difficulty.

"You're lovely."

"Sure." She forced a laugh. "My nose looks like a maraschino cherry and—"

"Don't joke, Shelly. I mean it." His voice was gruff, almost harsh.

"Then thank you."

He removed his glove and placed his warm hand on her cold face, cupping her cheek. The moment was tender and peaceful, and Shelly swallowed the surging emotion that clogged her throat. It would be the easiest thing in the world to walk into his arms, lose herself in his kiss and love him the way he deserved to be loved.

As if reading her thoughts, Sampson shifted, bumping Shelly's back so that she was delivered into Slade's arms. He dropped the hot chocolate and hauled her against him like a man reaching out a desperate hand in need.

"I told myself this wouldn't happen again," he whispered against her hair. "Every time I hold you, it becomes harder to let you go."

Shelly's heart gave a small leap of pleasure at his words. She didn't want him to let her go. Not ever. Everything felt right between them. Too right and too good.

How long he held her, Shelly didn't know. Far longer than was necessary and not nearly long enough.

Each second seemed elongated, sustaining her tender heart for the moment she must bid him farewell.

Not until they broke apart did Shelly notice that it was snowing again. Huge crystal-like flakes filled the sky with their icy purity.

"What should we do?" Slade asked, looking doubtful.

Her first instinct was to suggest that they return to the house, but she hesitated. Delaying the inevitable became more difficult every minute.

"We're going back," he said, answering his own question.

"Why?"

"I'm not leaving you and your father to deal with the horses. It's bad enough that I dragged you this far." Placing his foot in the stirrup, he reached for the saddle and mounted the Appaloosa. "Come on, before this snow gets any worse."

"But we can make it to the Wilkens's."

"Not now." He raised his eyes skyward and scowled. "It's already getting dark."

Grumbling, she tugged Sampson's reins free of the tree trunk and lifted her body onto his back with the agile grace of a ballerina.

The house was in sight when Slade spoke again. "After you call the Wilkens's, I need to contact Margaret. She's waiting for my phone call. I told her I'd call Christmas Eve."

Shelly's heart constricted at the mention of the other woman's name. Unless Shelly asked about his fiancée, Slade hadn't volunteered any information about Margaret. Now he freely thrust her between them.

"Naturally, I'll use my credit card."

He seemed to feel her lack of response was due to the expense. Shelly almost preferred to think that. "Naturally," she echoed.

"She's a good woman."

Shelly didn't know who he was trying to convince. "I don't think you'd love a woman who wasn't."

"I've known Margaret a lot of years."

"Of course you have." And he'd only known Shelly a few days. She understood what he was saying. It was almost as if he were apologizing because Margaret had prior claim to his loyalties and his heart. He needn't; she'd accepted that from the beginning.

When they left the cover of the woods, Shelly spoke, managing to keep her voice level and unemotional. "You use the phone first," she said, surprised that her voice could remain so even. "I'll take care of the horses so you can make your call in private."

"I won't talk long."

Shelly didn't want him to tell her that. "Don't cut the conversation short on my account."

He wiped his forearm across his brow. The movement brought her attention to the confusion in his eyes. "I won't."

At the barn Shelly dismounted slowly, lowering both booted feet to the ground. She avoided his gaze as she opened the barn doors and led the horses through. The wind followed her inside the dimly lit area. The cold nipped at her heels.

With a heavy heart she lifted the saddle from Pokey's back before she noticed Slade's dark form blocking the doorway. Her hands tightened around the smooth leather of the saddle. "Is there a problem?"

"No."

After leading Pokey to her stall, Shelly turned back to Slade only to find that he'd left.

Taking extra time with the horses, she delayed entering the house as long as possible. Removing the gloves from her hands one finger at a time, she walked in the back door to discover Slade sitting in the living room staring blindly into the roaring fire. She walked quickly to the phone and called the Wilkens's. Connie was glad to hear from her. After a full day driving neighbors around in the snow, Ted was exhausted. Shelly assured her friend that Slade had changed his mind anyway.

"I don't know about you," she called out cheerfully after hanging up the phone, "but I'm starved." The tip of her tongue burned with questions that pride refused to let her ask. Shelly possessed the usual female curiosity about Margaret and what Slade had said, if anything, about his current circumstances.

"How about popcorn with lots of melted butter?"

Slade joined her, a smile lurking at the edges of his full mouth. His eyes were laughing, revealing his thoughts. He really did have wonderful eyes and, for a moment, Shelly couldn't look away.

"I was thinking of something more like a triple-decker sandwich," Slade inserted.

"You know what your problem is, Garner?" It was obvious he didn't so she took it upon herself to tell him. "No imagination."

"Because I prefer something meatier than popcorn?"

Shelly pretended not to hear him; her head was buried in the open refrigerator. Without comment she brought out a variety of fixings and placed them on the tabletop.

Peeling off a slice of deli ham, she tore it in two and gave Slade half. "How about a compromise?"

He looked dubious, sure she was about to suggest a popcorn sandwich. "I don't know..."

"How about if you bring in the tree while I fix us something to eat?"

"That's an offer I can't refuse."

Singing softly as she worked, Shelly concocted a meal neither of them was likely to forget. Sandwiches piled high with three different kinds of meat, sliced dill pickles and juicy green olives. In addition, she set out Christmas cookies and thick slices of fudge that her father had sitting around the kitchen.

Slade set the tree in the holder, dragged it through the front door and stood it in the corner. "The snow's stopped," he told her when she carried in their meal.

"That's encouraging. I was beginning to think we'd be forced to stay until the spring thaw." Shelly wouldn't have minded, and her smile was a mixture of chagrin and ruefulness.

Sitting Indian style in front of the fireplace, their backs resting against the sofa, they dug into the sandwiches. But Shelly discovered that she had little appetite. Never had she been more aware of a man. They were so close that, when she lowered her sandwich to the plate, her upper arm brushed against his. But neither made any effort to move. The touch, although impersonal, was soothing. She paused, wishing to capture this moment of peacefulness.

"This has been a good day," Slade murmured, his gaze following hers as he stared out the living room window.

"It's certainly been crazy."

Slade's hand reached for hers, entwining their fingers. "I don't know when I've enjoyed one more." His dark gaze flickered over her and rested on her mouth. Abruptly he glanced away, his gaze moving to the piano at the far side of the room. "Do you play?"

Shelly sighed expressively. "A little. Dad claimed that my playing is what kept the mice out of the house."

A dark brow lifted with a touch of amusement. "That bad?"

"See for yourself." Rising, she walked to the piano, lifted the lid of the bench seat and extracted some Christmas music.

Pressing her fingers to the ivory keys, the discordant notes were enough to make her wince and cause Ol' Dan to lift his chin and cock his head curiously. He howled once.

"I told you I wasn't any good," she said with a dramatic sigh. Staring at the musical notes a second time, she squinted and sadly shook her head.

Slade joined her. Standing directly behind her, he laid his hands on her shoulders, leaning over to study the music.

"This may be the problem," she stated seriously. Dimples formed in her cheeks as she tried not to smile.

Turning the sheet music right side up, she leaned forward to study the notes a second time and tried again. This time the sweet melody flowed through the house.

Chuckling, Slade's hands compressed around her shoulders, and spontaneously he lowered his mouth to her cheek. "Have I told you how much fun you are?"

"No, but I'll accept that as a compliment."

"It was meant as one."

Shelly continued to play, hitting a wrong note every once in a while and going back to repeat the bar until she got it right. Soon Slade's rich voice blended with the melody. Shelly's soprano tones mixed smoothly with his, although her playing faltered now and again.

Neither of them heard the front door open. "Merry Christmas Eve," Don announced, looking exhausted. His pants were caked with mud and grit.

Shelly rested her hands above the keys. "Welcome home. How's the Adler's horse?"

Don wiped a weary hand over his face. "She'll make it."

"What about you?"

"Give me a half hour and I'll let you know."

"There's a sandwich in the kitchen if you're hungry."

"All I want right now is a hot bath." He paused to scratch Ol' Dan's ears. "Keep playing. You two sound good together."

"I thought we were scattering the mice to the barn," Slade teased.

Don scratched the side of his head with his index finger. "Say that again?"

"He's talking about my piano playing," Shelly reminded her father.

"Oh, that. No, by herself Shelly doesn't appear to have much talent. I don't suppose you play?" He directed the question to Slade.

"As a matter of fact, I do."

"You do?" Shelly was stunned. "Why didn't you say something earlier? Here." She slid off the bench. "Trade places."

Slade claimed her position and his large, masculine hands ran over the keys with a familiarity that caused Shelly's heart to flutter. His hands moved over the keys with deep reverence and love. Stroking, enticing the instrument until the crescendo of the music practically had the room swaying. Music, wrapped deep in emotion, so overwhelmingly breathtaking that Shelly felt tears gather in the corner of her eyes. Slade didn't play the piano; he made love to it.

When he'd finished, he rested his hands in his lap and slowly expelled his breath.

Shelly sank into the cushioned chair. "Why didn't you tell me you could play like that?"

A smile brightened his eyes. "You didn't ask."

Even Don was awestruck and, for the first time in years, at a complete loss for words.

. "You could play professionally. You're magnificent." Shelly's soft voice cracked with the potency of her feelings.

"I briefly toyed with the idea at one time."

"But..."

"I play for enjoyment now." The light dimmed in his gaze, and the sharp edge of his words seemed to say that the decision hadn't come easy. And it certainly was not one he was willing to discuss, even with her.

"Will you play something else?" Don requested, not moving.

From his look Slade appeared to regret admitting that he played the piano. Music was his real love, and he'd abandoned it. Coming this close again was pure torture for him. "Another time, perhaps."

There wouldn't be another time for them. "Please," Shelly whispered, rising and standing behind him. She placed her hands on his shoulder in a silent plea.

Slade's hand covered hers as he looked into her imploring gaze. "All right, Shelly. For you."

For half an hour he played with such intensity that his shoulders sagged with exhaustion when he'd finished.

"God has given you a rare and priceless gift," Don said, his voice husky with appreciation. He glanced down at his mud-caked clothes. "Now, if you'll excuse me, I'll take a bath before I start attracting flies."

Shelly could find no words to express herself. As Don left the room, she moved to Slade's side, sitting on the bench beside him.

Lovingly her fingers traced the sculptured line of his jaw as the tears blurred her vision. The tightness in her chest made her breathing shallow and difficult.

Slade's hand stopped her. Lifting her fingers to his lips, he gently kissed the inside of her palm. Shelly bit her bottom lip to hold back all the emotion stored in her heart.

A lone tear escaped and trickled down her pale cheek. With his thumb Slade gently brushed it aside.

His finger felt cool against her heated skin. He bent down and found her mouth with his. Without speaking a word, Shelly realized that Slade was thanking her. With her he'd allowed his facade to crumble. He opened his heart and revealed the deep, sensitive man inside. He was free now, with nothing more to hide.

Wrapping her arms around him, she kissed him in return, telling him the only way she could how much she appreciated the gift.

"Merry Christmas, Shortcake," Don greeted on the tail end of a yawn.

Shelly stood in front of the picture window, her hands cupping her coffee mug. Her gaze rested on the sunrise as it blanketed the morning with the bright hues of another day. She tried to force a smile when she turned to her father, but it refused to come. She felt chilled and empty inside.

"Where's Slade?" Don asked.

"The snowplows came during the night," she whispered through the pain. "He's gone."

Chapter Eight

"Gone? Without saying goodbye?" A look of disbelief marred Don's smooth brow.

"He left a note." Shelly withdrew it from her pocket and handed it to her father. The message was no more than a few lines. He thanked them for their hospitality and wished Shelly and her father much happiness. He said goodbye. Without regrets. Without second thoughts. Without looking back.

Don's gaze lifted from the note and narrowed as he studied his daughter. "Are you okay?"

"I'm fine."

He slowly shook his head. "I've never seen you look at a man the way you looked at Slade. You really liked him, didn't you?"

I love him, her heart cried. "He's a wonderful man. I only hope Margaret and that computer firm realize their good fortune."

"They don't, you know," Don whispered, coming to her side. He slipped an arm over her shoulder and hugged her close. She offered him a feeble smile in return.

"He might come back."

Shelly knew differently. "No." He'd made his choice. His future had been charted and defined as precisely as a road map. Slade Garner was a man of character and strength. He wouldn't abandon Margaret and all that was important to him for a two-day acquaintance and a few stolen kisses. He'd shared his deepest desires and secrets with her, opened his heart and trusted her. Shelly couldn't have wished for more. But she did. She wanted Slade.

Christmas day passed in a blur. She flew back to San Francisco the following afternoon, still numb, still aching, but holding her head up high and proud.

Her tiny apartment in the Garden District, although colorful and cheerfully decorated, did little to boost her drooping spirits.

Setting her suitcase on the polished hardwood floor, she kicked off her shoes and reached for the phone.

"Hi, Dad." Taking the telephone with her, she sank into the overstuffed chair.

"How was the flight?"

"Without a hitch."

"Just the way you like them." Don chuckled, then grew serious. "I don't suppose—"

"No, Dad." Shelly knew what he was asking. Don seemed to feel that Slade would be in San Francisco waiting for her. Shelly knew better. Slade wouldn't want to think of her. Already he'd banished any thought of her to the furthest corner of his mind. Perhaps what they'd shared was an embarrassment to him now.

Shelly spoke to her father for a few minutes longer, but neither had much to say. When they'd finished, she sat with the telephone cradled in her lap, staring blindly at the wallpaper.

For her part, Shelly worked hard at putting her life back on an even keel. She went to work each day and did her utmost to forget the man who had touched her so profoundly.

Her one resolution for the New Year was simple: Find a man. For the first time since moving to San Francisco, Shelly was lonely. Oh, there were friends and plenty of invitations, but nothing to take away the ache in her soul.

Two days before the New Year, Shelly stepped off the bus and on impulse bought flowers from a vendor on the street corner. One of her shoes had caused a blister on her heel, and she removed the offending pump once inside her apartment building.

The elderly woman who lived across the hall opened her door as Shelly approached. "Good afternoon, Mrs. Lester," Shelly said, pulling a red carnation from the bouquet of flowers and handing it to her neighbor.

"Now, isn't that a coincidence." Mrs. Lester chuckled. "I've got flowers for you."

Shelly's heart went still.

"The delivery boy asked me to give them to you." She reached back inside, then handed Shelly a narrow white box. "Roses, I suspect."

"Roses?" Shelly felt the blood drain from her face. She couldn't get inside her apartment fast enough. Closing the door with her foot, she walked across the room and set the box on a table. Inside she discovered a dozen of the most perfect roses she'd ever imagined. Each bud was identical to the others, their color brilliant. They must have cost a fortune.

Although she went through the box twice, she found no card. It would only be conjecture to believe that Slade had sent them. Unlikely, really. He wouldn't be so cruel as to say goodbye only to invade her life again. Besides, he'd claimed roses were expensive. She couldn't argue with that. They were.

The thought had just formed when the doorbell rang, and a delivery boy handed her a second long narrow box, identical to the first.

"Sign here." He offered her his ballpoint pen.

Shelly scribbled her name across the bottom of the delivery order and carried the second box to the kitchen table. Again she'd received a gift of a dozen red roses, and again there was no card.

No sooner had she arranged the flowers in her one and only tall vase when the doorbell chimed a third time. It was a delivery boy from another flower shop with a dozen roses.

"Are you sure you have the right address?" she questioned.

"Shelly Griffin?" He read off her street and apartment number and raised expectant eyes to her.

"That's me," she conceded.

"Sign here."

Again Shelly penned her name. And for a third time there was no card.

Having no vase to arrange them in, she emptied her jar of dill pickles onto a plate, rinsed out the container and used that. These she carried into the living room.

Whoever was sending her the roses was either very rich or else extremely foolish, she thought.

Hands pressed against her hips, she surveyed the small apartment and couldn't decide if it resembled a flower shop or a funeral parlor.

When the doorbell chimed again, she sighed expressively. "Not again," she groaned aloud, turning the dead bolt and opening the door.

But instead of opening it to a delivery boy as she expected, Shelly came face-to-face with Slade. He was so tall, dark and so incredibly good-looking that her breath became trapped in her lungs.

"Slade."

"Hello, Shelly." His eyes delved into hers, smiling and warm. "Can I come in?"

"Oh, of course." Flustered, she stepped aside.

"Do you realize you only have on one shoe?"

She looked down at her nylon-covered foot. "I forgot. You see, they're new and I wore them for the first time today so when—" She stopped abruptly. "Why are you here?" she demanded. With her hands behind her back, she leaned against the closed front door desperately wanting to believe everything she dared not even think about.

"I've missed you."

She closed her eyes to the tenderness that lapped over her in gentle waves. Few words had ever been sweeter. "How did the meeting go?"

"Fine. Better than expected."

"That's nice." Her gaze studied him, still unsure.

"I got a hefty bonus for my part in it, but I may have offended a few friends."

"How's that?"

"They were hoping I'd accept a promotion."

"And you aren't?" This sounded like something Margaret would love.

"No, I resigned this afternoon."

"Resigned? What did...Margaret have to say about that?"

"Well—" he took a step toward her, stopping just short of her but close enough to reach out and touch her if he desired "—Margaret and I aren't exactly on speaking terms."

"Oh?" Her voice went incredibly weak.

"She didn't take kindly to some of my recent decisions."

I'll just bet, Shelly mused. "And what are those decisions... the most recent ones?"

"I decided to postpone the wedding."

Shelly couldn't fault his fiancée for being upset about that. "Well, I can't say that I blame her. When—when's the new date?"

"Never."

"Never?" Shelly swallowed tightly. "Why not?"

"Why?" He smiled. "Because Margaret doesn't walk around with one shoe missing. Or haul sourdough bread across the country or laugh or do any of the things that make life fun."

Speechless, Shelly stared at him, love shining from her eyes.

"Nor does she believe I'll ever make a decent living as a pianist," Slade continued. "Hell, I'm over thirty now. It could be too late."

"But...?"

"But—" he smiled and reached for her, bringing her into the loving circle of his arms "—I'm going to give it one hell of a try. I'm no prize, Shelly Griffin. I don't have a job, and I'm not even sure the conservatory will renew their offer, but for the first time in a lot of years, I've got a dream.''

"Oh, Slade," she whispered and pressed her forehead to his broad chest. "I would consider it the greatest honor of my life to be a part of that dream."

"You couldn't help but be," he whispered, lifting her mouth to his. "You're the one who gave it to me."

*   *   *   *   *

A Note from Debbie Macomber

A Christmas tradition in our family is hand-dipping chocolates. Everyone gets involved, and by the time we've finished it's
debatable how much chocolate actually gets dipped and how
much is consumed. The chocolates and other Christmas goodies are the way our family chooses to thank the special people
who have touched our lives: teachers, coaches, the mailman and
several others.

However, with everyone more health and diet conscious—
including me—I decided the time had come to try my hand at
something new. So last year, for the first time, I decorated
candy canes.

My artist friend, Judy Grimes, has been decorating candy
canes at Christmas for years and she agreed to teach me. We use
a method called "figure piping." With the Royal Icing recipe—which is included—we create our own version of cartoon
characters climbing up candy canes. There's a Care Bear,
Snoopy, Mickey Mouse and, naturally, Santa.

Anyone who wishes to try this will require several virtues,
including patience, a sense of humor and a steady hand. For the
characters such as Santa, Snoopy and the Care Bears, we use a
variety of frosting colors. Frosting gels or pastes are readily
available at craft stores, as are the frosting bags and icing tips.

Once the icing is mixed and colored and the bags filled, you
have to work quickly before the mixture softens. This isn't a
major problem. If the frosting becomes runny, simply place it
in the freezer for a few minutes.

I will admit, however, that my artistic talents are limited. This
project would be unthinkable without Judy. My Snoopys look
like Droopys and my Care Bears couldn't care less. But by the
time we're finished, there are candy canes draped across the
kitchen and Judy and I are laughing hysterically, wondering why
we don't get together more often.

My wish for each of you this Christmas is that the Lord will
fill your life with special people like my friend Judy.

Debbie Macomber

Starbright

Maura Seger

MAURA SEGER'S
FAVORITE CHRISTMAS FRUITCAKE

I bake this cake immediately after Thanksgiving and serve it
between Christmas and New Year's Day.

> *1 cup dried apricots*
> *1¼ lb candied fruit*
> *1 cup dark or light raisins*
> *⅓ cup slivered almonds, walnuts or pecans*
> *2 (approx) cups all-purpose flour*
> *¾ cup butter*
> *1 cup granulated sugar*
> *4 eggs, separated*
> *1 teaspoon lemon peel or lemon extract*
> *1 teaspoon salt*
> *½ teaspoon baking soda*
> *½ cup (approx) Irish whiskey or rum*

In a saucepan, cover apricots with cold water and bring to
boil; boil for one minute, drain and chop coarsely.

Dust candied fruit, raisins and nuts with flour to prevent
them sticking and sinking to bottom of cake.

In large mixing bowl, cream together butter and sugar. Beat
in egg yolks, lemon peel and apricots until mixture is light and
fluffy. (If you have one, use a food processor.) Stir in candied
fruit, raisins and nuts.

Beat egg whites until stiff. Sift together 2 cups of flour, salt
and baking soda. Add dry mixture to batter alternating with egg
whites, beating well after each addition.

Pour batter into a well-greased 8-cup casserole; cover. Place
casserole in a large pan. Pour in enough water to reach 2 inches
up side of casserole. Bake in 275°F oven for one hour. Remove
casserole from water and bake cake for one hour longer or until tester inserted in center of cake comes out clean. (If desired,
pour batter into two 4-cup casseroles or 4 small loaf pans;
shorten cooking time accordingly). Let cake cool on wire rack.

After cake has cooled, remove from casserole, wrap in
cheesecloth and place in a cake tin (loaf cakes can be left in the
original pans). Pour a "goodly" measure of Irish whiskey over
cake and allow to season before serving. Store in a cool, dark
place.

Chapter One

Who says you can't go home again? Mollie Williams was determined to do so. For days she had thought of nothing except getting out of Manhattan before Christmas, escaping the jam-packed streets, the brittle gaiety, the strained attempts at joviality that characterized the city during the holidays.

Not that she hadn't once seen it differently. There had been a time when she had thought New York the epitome of glamour, even of magic. Nothing, she had been sure, could ever come close to it. Not even the stars above could compete with the glitter of millions of lights, the aura of wealth and elegance, the pervasive sense of excitement and accomplishment.

When exactly her view had changed she didn't know, but change it had, and now to remain in the city an hour, a moment longer was intolerable. Not even the knowledge that she could spend the holidays with friends who were truly dear to her could make her linger. She wanted to be gone, far faster than the sluggish traffic and the stubborn lights would allow.

With an exclamation of mingled disgust and impatience she slumped behind the wheel of her BMW. That morning on the radio there had been a gridlock warning. Looking out at the impenetrable traffic along Fifth Avenue, she could see it had been warranted.

Horns honked; drivers hollered; harried traffic cops tried to keep order. Pedestrians loaded down with packages swarmed around and between the stuck cars. When the light changed again it was impossible to move forward without running over a dozen oblivious people who went on their way with the insulated arrogance of true New Yorkers.

At last, after what seemed like hours, the cars lurched forward and she was able to turn onto a side street. It took Mollie "only" fifteen minutes to reach the next avenue. Within half an hour she had attained the F.D.R. Drive, which ran along the East River, and entered the stream of traffic heading north.

After that it wasn't too bad. Settling back in the seat, she turned on the radio, flipped past the stations playing Christmas carols and found herself some mellow music to while away the time. Vermont was, she estimated, eight hours away. If she drove straight through, she should be there in time for an early dinner.

Thoughts of the inn where she would be staying made her smile. There she would find peace and quiet, but even more importantly, she hoped to recapture a sense of the person she had once been, before life's often tumultuous, always unpredictable events engulfed her.

It didn't seem possible that she had turned thirty a few weeks before. As she had said to Joanna Wilkes, her neighbor and friend, "Last time I checked, I was twenty-three. What happened?"

The years had sped by so quickly. What she had once thought of as a substantial block of time had turned out to be as ephemeral as the glowing colors of a sunrise or a radiant autumn, difficult to hold even in memory. She could list the accomplishments of those years, and the defeats, but she had no real sense of where they had gone. And that troubled her, especially when she looked ahead and saw only more of the same.

Which was a good reason not to dwell on the future. For the first time in far too long she was actually taking a vacation, away from the ringing telephone, the constant meetings, the nonstop crises that typically plagued a new and rapidly growing business. She was getting away, feeling as guilty as a schoolchild playing hooky and at least as delighted. Never mind if it was only for a few days, she was going where she wanted to be.

"Williamstown, Vermont?" Joanna had said when Mollie told her of her plans. "Never heard of it."

"Neither have most people. It's a small town, actually a village, serving a farming community."

"Oh...that sounds very...nice." Trust Joanna to feel that way. The tall, willowy blonde left New York only for Paris, London and other cities of that ilk, or—if she really wanted to commune with nature—an exclusive Caribbean resort. Otherwise she claimed that being further than walking distance from Saks gave her a rash.

"You don't have to be polite about it," Mollie had assured her. "Lots of people would never give Williamstown a second look, but I love it, and I've been wanting to go back for quite a while."

Joanna had accepted that with a gesture conveying her abiding tolerance for human foibles. She had wished Mollie a good trip and gone back to buffing her nails. Joanna was a former model and newly minted actress with a role on a popular soap. The endless plot complications fascinated Mollie, who taped the show every day while she was at work and usually caught up in an orgy of watching on a weekend afternoon. Joanna's character was currently involved with daytime TV's latest heartthrob, Derek Eberhard, who played a ruthless, virile, and irresistible tycoon. The interaction between them was an unabashed mixture of sex and romance.

Remembering some of the more recent scenes—the ones that had threatened to send steam out of the TV set—Mollie sighed. She hated to admit it, but lately the lack of anything remotely similar in her own life had begun to trouble her.

Her hands tightened on the steering wheel. After Padraic, she had absolutely sworn that she was through with men. Better to be alone the rest of her life than to have to put up with the craziness, the arrogance, the sheer bullheadedness of the male of the species. Any woman with her head on straight knew they were only good for one thing, and Mollie could live well enough without that, thank you very much.

Or at least she had thought she could. What she was beginning to discover was that while life without sex wasn't so bad—not great, but not terrible, either—life without love was barren.

A red MG darted in front of her. She slammed on the brakes, blared the horn and shot the offending driver an angry look, all without interrupting her train of thought.

Had Padraic ever really loved her? Her full mouth tightened as remembered pain darkened her sapphire-blue eyes. What difference did it make, anyway? If what she had received from her ex-husband had been love, then that emotion was singularly overrated.

The proof was to be found in how well she had done since their separation and subsequent divorce. Only when she was free of him had she been able to fulfill her own dreams, to find within herself the strength to build a highly successful fashion company turning out a line of clothes that women across the country adored.

A Mollie Williams original—or, better yet, several of them—was the foundation of every savvy woman's wardrobe. Her elegant, feminine, versatile creations showed up in corporate boardrooms and luxurious restaurants, but they were also immensely popular with women who had to scrimp to afford them but thought the sacrifice well worthwhile. Very simply, Mollie knew that her clothes made women feel *more*— more beautiful, more sophisticated, more confident, more at ease wherever they went and whatever they did. That gave her an immense sense of satisfaction, enough so that until lately she had truly believed she had everything she wanted.

She sighed again and, as traffic narrowed to a single lane that moved at a crawl, tilted her head back against the seat. She'd meant to get a haircut before leaving town, but there had been no time. Her mane of wild cinnamon-hued waves billowed out over her shoulders. "The soul of you," Padraic had called it, "trying to escape."

He was always saying things like that—dramatic, evocative, thrilling. But then, words were his business, and he knew how to use them. Or at least he had. She had no idea what he was doing these days and, she told herself, she didn't care. Geniuses like Padraic commonly burned themselves out early; if that had been his fate, she'd just as soon not know the details.

Past the outer edge of the city traffic at last smoothed out and she was able to pick up speed. It had snowed the previous day, a dusting that etched the barren trees and softened the frozen ground. Mollie remembered the white Christmases of her childhood and smiled wistfully. How kind Grania and Da had been. Both in their sixties when she had come to live with them, they nonetheless received her with all the devotion any child could want. The tragic death of their only child, Mollie's mother, in the same car accident that killed her husband was a blow from which they never fully recovered. But that did not prevent them from giving Mollie a home filled with love and laughter.

How she missed them. Grania's death some eight years before had been hard enough to bear, but when Da followed scant months later it had been almost more than she could stand. Looking back, she realized that she had still been numb with grief when she met Padraic. The passion they found together had, in a very real sense, brought her back to life. Perhaps that accounted for the extraordinary intensity of their relationship, which had progressed from first meeting to marriage in no more than a few weeks.

Her friends had thought it all wildly romantic. Padraic had already been a figure of near legendary proportions within the theater world, and well known beyond it. "The mad Irishman," he was called, not inaccurately. Directors, theater owners, backers, all threw up their hands in despair when they had to deal with him. Yet they were always willing enough to come back for more. Actors and actresses adored him, knowing as they did that each character that sprang from his incredible imagination was as rich a part as they would ever get.

He had been immensely talented beyond the understanding of most people, and to add to all his other gifts, he had even possessed the discipline needed to transform potential into actuality. Mollie had admired all that unstintingly, but she thought she could be forgiven for also sometimes wishing that he could be just a bit more human, more tolerant of her needs, more willing to put her ahead of his work some of the time.

As it was, she had always known exactly where she fitted into Padraic's life—in bed. They had never had any problems there, despite the fact that she had been a virgin when they met and shy about matching his passion with her own. For a while the pleasure they found together had been enough. Then it hadn't. She still didn't know when the transition had occurred, or why. All she was sure of was that she could never go back to the way she had been.

Not that she would ever have the opportunity. Men like Padraic Delaney were few and far between, all the more so since he had dropped out of sight.

Halfway to her destination Mollie pulled over at a gas station, stretched her limbs, bought a Coke and made a call to the office. Her assistant, Billy Barnes, twenty-four going on fifty, told her in no uncertain terms that everything was fine and she needn't given them another thought.

"We're peachy here," he said blithely. "The new Bombay silk is in and looks yummy. You're going to love it. Jennifer's talking to Wilbur again, so peace reigns in the cutting room. And they've added croissants to the coffee wagon."

"Sounds like I should go away more often."

"Well, of course we all miss you," Billy assured her. "But you need a break, so just relax and enjoy yourself. Oh, and Merry Christmas."

Mollie muttered her thanks, hung up, finished the Coke and tossed the can over her shoulder into the trash. She grinned at the appreciative whistle of the mechanic and got back in the car. Moments later she was on the road again, heading north.

Wasn't it great that everything was okay at the office? In fact, better than okay, considering how long Billy had been griping about the stale Danish and yucky donuts on the coffee wagon. Now he would have to find something else to complain about. Which wasn't fair, not even as a passing thought. He was a perfectly nice, hardworking, intelligent person whom she was lucky to have as an employee. Just as she was fortunate to have found all the people who worked for her. They were a great team, and she knew perfectly well they were responsible in large measure for her success. None of which explained why she was ticked off that they could get along without her.

Must be separation anxiety, she thought. This was the first time she had been away from the office for more than a couple of days since starting the company. At first she had slept on a cot beside her desk, working seven days a week, eighteen hours a day. Lately it hadn't been anywhere near that bad, but she still felt funny taking a whole week off.

Still insecure, Williams. Still not quite able to accept your success and believe it will last. Padraic had warned her about that, during their last huge fight. He'd said her biggest problem was a lack of faith in herself. He'd accused her of looking to him to provide her with a sense of identity and purpose, and made it quite clear that he had no intention of doing so. She'd hurled back her own set of charges—that he was insensitive, egotistical and uncaring. That he thought of nothing except his writing and sex. That he expected her to be there when he wanted the latter, and to be invisible the rest of the time. Most of all, she had hurled angry words at him about Jessica. Words he had not bothered to refute.

So that had been that. She'd gone on her own, founded Mollie Williams Fashions, worked like a Trojan to make it a success, and was now basking in the glory of her own accomplishments. Supposedly. Maybe going home would help her work that out.

Home. Such a lovely word. Barely had she reached the outskirts of Williamstown, the settlement founded by her ancestors some two hundred years before, than she began to recapture the wonderful sense of belonging she had once known there.

But then why wouldn't she, when Williamses had lived in the village in an unbroken line stretching back to the original founders? She was the last of them, and it wasn't until she had left that there were no more Williamses in Williamstown.

Leaving had been almost the toughest thing she had ever done. Only her parting from Padraic had cost her more. But she'd had no choice, not when she needed every penny she could get her hands on to start her business. The old farmhouse she'd inherited from her grandparents had been her only tangible asset.

During the divorce proceedings Padraic had suggested that he'd be willing to put up the money to help her get started. Mollie truly believed she would have died before accepting it. As it was she'd had barely enough to rent dingy office space and buy materials. But that was all behind her now, and she wasn't going to dwell on it. Not when she was finally beginning to feel really excited about being back.

It seemed that nothing had changed in the village. Main Street was still lined with Colonial-style buildings, many of which dated from the previous century, while the rest looked as if they did. The maple trees planted decades before at regular intervals along the street were decorated with small, twinkling lights. Pine wreaths hung on every door, their scent filling the air.

It was snowing lightly, soft flakes dancing past her windshield. She turned a corner, then another, and came at last to the Rooster Inn, a rambling roadside stopping place added onto over many generations and set on a slight rise overlooking the rest of the village. Mollie parked the car, got out, and stood for a moment looking at the comfortable old building. It was so well remembered from her childhood that she could hardly believe that it, too, hadn't changed. But then, she supposed that Jeremiah Withers, who had inherited the inn a few years before, took great pride in keeping it in top condition.

Gathering her mink coat more closely around her— it had been her thirtieth birthday present to herself— she walked up the flagstone path. In her hand was a Gucci suitcase holding the essentials she expected to need during the next week. Bells jangled as she opened the door and stepped inside.

Mollie stopped in the hall and looked around appreciatively. All her senses were alert to the pleasures surrounding her. Collector's pieces of Early American and Shaker furniture glowed in the late-afternoon sunlight, the rich patina of their woods turned to burnished gold and copper. The mingled scents of a wood fire and baking bread settled over her like a featherlight blanket of down. She could hear a piano being played nearby and a handful of voices, untrained but charming, raised in song.

Eagerly she moved on to the room from which the music came. A dozen or so people were there, most gathered around the piano, the rest seated at the long wooden bar or at the tables scattered around the room. Over the large fireplace stretched a magnificent pair of elk's antlers topped with Christmas wreaths. Behind the bar, wiping it down with a white cloth, was Jeremiah Withers.

Mollie approached him with a broad smile. "Jerry, it's good to see you again. You haven't changed at all." That was true. He was still the same tall, lanky man with the shy eyes and the gentle manner that she remembered. What did surprise her was the sudden blush that spread across his cheeks when he saw her.

"Mollie . . . it's you. . . ." he said, the cloth abruptly halting in midair.

"Why . . . yes, it is. You sound so surprised. Have I changed that much?" It had been five years since she'd last been in Williamstown, and a great deal had happened in that time, but surely not enough to justify his reaction. He seemed almost embarrassed, which made no sense at all.

"No," he said, hastily folding the cloth and tucking it under the bar. "That is, you look great."

"Thanks," she said dryly, aware that they had become the objects of interest of the other people in the bar, who were looking at them curiously. "You did get my letter?"

"Letter?"

"About the room." He must have received it; she had a confirmation of her reservation in her pocketbook.

"Oh . . . that. Oh . . . listen, Mollie, I'm awfully sorry about this, but there's a problem. I guess maybe I should have called you."

"Problem?" Her voice had dropped, becoming tight. The last thing she wanted to deal with was a problem of any sort, certainly not one that involved her long-awaited vacation.

"Yes . . . you see, we have some other people staying here, and they were supposed to check out, only they haven't, and I can't very well . . . that is, I could ask them to leave, but it doesn't seem right. Not with Christmas and all. You know, just to throw them out on the street."

"All right, I'll take another room."

"That's just it." He glanced away abashedly. "There aren't any."

"I don't understand. . . ." He couldn't be serious. She hadn't come so far, all the way home, to be turned back now.

"I'm sorry," Jeremiah said gently. "But all our rooms are filled. There's no place for you to stay here."

"But . . ." She shook her head disbelievingly. Jeremiah had been her friend; surely he must have some idea of what coming back meant to her. How could he simply turn her away? "Maybe . . . there's someplace else. Another inn?"

"I'm afraid not. The Rooster's still the only one in town."

He didn't even look particularly sorry about that. In fact, he'd returned to wiping the bar, as though expecting her to simply leave.

Instead Mollie drew herself up to her full five feet eight inches and faced him squarely. "Now look here, Jeremiah, I won't be treated like this. I've had a long trip, I'm tired, and I want a room. It's all very well for you to say that—"

"There's nothing I can do," he insisted.

"There has to be."

"'Fraid not. Of course, you might be able to find a room in somebody's house, though I expect most people are full up already with relatives and friends."

"I don't want to stay with strangers."

"Then stay with me."

At the sound of the deep, smooth voice coming from behind her, Mollie whirled around. Her eyes widened in disbelief. She couldn't possibly be seeing what she seemed to be....

Padraic Delaney looked back at her imperturbably, a sardonic smile curving his lean mouth and an unholy light burning in his emerald eyes.

Chapter Two

"What are you doing here?" Mollie demanded, only half expecting the apparition before her to reply. Padraic couldn't possibly have just walked back into her life as though he had never left it, offering her a place to stay and acting as though there was nothing at all untoward about his sudden reappearance.

"Having a drink," he said. "Care to join me?" Before she could respond, other than to open her mouth and stare, he signaled to Jeremiah. "Two brandies, please, Jerry. We'll have them by the fire."

"We will not," Mollie said, finally regaining her voice. "You do what you want, but I'm leaving."

"And going where?" He spoke softly, but the rough timbre of his voice vibrated clear through her. As it always had, especially at night when they'd lain in bed together after making love, speaking softly of the things lovers talk about.

Stop that! She was crazy to be indulging in such memories, especially now, when the man who starred in them was standing right in front of her. He really was there, she realized with a deadening sense of inevitability. It wasn't her imagination playing crazy tricks on her.

There were the same broad shoulders and powerful chest, the narrow waist and lean hips that she remembered so well. His hair was still thick and black, though faintly touched by silver now. His broad, craggy face—too powerful to be called handsome— hadn't changed, except perhaps to acquire a few more character lines that only added to his appeal. His green eyes, deeply set and thickly lashed, were still riveting. And his slanted brows remained a barometer of his mood, expressing both challenge and skepticism, as though daring her to walk out the door and prove to him that she didn't have the courage to spend even a few minutes in his company.

"All right," she snapped. "I'll have a drink, but that's all. Then I have to find someplace to stay." There were several motels outside of town; she'd spend the night at one of them and head back to New York the next morning. Hardly the way she had imagined spending the holidays, but that was just too bad. Obviously fate had never intended her to return, so the sooner she left the better.

"You already have a place," Padraic said as he took her elbow and steered her toward the fire. The touch of his hand, even through the layers of her fur coat and the soft wool dress she wore beneath, was electrifying. She jerked away as though stung and glared at him.

"You can't be serious. There's no way I'd share your room." She presumed he was staying at the inn, though she couldn't imagine why. The few times she had managed to get him up to Williamstown he had been thoroughly bored and anxious to return to the city.

"You don't have to," he said as he took the two snifters of brandy from Jeremiah and set them on a low table near the fire. "It's a good-sized house I have, with plenty of room for you."

Dimly Mollie remembered that whenever he was particularly anxious about something he had a tendency to slip back into the speech rhythms of his Dublin childhood. That he had just done so puzzled her, though she didn't care to dwell on it. Other matters were more pressing.

"A house? You mean you're actually living here?" Padraic? The man who claimed there was no civilization outside the city and that being exposed to large chunks of sky undivided by buildings made him dizzy?

"A man's entitled to change, wouldn't you say?" he inquired. "I've decided I like the country. It's very... inspiring."

Gingerly Mollie sat down across from him and reached for her brandy. She took a sip, eyeing him over the rim of the glass. "You're writing again?"

He frowned slightly. "What makes you think I ever stopped? Heavens, woman, you ought to remember writing's like breathing to me."

"I thought it was," she agreed, "but there's been nothing from you in so long." Padraic's last play, *Winners and Losers*, had premiered shortly after their divorce to critical acclaim and a slew of prizes. It was still running three years later, a feat almost unheard of for a nonmusical. But since then there had been only silence.

"That doesn't mean I'm not working," he assured her. Leaning back in the chair, his big body apparently at ease, he looked perfectly at home in an environment where he had once been anything but. The blue chambray shirt stretched over his broad chest, the khaki trousers covering his long legs and the tweed jacket hung over the back of the chair were all well made but casual. He sat with one leg crossed over the other, a foot resting on the opposite knee, giving her a view of worn work boots with a few clumps of dirt clinging to the cleated soles.

Looking at him more closely Mollie saw that he was lightly tanned, and that the skin over his high cheekbones was ruddy, as though frequently exposed to sun and wind. His large hands, with their long, blunt-tipped fingers, were slightly chapped and, when he reached for his glass, she saw calluses on his palms.

"What have you been doing?" she asked. "Besides writing."

"This and that. You know what it's like living in the country; there's always something that needs seeing to."

True enough, except that she had a hard time picturing Padraic chopping wood, repairing a stone wall, milking a cow, or doing anything else of the sort. His idea of exercise had always been either a long, solitary run in the park or a savagely paced game of racquetball.

"Enough about me," he said. "I hear your company is a great success. Congratulations."

"Thanks," Mollie replied, a bit unsteadily. She was surprised, not to say disconcerted, that he knew anything at all about what she had been doing. Not only that, but he seemed genuinely happy for her, which severely diminished any chance she might have had to say "I told you so." Not, of course, that she would have indulged in anything so childish. It was only that she might have enjoyed pointing out to him how well she had done on her own.

Padraic watched the play of emotion across her face and repressed a smile. After the first shock of actually seeing her again he had settled down enough to drink in the sight of her. She was even more beautiful than he remembered. There was a piquancy about her delicate features that never failed to take his breath away.

Her unusually large blue eyes had always dominated her face, not only because of their size and loveliness, but because of the soul that shone through them. When she was happy they sparkled with silver lights. When she was sad or upset, as he sensed she was now, the glow was dimmer, as though a veil had fallen between her and the rest of the world.

The first time he had seen her, she had made him think of a forest sprite wary of being caught by the eye of man, let alone touched by him. Back then, when she was twenty-two and he was thirty, she had been all coltish angles and half-formed curves, the promise of a woman not yet fulfilled.

Now that was changed. From the top of her wild hair, in which the glowing whisper of the fire was caught, to the bottom of her slender feet, shod in the softest of leather pumps, she was a remarkably lovely thing. She had removed her coat when they sat down, revealing an elegantly draped dress of sapphire wool, one of her own designs, he guessed. It lightly skimmed her tall, slender body, managing at once to be both utterly proper and devastatingly sensual—not unlike the woman herself.

Padraic swallowed a large portion of his brandy and bade the memories stay away. He'd had enough of them over the long years. To be confronted with them again at the same time that he was looking at the cause would be too much.

"It's a remarkable coincidence," Mollie said slowly. "Our both turning up here at the same time."

Padraic shrugged. "These things happen. Besides, if you think about it, it really isn't all that remarkable. After all, I live here and you used to, so why shouldn't we run into each other?"

She didn't have an answer to that. Surely he must be right. The alternative, that the meeting had somehow been arranged, was ridiculous. Had Padraic needed to get in touch with her, he could have done so easily enough through her lawyer. Not that she could think why he would want to. Whatever they had once shared was long since over and done with.

Uneasy at his steady scrutiny, she glanced out the window. "It's starting to get dark. I'd better be going." Despite herself, the reluctance she felt as she contemplated the ruin of her plans was evident.

"Forget about finding a motel," Padraic urged. "You'll be more comfortable staying with me."

His weren't the only eloquent eyebrows; hers bespoke skepticism fluently. "I doubt that very much."

"Why? Surely we're long past the stage when we couldn't be pleasant to each other. You need a room, I have a spare, so why shouldn't you use it?"

"It's not that simple."

"It is if we want it to be," he insisted.

Mollie was tempted. The chance to spend a little time with Padraic was all but irresistible. That worried her. She fervently wished that she could feel nothing for him, but watching the play of light and shadow across his rugged features, she knew that wasn't the case.

Once she had loved him with all her heart and soul. Then, for a brief time, she had truly hated him. After that there had been only numbness, which now seemed to be fading with dangerous swiftness as pinpricks of awareness and need darted through her. She shifted uneasily in her chair and looked at him closely.

"Why are you being so nice to me?"

He lifted his eyes to heaven. "What a question to ask. Aren't you used to people being nice?"

"Sometimes . . . but not you. You're wonderful or you're terrible, never anything in-between."

He was silent for a long moment before he said, "I suppose I do tend toward extremes."

He sounded so regretful that Mollie couldn't stop herself from reaching out to him. Her hand touched his lightly. "That's just the way you are. There's no reason to wish otherwise."

"No?" His fingers curled around hers, warm and strong. "I could think of several reasons, but never mind. Shall we get started?"

"You're presuming I'll come with you."

He shook his head. "I'm presuming you're too kindhearted not to accept my offer in the spirit in which it's given."

"And that is?" she asked.

"Friendship, nothing more. Perhaps we won't be able to manage it, but I'd at least like to try."

While she thought it over he settled up with Jeremiah, who was doing his best not to look at either of them. The innkeeper murmured something Mollie didn't quite catch. She was too preoccupied, trying to come to terms with the idea of being friends with Padraic. They had never been that. Lovers, yes, sometimes adversaries, but never friends. There had always been far too much passion between them to allow for calm affection.

Yet it might still be possible. Time was, after all, supposed to heal all hurts. After three years it was important to her to believe that she could take Padraic in stride.

"All right," she said suddenly. "I'll stay with you, but only for tonight. Tomorrow I'm heading back to the city."

"Why?" he asked as they left the inn. It had begun to snow more heavily. Fat flakes drifted past them in the gathering twilight. An inch or so had already accumulated on the ground. Instinctively Mollie accepted Padraic's arm to keep herself from slipping.

"Surely there's no reason for you to rush back," he said as they reached her car. "Hadn't you planned to spend Christmas here?"

"At the inn. Since that isn't possible I may as well go back and get some work done."

His brows drew together in a dark scowl, and for a moment she thought she was about to witness an eruption of the famous Delaney temper. That faded as quickly as it had come, and he smiled mildly. "Why don't we talk about that in the morning?" Before she could answer he held open the car door for her, helped her in and closed it carefully. "I'm driving a red pickup," he said. "You shouldn't have any trouble following."

Mollie didn't, at least not at first. It wasn't until they turned off onto a dirt road running deep into the forest that she began to think there had been some mistake. The route they were following was all too familiar to her, though she had thought never to take it again. That she might had briefly occurred to her when she was planning her trip, but she had deliberately put the idea out of her mind.

It was one thing to return to her hometown for a few days; it was quite another to deliberately subject herself to all the memories, and all the regrets, that would come if she ever again set foot in the beloved farmhouse that had been her grandparents, and that she had been forced to sell in order to realize her dreams.

Yet it now appeared that was exactly what she was expected to do. Mollie's throat grew tight again and her heart pounded painfully when she drew up behind the red truck parked in front of the two-story house set in a clearing surrounded by ancient oak and maple trees. A stream ran nearby, and off to one side she could see the old stone well, long since boarded over. On either side of the porch rhododendron bushes had their leaves folded against the cold. The lawn was covered with snow on which she could see the tracks of a few late-foraging birds and squirrels.

Padraic had gotten out of the truck. Hastily, before he could get too close, she slipped from the car and stood staring at the house. For all her absorption, she was well aware of him when he came to her side.

"How long..." Her voice sounded like sandpaper on old wood. She stopped, cleared her throat, and tried again. "How long have you been renting it?" Please let it only be for a week or two; please let him be quickly on his way back out of her life.

"I haven't. I bought the house when you put it on the market three years ago."

Mollie turned and faced him squarely. "Why?"

He shrugged and let his gaze fall away. "Why not?" At her sharp intake of breath, signaling as he well knew the end of her patience, he went on quickly. "I'd decided to get out of the city, and I needed a place to live. Williamstown was the only small town I knew of, so it was only natural to start looking here. When the real estate agent told me the farmhouse was on the market I grabbed it."

She tugged her coat more closely around her, trying to shut out a chill she knew came from deep inside. "That doesn't make any sense. You hated the house. I was only able to get you to visit a couple of times, and you made it quite clear you didn't enjoy yourself."

"Yes... I suppose I did." His eyes were hooded as he jerked his head toward the porch. "The snow's getting heavier, and it's cold. Let's go inside."

Mollie didn't want to. Every instinct for survival that she possessed told her to get back into her car and put as much distance as she possibly could between herself and her ex-husband. He was altogether too compelling, and too dangerous. With very little effort he could make her forget all the staunch resolutions that guided her in her new life.

Except that she couldn't quite muster the strength to walk away, not from both Padraic and her grandparents' house. She might have been able to resist them separately, though she suspected that was debatable, but together they were too potent a reminder of her past to be ignored.

Besides, she was all but overwhelmed by curiosity to see what he had done to the place. With any luck he had ruined it, in which case she could leave with a clear conscience.

Luck, it seemed, wasn't with her. Barely had she stepped into her childhood home than she realized it had been receiving tender, loving care. Although much had changed—the walls were freshly painted; the floors and staircase had been sanded; the heavy, rather dour furniture she remembered was gone—much had also remained the same. Most importantly the sense of warmth and welcome she had always associated with the house was not only intact but stronger than ever.

She managed a shaky laugh. "I'm surprised."

"I realize it isn't exactly the same...."

"No, it isn't that. It's lovely. If I'd been able to keep the house I had all sorts of plans about what to do with it. Plans you seem to have carried out, yet..." She turned to him, her blue eyes filled with bewilderment. "I never told you about them, did I?"

He shook his head. "No, we never discussed that. Perhaps I just picked up some of your feelings for the old place."

She had never considered Padraic to be particularly sensitive to her feelings, let alone any so private as her love for the house he had disparaged. Yet there must be something to what he was saying, because he truly had captured her vision of what might have been.

How disconcerting to discover that what she had thought was locked forever in her mind existed quite firmly in reality. How disturbing to wonder what else she had long since come to think of as impossible might actually be within her grasp.

Chapter Three

"You look tired," Padraic said gently. "Why don't you go upstairs and get settled in while I see about dinner?"

Mollie nodded absently. She was still struggling to come to terms with being in the house. Climbing the stairs, she noted that they still creaked in all the same places. At the top she suddenly thought of something and turned around, surprised to find Padraic still standing in the hall looking up at her.

"How will I know which is the guest room?"

"It's your old room. I took your grandparents'."

Of course, she should have expected that. The only other room on the second floor, besides the bath, was a tiny cubicle under the eaves that Grania had used for sewing. Telling herself that it didn't matter, she walked down the short corridor and gingerly opened the door she knew so well. A sigh of relief escaped her as she realized that her former room, like the rest of the house, had been redecorated.

The narrow oak bed she had slept in was gone, as were the battered pine dresser she had used and the old school desk where she had done her homework. In their place was a delightful four-poster bed of shaker design covered with a traditional Lone Star pattern quilt in white and blue. A braided rag rug in the same colors covered the floor. White lace curtains hung at the windows. A golden pine armoire took up most of one wall, with a matching dresser opposite it. On the dresser a poinsettia plant in a wicker basket added a festive touch.

Much of the tension Mollie had been feeling ever since she walked into the inn and discovered her plans had gone awry began to ease. She unpacked quickly, placing her few toiletries on the dresser. The lacy underwear she favored and two equally feminine nightgowns went into a drawer. In the closet she hung the slacks, shirts and sweaters she had brought, along with the long black evening skirt she had added at the last minute. On the back of the door she hung her wooly white robe, chosen more for practicality than looks. She had expected the inn to be drafty, and while the house was less so, it too had its cold patches.

That done, she ran a brush through her hair in a futile effort to give it some sense of order. The gesture was made out of habit; no matter how many times she had tried to tame the riot of cinnamon waves she had never even come close to succeeding. Admitting defeat yet again, she left the brush on the dresser and went back downstairs.

Padraic was in the kitchen, standing in front of a six-burner stove that looked as though it belonged in a gourmet restaurant. He was stirring a large pot from which tempting aromas wafted.

She was about to comment on the incongruity of the situation, having never seen him so much as boil water before, when two things simultaneously captured her attention. One was the large, beautifully decorated Christmas tree in the far corner of the kitchen, near the fireplace. The other was the Irish wolfhound that had just hurled itself at her and was busy licking her face.

"O'Casey!" she exclaimed with delight, prompting his tail to wag all the more fiercely and his tongue to scrub all the more devotedly. They had been great pals, she and O'Casey, in the years she was with Padraic. The dog had been little more than a pup when she first met him and, though devoted to his master, he had wholeheartedly accepted her as the second most important person in his life. Apparently he hadn't forgotten.

"Down boy," Padraic said with gentle firmness. The dog obeyed instantly, but sat on his haunches scant inches from Mollie's feet, his eyes on her adoringly and his tongue lolling at the ready.

"I've missed O'Casey," she said as she scratched the dog behind his ear.

"At least that's something."

"What?"

"Never mind. Dinner's almost ready. That is, if you still like bouillabaisse."

Mollie assured him that she did. The spicy seafood stew had always been one of her favorites. "Don't tell me you just whipped this up," she teased as, following his directions, she took French bread from the oven where it had been warming and sliced it.

"I made it this morning. It's better when it's had a chance to sit for a few hours."

"When did you learn to cook?"

"After I moved up here. It was that or starve." He smiled as he ladled two large bowls full of the stew. "You know how it is here, everyone's expected to be self-reliant."

"True, but you could have hired someone to come in to help."

"I preferred to be by myself for a while."

That was all he said, but Mollie got the feeling there had been a great deal more to his decision to isolate himself in the country than he was saying. Even if she had felt up to questioning him further, there was no opportunity as he neatly changed the subject.

"What do you think of the tree?"

"It's lovely, just like the ones I remember from..." She stopped and, at the quick flash of acknowledgment in his eyes, peered more closely at the decorations. Wooden soldiers in gaily painted uniforms, sparkling birds with golden beaks and shimmering glass ornaments danced in front of her eyes. On the top of the tree was a white dove. Nestled within the branches was a very old, fragile angel holding a lyre.

"H-how... how did you get these?"

"They were in the attic," Padraic said as he set the bowls on the table. "You must have left them here after our last Christmas together."

She had done exactly that, and had managed not to think of them since. They were the decorations from her childhood, except for the dove, which she had purchased herself. How well she remembered that day. She and Padraic had had yet another fight, and she had gone off by herself so that he wouldn't see her tears or her pain.

Wandering through the streets, feeling sorry for herself because Christmas was coming even as she suspected her marriage was ending, she had spied the dove in a store window. Some impulse, perhaps lingering hopefulness, had driven her to buy it, and later to return to their apartment and persuade Padraic to come to Williamstown with her for the holiday.

He'd gone along despite the fact that the one other trip he'd made there had not been a success. Buoyed by her own enthusiasm, Mollie hadn't noticed the lack of his until it was too late. Only afterward did she realize that he had been in the throes of writing an extremely difficult play, one that he hadn't been sure he would ever be able to finish.

Genius was a harsh taskmaster. Padraic put more of himself into what he did than anyone she knew. Unfortunately, that had left very little for anything else, including their relationship.

Despite her best efforts the holiday had turned out to be tense and cheerless. Before it was over they had fought again and gone back to the city separately. One of the last things she had done before leaving was to pack up the Christmas ornaments and put them away in the attic.

"I'm surprised you bothered with a tree," she said as he held her chair for her and she slipped into it. "That sort of sentiment never seemed to appeal to you."

He took his place opposite her and reached for the wine to fill both their glasses. "I did manage to give you that impression, didn't I?"

"Are you saying it wasn't true?"

"No, only that it was incomplete." At her puzzled look he explained, "I never let you see why I didn't like holidays, all the excitement and the expectations. But then, there's so much I never let you even glimpse."

Mollie had always suspected as much, but she was astonished to hear him admit it. Early on in their marriage she had tried hard to get to know Padraic as he truly was beneath the facade of sophistication and brilliance. Her every attempt had been adroitly blocked, until she had finally given up, thinking that perhaps there really wasn't anything more. But always she had known better.

"Tell me," she said softly.

He took a deep breath and let it out slowly. "You know I grew up in Dublin and came to this country when I was eighteen. What I never told you was how damn poor my family was. Tinkers, we were called, and I suppose Tinkers we were, since we were always moving from one place to another trying to stay ahead of the rent collector. Dad worked when he happened to be in the mood; more often than not he preferred spending his time at the bottom of a bottle. Ma did the best she could, but it was too much for her. She walked out when I was ten, and that's the last any of us saw of her."

"Oh, Padraic... I'm so sorry...."

His face hardened for an instant, then relented. She could almost see him fighting against the instinct to close her out. For the first time she glimpsed where that came from.

"I got over being sorry about it a long time ago," he said. "Around the time I began to realize that this gift I have...or curse, whichever seems more apt at the moment...wouldn't be the same if I'd grown up in a nice genteel family. Self-pity isn't my problem, thank God, but I do seem to have a problem with looking on the brighter side of life and really believing it exists."

"I can see why now." Hesitant about probing too far, but anxious to know more, she asked, "Why did you decide to come to the States?"

He smiled wryly. "Mainly because that's where the ship I was on happened to dock. I signed up on a freighter when I was fifteen. They weren't too particular about papers, and I was big for my age. In the next three years I saw most of the world. By the time we hit New Orleans with a load of pipe fittings, I was ready to move on."

"You never mentioned any of that, either."

"I was ashamed of it," he said bluntly. At her incredulous look he went on. "Try to see it from my point of view. There you were, the sheltered granddaughter of two fine, loving people, and there I was, ex-tinker's brat, ex-stevedore, ex-jack-of-all-trades turned playwright. I was eight years older than you, but there seemed to be at least a couple of centuries between us in experience. I was terrified of hurting or disillusioning you, and in the end I managed to do both."

"Knowing the truth about you wouldn't have caused either," she murmured. "It was being kept in the dark that led to problems."

"I'm sorry, Mollie."

"Don't be," she said. "If there's anything I've learned over the last few years its that regrets are always futile." Her eyes met his across the table. "I think you know that, too."

"I do," he agreed, "but there are still times when I wish things had been different between us."

So did she, but she had meant what she said about not looking back. How much better it was to concentrate on the present. With a smile she picked up her spoon and began to eat the bouillabaisse, pausing only to compliment him on it. After a moment Padraic followed suit.

The fire sent a warm glow through the room. O'Casey lay at their feet, his long snout resting on his paws. Tiny lights on the Christmas tree twinkled brightly. Outside the snow continued to fall, heavier than before, but inside there was peace and comfort.

After dinner Padraic and Mollie cleared up, then settled in front of the fire with their glasses and the remains of the wine. Mollie had kicked off her shoes and curled her long legs under her. She was feeling pleasantly drowsy, but not yet ready for sleep.

"This is very nice," she murmured, almost to herself.

Seated beside her, close though not touching, Padraic smiled. "It is that. I can't remember the last time I felt so relaxed."

"Me either." The world she had left only a few hours before—of crowded city streets, the constant demands of her business, her own persona as a self-made professional—all seemed very far away. She viewed it with some befuddlement, as though unsure whether it was real or a briefly imagined dream.

That was nonsense, of course. Undoubtedly the product of her fatigue, the wine, the shock of being with Padraic. If anything, this was the dream. She would be only half surprised to wake up in her apartment and discover that she had never left New York.

"What are you thinking about?" Padraic asked.

"Dreams. How lovely they are...exciting, but safe."

"Is this a dream?"

Mollie frowned slightly. "Don't you know?"

"Logically it's real. But what has logic to do with anything?"

She looked into the fire, than back to him. "Too complicated. Either it is a dream or it isn't."

"And if it is?" He had moved closer. She could feel the warmth of his big, hard body reaching out to her, supplanting the warmth of the fire, which seemed somehow to be growing hazy and far away. The couch they sat on was wrapped in shadows, giving it an insubstantial form well suited to dreams.

If it was...? How would she feel then? To throw off the shackles of reality was an enticement she could scarcely resist. After so many years of having to be relentlessly pragmatic, the chance to indulge long-suppressed needs beckoned seductively.

Her lips parted soundlessly and, without knowing, she moistened them with the tip of her tongue.

Padraic's mouth tightened. He reached out and took her glass from her unresisting hand, setting it on the table beside his own. "Mollie, do you have an idea what it's doing to me to be so close to you and not know if I should . . . ?''

"Should what?'' Was that her voice, so soft and caressing? She put a hand to the back of her neck and absently lifted the thick weight of her hair. How green Padraic's eyes were. She could fall into them forever and never land. Like Alice through the looking glass, into another time and place. A dream.

A low groan broke from him. He bent his head, and his mouth touched hers, hot and yearning, savoring the softness of her lips. Unthinkingly she responded. Her hair drifted again over her shoulders as she reached out to him, cupping the back of his head, fingers tangling in rough ebony silk, drawing him closer.

Well-remembered and long-missed pleasure rippled through her. She knew what was happening was crazy; she should call a halt immediately. But somehow she couldn't bring herself to do it.

What was the harm, really? She wasn't involved with anyone else, hadn't been since her divorce, despite sporadic attempts to feel something for another man. And there was no evidence of another woman in Padraic's life; if there was one, at least she wasn't living with him.

Who would be hurt if they made love, just this once? His mouth had drifted down to her long, slender throat, and against his lips he felt the ripple of her laughter. His head jerked up. "You find this funny?''

"No, not exactly. I was only thinking that we should wait for New Years. You know, for auld lang syne."

"I don't want to wait," he said. "And I don't think you do, either." As though to prove his point his big hands cupped her breasts, feeling through the soft wool of her dress and the lace of her bra the hardened proof of her arousal.

"Did you know," he went on silkily, "that I was always fascinated by your nipples? They're such a delicate shade of pink and so incredibly responsive."

Mollie could feel herself blushing all the way down to the part of her in question. In an effort to right the balance she ran her hands over his chest and nipped lightly at his chin. "I could go on about how fascinated I was by your body, but I wouldn't want to embarrass you."

"That's all right," he assured her hastily. "I can stand it."

"Well then..." The words she murmured in his ear, contrary to his assurances, made him flush darkly. Before she had said all that was on her mind he grasped her waist and lowered her onto the couch.

Giddy with hunger and the intoxicating sense of her own power, Mollie smiled up at him. "I'll have you know we're in the process of crushing a very expensive dress."

"Can't have that," Padraic said, his voice low and raw with need. Before she could take another breath he had adeptly unzipped the dress and lowered it from her shoulders. "Sit up a little."

Mutely she obeyed, and the garment was stripped from her and tossed over the back of a chair. When she had dressed that morning it was with no expectation that anyone would see her half-naked. The bra and panties she had chosen were delicately feminine, as always. But she was also wearing panty hose, which she knew Padraic hated.

"I haven't changed my mind about these things," he said as he took hold of the waistband and pulled them down over her hips and thighs. He stopped for an instant, giving her a chance to object to his handling of her. When she did not, he finished removing the panty hose and tossed them on the floor.

Looming over her, he began to unbutton his shirt. She lay against the cushions and watched him, aware that her breath was coming fast and hard, causing her breasts to rise above the narrow cups of her bra and threaten to spill over.

Padraic was equally aware of the danger, and the temptation. He managed to withstand it long enough to get his shirt off and undo his belt, but then he had to pause and give his driving need release.

"This thing isn't locked, is it?" he demanded as he reached behind her to fumble with the catch of her bra.

"I don't think so," she assured him breathlessly. When it still wouldn't give after a moment she raised herself slightly and, replacing his hands with hers, undid the clasp. The lacy fabric fell away from her, revealing her breasts to his hungry eyes.

"Lord," he whispered, "you're every bit as beautiful as I remember."

"You aren't bad yourself," she managed huskily. Hardly aware of what she was doing, she rubbed against him, feeling the rough texture of his chest hair on her swollen nipples.

"I can't stand much more of this," he murmured.

"Then don't."

Their eyes met, his questioningly, hers still with a hint of uncertainty, but also with conviction. Whatever happened afterward, whatever the regrets or consequences, she could not leave him now any more than he could leave her.

Standing up swiftly, he removed the rest of his clothes and stood before her proudly naked. The sheer strength of him gave her a moment's pause, but that faded instantly and she reached out to him.

With a groan he came to her, his head burrowing into the warmth between her breasts even as his hands removed her last garment. When the final barrier was gone they moved together artlessly.

Their joining was swift; neither could bear to wait a heartbeat longer. But for Mollie it was also slightly painful. Padraic felt her flinch and stopped, lifting himself above her. His eyes were dark, clouded with mingled desire and concern, as he stared into hers.

"Mollie . . . are you all right?"

"Yes," she assured him quickly. "It's just that I haven't . . . that is, it's been a long time for me."

"How long?" The words were out before he could stop them. Even as he cursed himself inwardly, knowing that he had no right to ask, he couldn't help being filled by a burgeoning sense of elation.

"Since you," she said, and gasped when he reflexively moved within her. "I tried, God knows, but I couldn't."

"I'm glad," he said fiercely. "Forgive me, but I am." Then he moved again, and she forgot everything except the overwhelming pleasure he was bringing her and, at its end the blinding joy of absolute release.

Chapter Four

The first thing Mollie saw when she opened her eyes the next morning was the poinsettia on the dresser. She stared at it blankly for several moments until the implications of where she was sank in. Then she sat up abruptly.

The covers fell away to reveal that she was naked. She grabbed for them hastily, even though she was alone and likely to remain so. Padraic had seemed to understand the night before that she needed time by herself to come to terms with what had happened. He had acquiesced to her sleeping in the guest room, though she knew he would have preferred her to share his.

Had she done so they would undoubtedly have made love again, which would only have left her with more problems to sort out.

She had more than enough as it was. Wrapped in her robe, she slipped out the door, listened for a moment, then hurried into the bathroom. A hot shower helped to restore her equilibrium a little, but nothing could banish the sense of unreality that pursued her from the night before.

When she returned to her room and dressed in a pair of warm wool slacks and a bulky sweater, she knew that she was choosing the clothes as much for their lack of allure as their practicality. That done, she began to brush her hair, only to break off when her glance fell on what lay beyond her windows.

Snow. A great deal of it. Stretching as far as the eye could see, weighing down the trees, gathering in immense drifts, blowing on the brisk wind, and still falling. A blizzard's worth, firmly ending any tentative idea she might have had about staging a quick exit.

With a harried grimace she went downstairs. The sounds she'd heard earlier had stopped, and now there was only silence in the house. Puzzled, she poked her head into the kitchen and found it empty. A coffeepot sat on a low flame on the stove; otherwise there was no sign of Padraic.

O'Casey's ecstatic woof drew her to the back door. She opened it and peered out. A path had been shoveled from the kitchen to the woodshed a short distance away. As she watched Padraic appeared from around the other side, wheeling a cartload of logs. When he saw her, he stopped and frowned.

"You shouldn't be standing in the door like that. It's too cold. Go back inside."

Mollie bristled at his authoritarian tone. It grated on her independent nature, not to mention providing a severe letdown from his loving behavior of the night before. "I'm fine," she informed him tartly. "I see it snowed."

"Very good," he drawled. "Ever think of becoming a meteorologist?"

She flushed and whirled around, storming back inside and slamming the door behind her. Where did he get off being so sarcastic with her? Furiously she blinked back tears, telling herself that she was a fool to care what he thought. But after what they had shared his derision was even harder to take than she could have imagined.

She was still trembling when the door opened behind her, and a moment later she felt a warm, firm hand on her arm. "I'm sorry, Mollie. I don't know what got into me."

Refusing to look at him, she shrugged. "It doesn't matter."

"Of course it does." Insistently, despite her half hearted resistance, he turned her around and gently lifted her chin so that she had no choice but to meet his eyes. "What happened last night was so beautiful that it threw me. I woke up this morning not sure of anything except that I wished we could have gone on as we were forever. That scared the hell out of me, and I took it out on you the first chance I got."

His honesty soothed her, enough so that she was driven to match it. "I was scared, too."

He laughed softly. "We're a pair."

An odd choice of words, she thought, but undeniably apt. Or at least it had been during the five years of their marriage, and again last night. But that was all, she reminded herself. What had passed between them in the hours of darkness had been a dream, nothing more. To forget that would be to open the way for pain greater than any she had yet experienced.

"Are we snowed in?" she managed to ask.

He nodded. "The electricity and phone are out. We can figure it will be at least a couple of days before the roads are cleared." At her quick look of concern he added, "There's nothing to worry about. We've got plenty of food, and there's an auxiliary generator to run the water pump. As far as keeping warm goes," he said smiling, "we'll have to use our ingenuity."

"Let's use that wood you brought in instead," she suggested with some asperity.

He chuckled, but didn't press the matter, and a few minutes later she saw him feeding bits of tinder into the cast iron stove that stood at the opposite end of the kitchen from the fireplace. "This will work better than an open fire," he explained, "though I'll start that, too."

Mollie nodded, but otherwise didn't respond. She was afraid that if she tried to speak her voice would give away the fact that she had been surreptitiously watching him while she prepared breakfast. The graceful movements of his large, muscular body had never failed to fascinate her. When he straightened up and brushed off his hands she hastily looked away.

"Breakfast is ready."

"Good," he said. "I'm starved."

So was she, though she told herself it was because of the cold. In fact she knew perfectly well that vigorous lovemaking had always increased her appetite. Padraic knew it, too; he grinned as she helped herself to a second slice of toast and liberally spread it with raspberry jam.

"Hungry?" he asked mildly as he held out the plate of crisp bacon.

"A little." To substantiate that claim she forced herself to take only one strip instead of the three or four she would have liked. Since she had cooked so much that left a considerable pile on the plate, but Padraic made short work of that, as he did of the toast and the fluffy scrambled eggs—to which she had added a hint of dill before realizing that she had done so because he liked them that way.

"You were always a great cook," he said as he sat back, replete at last.

"I managed. Are you sure you had enough?" She looked pointedly at the array of empty plates. He had a nerve being able to eat like that and not put any weight on.

"Worrying about your waistline?"

His uncanny ability to read her thoughts had always disconcerted her, but never more so than now. "No," she said as she stood up and began to clear the table.

Padraic rose and gestured her back into her chair. "I'll do it. Have another cup of coffee and relax."

She wanted to say that she couldn't possibly relax with him so near, but stopped herself in time and managed to feign interest in an old magazine while he tidied up the kitchen. When he had finished he returned to her, saw what she was doing and shook his head. "I had no idea you were interested in commodities futures."

"What?"

"The article you're reading. It's about commodities trading, specifically futures." Lights danced in his emerald eyes as he realized he had caught her out. "I tried to make sense of it myself a few weeks ago without much luck. Maybe you could explain it to me."

"I'm afraid not. Padraic . . ."

He pulled out his chair and sat down beside her. "Yes?"

"We can't go on like this, dancing around each other." She took a deep breath. "Perhaps what happened last night shouldn't have, but I can't bring myself to really regret it. If you do, I'm sorry."

"I don't."

He spoke so softly that it took her a moment to understand what she had heard. Her eyes flew to his face. "Really?"

Padraic nodded somberly. "I'm glad it happened. No woman has ever meant as much to me as you do, and now I'm sure none ever will."

"I don't understand." He had spoken as though he still cared for her, as though no one else had ever mattered. But she knew that couldn't possibly be true. "What about Jessica?"

He flinched, and for a moment she thought he didn't mean to answer, but at length he said, "Jessica was . . . a mistake."

Mollie choked back a humorless laugh. "I suppose that's as good a word as any."

"I mean it. I used her to hurt you, because I was angry that you didn't trust me. As soon as I'd done it, I knew it was wrong, but it was already too late."

"I don't want to talk about it anymore." The mere thought of Jessica Peters—the beautiful, sensuous actress who was the toast of both Broadway and Hollywood—made her stomach twist painfully.

"I think we'd better."

"No." She started to rise, thinking only of getting away.

His hand lashed out, closing over her wrist in a grip that would have hurt if it hadn't eased so quickly. "Please, Mollie, give me a chance."

More even than the words, the anguish in his voice reached her. He was a proud man who had never begged for anything, yet she sensed that he would do so now if that was what it would take to make her listen. Humbled by his willingness to make so great an effort, she relented.

"It wasn't what you thought," he said when she sat down again. "Jessica was never my mistress."

"Are you saying you never slept with her?" Mollie demanded incredulously.

"No, I'm not. I slept with her, all right. What I'm saying is that I never made love with her, or had sex, or got involved, or however else you want to put it."

Mollie didn't believe him. She simply couldn't, after so much pain and disappointment. Yet neither could she completely ignore the ring of truth in his words. Whatever else Padraic might have been, he had never been a liar. Truth shone from the man himself as it did from his prose. Could that have changed, or was there a chance she had misjudged him?

"Tell me," she said, knowing even as she spoke the words that they should have uttered years before. "The night you spent with her, what happened?"

"You remember we were rehearsing *Winners and Losers*?" When she nodded, he went on. "The run-through went very late. Afterward we all went out to dinner. You and I had fought that morning about the same problem that had been at the crux of all our arguments. You wanted your own career; I wanted you to devote yourself to me. It was damn selfish on my part, I admit that. But at the time I didn't see it, and I was in no mood to start up with you again. Anyway, after the others left I stayed on at the restaurant with Jessica. After a while she suggested we go to her apartment.''

Good old Jessica, Mollie thought glumly. She could picture the other woman seeing her opportunity and not hesitating to grab it.

''Neither one of us was feeling any pain when we got to her place,'' Padraic said. ''We sat on the couch, still talking. She was easy to be with, beautiful, intelligent—'' he smiled slightly ''—admiring of me and my work. She took me very seriously, did old Jessie.''

''So you went to bed with her?''

''With the worst intentions. I fully planned to give her everything she wanted and them some. After all, it had been quite a while since you and I had made love, and I was more than ready.''

''I see,'' Mollie said. ''But then how can you claim that you didn't . . . ?''

''Because, sweet love, Mother Nature—no accident she's female—always has a few tricks up her sleeve where would-be wayward husbands are concerned. There I was, all primed for action, and suddenly, there I wasn't. If you get my meaning.''

Mollie did, though it took a moment. She had always found Padraic to be an incredible lover, strong, tender, giving, and unfailingly virile. Exactly as he had been the night before. To think that he hadn't been able to perform with a woman took some getting used to.

"Does this have anything to do with why you left New York?" she asked.

"Did I flee in horror of my lost manhood?"

She flushed, but nodded.

"No, it wasn't that at all. I left when I realized you were convinced I'd been unfaithful to you."

Her eyes closed briefly, reflecting hurtful memories. "Davey Benson called me that morning, after you'd been out all night. Remember him?"

"Vividly. Last I heard he was doing toilet cleaner commercials."

Mollie giggled. "That's about what he deserves. He loved every minute of telling me that you were with Jessica. He even gave me her address and said if I didn't believe him, I should go see for myself."

"So you did."

She nodded grimly. All too well she remembered the moment when Jessica had answered the door clad only in a sheer nightie and languidly beckoned her inside, just as Padraic walked out of the bedroom.

They had stared at each other for a long, agonizing moment before Mollie had turned and run for her very life.

"I should have waited," she murmured, "to hear what you had to say."

"I thought so, too, at the time, but since then I've come to see it in a different perspective. The fact that I hadn't actually made love to Jessica didn't mean that I hadn't failed you. I had, and in the process I'd failed myself." He laughed harshly. "With hindsight I even know why it all happened."

"Why?" Mollie said softly.

"For months I'd felt my life slipping away from me. I was being seduced by my own success and didn't realize it. What had once sustained me, the straightforward compulsion to tell a tale, was no longer enough. I wanted money, fame, adulation, and believed them all to be my right. Against all this stood you, with your own problems about my success, yet also a continual reminder that there was a great deal more to life."

"I didn't mean to hold you back in any way."

"You didn't. On the contrary, without you I would never have gone as far as I did. I found that out after we separated, when nothing seemed worthwhile. So I came here, first to lick my wounds, then to rediscover myself. I bought the farmhouse because I told myself it happened to be convenient. But in fact I missed you terribly and felt closer to you here."

Mollie closed her eyes against the tears that were threatening to fall. A piercing sense of sadness filled her. If only she and Padraic had been so honest with each other in the past, they would never have come to such a point. All the pain and regret of the last few years could have been avoided.

"Don't," Padraic said. He touched her cheek gently with the back of his hand in a gesture she remembered all too well. "There's no point in thinking about what might have been. The past is the only thing we can't change."

"It's just that..." She broke off and took a deep breath, fighting for control. What she had to say was hard enough without breaking down in the middle. "I was in love with you. Really in love. I thought we would be together for the rest of our lives, and when I realized that wasn't going to happen it was almost more than I could bear."

"You came out of it all right, though. The success you've had since shows that."

"Don't be fooled," she said. "I'm proud of what I've accomplished, but I know a lot of it happened because I felt driven to fill the enormous hole in my life after you were gone."

He shook his head in bewilderment. "I thought you'd always wanted your own business."

"So I did, but not quite to the extent I've achieved." She made a sound halfway between a laugh and a sob. "A claim could be made that I've overdone it."

"Is that how you feel?"

"I don't know," she admitted. "There are days when everything goes great and I'm on top of the world. Then there are times when there are loads of problems, but I feel a great deal of satisfaction in dealing with them. But once in a while—" she smiled wanly "—I wake up in the middle of the night wondering why on earth I'm bothering. What's the point?"

He nodded slowly. "I know what you mean. It's happened to me, too."

"How could it have? Your writing is your life."

"Was," he corrected. "Not anymore."

A chill ran through her. If Padraic had lost his tremendous gift, something truly important had gone out of the world. "But you said you were still working."

"I am, and the irony of it is that the results are better than ever. The difference is that they don't satisfy me the way they once did."

"Do you know why that is?" If he had found the answer, perhaps he could share it with her.

"Yes, I know."

"Why?"

He looked at her for a long moment, then smiled gently. "Later, sweetheart. We'll talk about it later. In the meantime, let's go out and play."

Chapter Five

"In the snow?" Mollie asked.

"Of course. How could we pass it up?" He rose and held out a hand to her. "We'll make angels and build a snowman. And if that isn't serious enough for you, we can put out food for the animals. With this bad storm, they'll need it."

Within an hour Mollie was flushed and laughing. Snowflakes clung to her eyelashes and the wisps of hair escaping from beneath the knit hat Padraic had insisted she wear. He had even rummaged around and found her a pair of mittens that looked vaguely familiar to her.

"I left these here, too, didn't I?" she asked when they were catching their breath after hauling out and spreading several bales of hay, as well as what seemed like at least half a ton of nuts and seed.

He nodded, his eyes glowing from the exertion and something else she didn't quite want to recognize. "They were in a drawer."

"Why didn't you throw them out?"

"Never got around to it, I guess."

Mollie didn't believe him, but that was all right. The snow was beginning to taper off, and patches of blue sky showed through the clouds. It was very cold, and the air had a crystalline quality that made every sound reverberate in a high, sweet way.

With much laughing and teasing they built a snowman who turned out to be slightly lopsided but still perfectly respectable. They made angels in the snow. Padraic had a hard time getting back onto his feet without mussing them; Mollie had to show him how. When she held out her hand, he took it and tugged.

"Oooff."

"Sorry, sweetheart, I couldn't resist."

Lying on her back, she stared up at him. His skin was ruddy with the cold, and his eyes gleamed brightly. A pulse beat in his jaw, which she suspected had nothing to do with their exertions.

Memories of the previous night flitted through her mind. She parted her lips and sighed softly.

He held himself above her a moment longer, big and hard, yet not in the least threatening. Her last coherent thought before his mouth covered hers with fierce demand was that she was a match for him.

His tongue searched her moist warmth with devastating thoroughness. He filled her with the taste and scent of him, evoking all the while an even more intimate possession. Through the barriers of their heavy clothes she could feel his arousal. A low, yearning moan broke from her as her hands tangled in his thick hair, holding him even closer.

When he moved she did not know, but one instant she was lying beneath him, pressed into the snow, and the next their positions had been reversed. She rested on his broad chest, looking down at him bemusedly. He smiled so tenderly that for a moment her heart stopped. Without thinking she initiated a kiss that in its own way was as powerfully sensual as the one they had just shared.

When it was over they were both breathing hard. Mollie felt taken aback, even embarrassed. Now that she thought about it, she realized that she had never been the aggressor in their lovemaking. Perhaps because of the difference in their ages and experience, that role had always fallen to Padraic. By the time they might have changed, the habit was solidly set.

He saw the hesitation in her eyes and stood up, without any difficulty this time, drawing her with him. They gave a great deal of attention to brushing the snow off each other's backs, which effectively did away with any unease and led to a mad chase back to the house.

"Hot chocolate," he announced when they were back inside. "In front of the fire. I might even be able to find a few marshmallows to toast."

"Who could ask for anything more?"

They did an off-key rendition of the song of the same name, making up most of the words as they went along. O'Casey lay down on the floor and eyed them mournfully.

"Sorry, boy," Mollie said, petting him apologetically. "We'll cut it out."

"Remember when we used to sing in the shower?" Padraic asked as he took a saucepan from the cupboard and poured milk into it.

"Uh...I suppose." She was blushing, but hoped he would think it was from the cold.

"Suppose? Those are some of the fondest memories of my life."

Mollie broke down and grinned. "There were times when I thought I was doomed to pruneyness."

"You made a terrific-looking prune, honey. Believe me."

"Hmm, you weren't so bad yourself. Now do you mind if we change the subject?"

"Yes, but I can live with it. How about some music?"

Mollie agreed, and he stuck a tape in the stereo. Soft Christmas music filled the room.

"Do you mind?" he asked.

"No, I guess I'm in more of a holiday mood than I thought."

"Me too."

"It's nice, isn't it?" she said, looking at the tree, but seeing him.

"Yes, I can see now why people do this regularly." He sat down beside her and handed her a steaming cup of cocoa.

She took a sip and giggled. "I was just thinking how angry I was at Jerry when he messed up my reservation at the inn, and now I'm glad he did."

"Uh . . . sweetheart, there's something I have to tell you about that."

She cast him a long look through her lashes. "Oh, really?"

"Since I've been living here Jerry's gotten to be a good friend."

"How nice."

"He knew I missed you."

"Did he by any chance mention I was coming up?"

"I believe he did. Only in passing, mind you."

"Funny thing," Mollie said, "about those people who decided to stay on longer than they'd planned. You know, the ones Jerry couldn't bring himself to put out."

"There weren't any."

"What's that?"

"The people, they didn't exist. I asked Jerry to tell you there was no room."

Mollie sighed and licked a trace of cocoa from her upper lip. "Devious of you."

"I was desperate."

"Never, not you."

"Really, I was. The moment I heard you were coming back I knew I had to see you, and more than that, I wanted us to really have a chance to talk. It seemed like a godsend until I realized you'd be staying at the inn and there was no reason for us to even run into each other."

"I have to tell you the truth, Padraic. I'm enormously touched that you went to such lengths."

"Really?"

She nodded solemnly. "It's very flattering."

"Well, good. I was afraid you might be annoyed."

"Because you manipulated me?"

He groaned softly. "You are annoyed."

The smile she gave him, soft and lingering, assured him that she was anything but. "You've turned into a romantic."

"My deep, dark secret and you blurt it out."

"I'm sure O'Casey is shocked."

He got up, tossed another log on the fire and returned to her. Silence reigned, except for the crackle and hiss of the flames. At length, without looking at her, he said, "I want you back, Mollie. I want us to try again."

She had always imagined that if she ever heard those words she would be on top of the world. What divorced woman didn't occasionally fantasize about a repentant ex-husband longing for a reconciliation? But that was all it was, the stuff of dreams, with no connection to reality.

Softly, she said, "We've changed a great deal, Padraic."

"For the better."

"Maybe, but we've done it separately. You're not the man I married, and I'm certainly not the woman you chose as your wife."

"We're still the same people," he insisted. "We've simply learned a few things along the way."

"It's true the last few years have been very... educational. For one thing, I've learned that I need a great deal of independence. I've gotten used to making my own decisions and going my own way without having to consider anyone else. Not only that, but I've discovered that I like that kind of freedom."

"You were telling me that you wondered sometimes if it was all worthwhile."

"Everyone has dark moments of self-doubt. I'm no different in that respect. What I'm saying is that I could never go back to the way I used to be, subordinating my own needs to someone else's."

"Namely mine."

Sadly, she nodded. "It wasn't your fault. For a long time I blamed you, but now I know better. I was so young, and so uncertain, that it was easiest for me to try to live through you."

"Plenty of women do that with their husbands."

"And I doubt if one of them has ever been truly happy. No, it wasn't for me. Wasn't and isn't."

"There's no reason to think it would happen again," he said.

"But the potential is there, and it scares the daylights out of me."

He put down his cup and turned to her, taking her face between his big hands and looking directly into her eyes. "Ask yourself this, mavourneen," he said, his voice taking on a soft burr. "Are you really afraid of me, or of yourself?"

Through stiffened lips she murmured, "Is this a trick question?"

He laughed and dropped a soft kiss on her mouth. "No tricks, not now and not ever. But I meant what I said. I hurt you, so it's natural for you to be afraid, but you have far more control over this situation than you think."

"Last night," she reminded him, "I had no control at all."

He sat back and regarded her steadily. "Is that what troubles you?"

"It was exactly as it had always been, you leading and me following. Not," she added hastily, "that I minded. It was beautiful and . . . thrilling."

"Thank you," he said gravely. "However, it can't have been a complete success if it left you with such doubts."

"Was that the purpose, to erase all my doubts and make me agreeable to anything you wanted?"

"In part," he admitted disarmingly. "I'm a man, not a saint. I want you, and I'm not overly scrupulous about how I get you."

"Thanks for the warning."

"As though you needed it. You understand me better than you think."

"It's true that I understand enough to be afraid," she said.

"Because of last night?"

When she nodded, he sighed deeply. "I didn't mean that to happen. I'd told myself that I'd be the soul of patience. But once you were actually here, so close to me, I couldn't restrain myself."

"Don't sound so regretful. As I said, it was good."

"Not if you're frightened off."

The music stopped. In the sudden silence Mollie could hear her heart thudding ominously. She was coming face-to-face with truths she wasn't necessarily ready to confront. Truths about herself even more than about Padraic. Honesty forced her to admit that was the true source of her fear.

"My grandparents," she said suddenly, "were very good to me."

"So you've always said."

"It's a shame they died before you could meet them. They would both have liked you, and I think you would have felt the same way about them."

"I'm sure I would have, but . . ."

"But what's that got to do with anything?"

"Obviously something. Will you explain it to me?"

She was willing enough to try, which was more than she had ever done in the past. Slowly she said, "You know my parents were killed when I was eight?"

He nodded. "In a car accident. A terrible tragedy."

"Yes, it was, and not only because they were my parents. They were also very good people, and so much in love." She smiled wistfully. "That's what I remember most about them, the love that was always present, a steady, constant glowing like a warm fire through all the days and nights."

"They were very fortunate, though I'm sure they worked at it."

"Yes," she said. "Looking back, I can see that they did. In a way I suppose their dying together was merciful, since they would have been utterly devastated apart. As Grania and Da were."

"They died shortly before we met?"

"That's right, within a few months of each other. And again I told myself it was for the best, because they also shared a great love. It was different in some ways from what I saw with my parents, probably since it'd had so many more years in which to ripen. But at bottom the effect was the same."

"Did you feel shut out by the love they shared?" he asked gently.

She shook her head, not offended by the question, because she had accepted that he was genuinely trying to understand. "There was never anything like that, either with my parents or with Grania and Da. I really believe that the more you love, the greater your capacity to do so. They lived at the center of a magic circle, and they didn't hesitate to let me in.''

The beginnings of comprehension shone in Padraic's emerald eyes. ''At least not until they died and the love went away.''

Why was she surprised that he had gotten the point so quickly? At the heart of his great talent lay an ability to uncover the most private and even painful sources of human motivation, to strip the soul bare and shine the light of reason on it. Once that had seemed so callous to her that she had instinctively shied away from ever being the object of his penetrating interest, but now she saw it in different terms, realizing that his understanding was not a threat but a gift.

''It took me years to see the problem,'' she said, ''and even then I refused to deal with it. I did love you, even though that filled me with fear, but when you seemed to withdraw from me, I accepted it without a fight because that was what I'd been expecting to happen all along.''

''And I was too obtuse to realize it,'' he said in self-disgust.

''It wasn't your fault,'' she insisted, reaching out to him. ''Perhaps if we'd been genuinely open with each other during our marriage I might have expected you to understand. But I'd done everything possible to keep you from really seeing inside me.''

''And I'd done the same.''

They exchanged a slow, sad smile. "As you said," she murmured, "we're a pair."

"None of which means things wouldn't be different if we tried again."

"I don't know, Padraic. After all this time, all that water under the bridge... Not to belabor the point, but we aren't the same people."

"Isn't that to our advantage?"

She didn't know. There was no easy answer to what he was asking. Knowing the source of her fears didn't mean that she had done away with them. She still remembered all too clearly how desperately hurt she had been, and she had a natural disinclination to risk such pain again. Especially with a man as overwhelming as Padraic.

"I have a friend," she said softly. "Her name's Joanna; she's a former model turned actress. Anyway, she has a theory that career women can't have successful relationships with men who are either their own age or older. She believes the conflicts are simply too profound and that it's smarter to get a younger man, one who's grown up with the idea of the liberated woman and has far fewer problems dealing with it."

"Does she practice what she preaches?" Padraic asked, the merest suggestion of a growl in his voice.

"She has, several times, but lately..."

"Yes..." He was smiling as though he already knew what she was going to say.

"She met someone older whom she really likes, too much, in fact, at least to hear her tell it. He's forty, a banker, very strong-willed, and no matter how hard she tries, she can't seem to tear herself away from him."

"Because he's a man," Padraic said succinctly, "not a pet. If you want fuzzy warm affection, get a dog. No offense, O'Casey. For anything more substantial you have to take some risks."

"I know all about risks." She couldn't help it, she was getting angry. He seemed intent on challenging her. "But there are good risks and bad, as with everything else in life. Only a fool ignores past experiences instead of learning from them."

He ran a hand through his hair, already unruly from the wind outside. She stifled an impulse to smooth the stray strands and kept her attention on the fire instead.

"Which leaves us where?" he said.

"I don't know." She wished to God that she did.

Padraic stood up and walked over to the windows. The light was beginning to fade, along with his hopes. "It's stopped snowing."

Her hand on his arm startled him; he hadn't heard her come to his side. "I'm sorry," she said softly. "I'd like nothing better to be able to tell you that all this has worked and I want us to start over again. But if I said that, I'd be pretending to be a lot more certain than I really am, which I don't think you would really want."

"No," he agreed, "I wouldn't, but don't imagine for a moment that I'm giving up."

"Never," she assured him. "I know how tenacious you can be."

"Especially when something very important to me is at stake."

Thrilled though she was by the sugge[...] wanted her so much, Mollie managed t[...] But the smile faded and was replaced [...] sion of puzzlement as she said, "List[...] that?"

For a moment he didn't; then his face, too, was wreathed in amazement. "Is that what I think it is?"

"Sleigh bells."

"It isn't even dark yet. What's Santa doing out this early?"

"Unless I miss my guess...." She opened the window and peered out, heedless of the brisk wind that was blowing the snow into fanciful swirls of glittering white. "Look," she said, pointing. "It's the old sleigh from the Rooster Inn. Jerry's father used to get it out every Christmas, but it's been in mothballs for years."

"Not anymore, apparently."

They both hurried to the door in time to see the large, horse-drawn sleigh pull up in front. A red-faced, slightly abashed-looking Jeremiah Withers waved a hand in greeting. "Hope I'm not interrupting anything."

"Not at all," Padraic assured him, staring in amazement at the prancing horses and the shiny sleigh. "That looks like fun."

"It is. Hop in."

"Us? But...?"

"No buts," Jerry said firmly. "I've been rounding up everyone for hours. You're the last. We're all getting together at the inn for caroling before church. It won't be the same without you."

stion that he
smile lightly.
by an expres-
n. Do you hear

...T

nged a startled look.
'Obviously you've never

..iy. "Doesn't matter. It's the
...its."

The horses shied, eager to be on their way. "Com-
ng?" Jerry asked.

"Who could pass it up?" Mollie said with a laugh.
Padraic hurried inside to get their coats, then helped
her into the sleigh. They snuggled together under a
blanket.

The last of the storm clouds had fled, and in the
crystal-clear sky they could see the first few stars announcing the arrival of Christmas Eve.

Chapter Six

By the time they reached the inn it was fully dark. The sky had turned into black velvet across which a giant hand had tossed an infinity of glittering diamonds. Snow crunched under their feet as they walked up the path. Inside, a roaring fire cast warmth over the crowd of people gathered around the piano. Mollie spotted several familiar faces. She waved in response to their greetings and joined Padraic at the punch bowl.

"I'd forgotten how much fun this is," she said. "It's wonderful."

He smiled down at her, the look in his eyes so warm and tender that she flushed. "You're as happy as a child, aren't you? Full of all the magic of the moment."

She nodded slowly. "I suppose I am. Does it seem foolish to you?"

"Not at all. In fact," he said as he glanced up at the ceiling, "I'm all for the holiday spirit."

Mollie followed the direction of his gaze and laughed. "Mistletoe. I might have known."

"You wouldn't want to fool with tradition, would you?"

She fluttered her eyelashes innocently. "Who, me? Wouldn't dream of it."

...en he touched her lips with
...increasing demand until the
...arty faded away and there
...n, afloat in a world of pure

...rt, not touching at any point
...t in the space between them a
powerful current .... Mollie had a dist.......
of electrified air, glowing with a force she ....t
define but felt she knew intimately.

When they at last broke apart, reluctantly, the
strange sense of ethereal contact went on, even after
they were both swept into the crowd of people around
the piano, who kindly did not joke about their preoc-
cupation with one another.

Years had passed since Mollie had last sung carols,
and she suspected Padraic had never done so. But
there was tolerance for rusty voices, and batches of
sheet music for faulty memories.

They sang all the old favorites, from the jovial
"God Rest Ye Merry Gentlemen" to the tender "Silent Night." In between the singing they drank punch
and eggnog, nibbled on Christmas cookies and fruitcake, and talked.

Mollie caught up on news from old friends. She
chatted with Mabel Porter, who ran a local gift shop
when she wasn't painting, and with Carly Phillips,
whom she had gone to school with and who had since
become a vet. Norris Daniels was there, another
schoolmate, who had followed his father into the
family law firm. There were others, too, easily a dozen
in all that she knew but hadn't seen in several years.

To her surprise they were all well acquainted with Padraic and accepted him as one of their own. He fitted in easily with the happy crowd, in some ways more easily than she did after having been away so long.

Shortly before midnight they all piled into the assortment of sleighs and sleds waiting outside the inn and made the short trek to the church. It was a small, white clapboard building, set in a copse of old oak trees, with a graceful bell tower and pretty stained glass windows. Built in the early eighteenth century, it had changed little over the years.

To Mollie the church had always possessed a special quality of peace and reassurance that she had never found anyplace else. As she stood within the carved wooden doors, looking down the long aisle toward the altar, she realized that had not changed. Even the small children, entering in their parents' arms or with their hands securely tucked in larger ones, were awed and subdued by the atmosphere. The golden light reflecting off mellowed oak and muted glass seemed to say that here all earthly cares were put aside and a higher purpose ruled.

Instinctively Mollie took Padraic's arm as they walked down the aisle. He put his hand over hers, and they exchanged a smile.

The minister was a young man with unabashed enthusiasm for his calling who was clearly deeply moved by the significance of this particular night. He eloquently shared that with his congregation as he spoke in simple but evocative terms of the meaning of the child born into the world so long ago and so far away.

Mollie had never thought of herself as an especially religious person. She had fallen out of the habit of attending church regularly, and had frankly felt no lack in her life as a result. Over the years she had come to take her faith so much for granted that she rarely gave it any thought.

Padraic was the same. There had been a time in his life when cynicism and general weariness with the world made him skeptical about all religion. He had turned away from it without a qualm, and for quite some time had congratulated himself on not needing what he had tended to regard as a crutch.

With the passing of the years and the painful acquiring of wisdom his views had changed. He now had a sense of something larger than himself that breached the barriers of human frailty and solitude, and imbued him with a strength that he was honest enough to admit he would not have had on his own.

When the notes of the last "Amen" faded away Mollie and Padraic remained where they were for a long moment. They did not look at each other, nor did they speak but between them there flowed a current of understanding that was startling in both its clarity and familiarity. Though neither had experienced it before, both recognized it as another and deeper ramification of the passion they had shared. It was a spiritual celebration of what they had known physically, and made clear to them for the first time the full rightness of the expression "making love."

But powerful and moving as it was, it did not completely banish all doubts. At least, not for Mollie. No sooner did she leave the cloistered atmosphere of the church than a deadening sense of fear and confusion settled over her.

"Padraic," she said softly as the others were making their plans to return to various homes for present opening and partying, "Let's go back to the house."

She didn't need to say anything more. Like her, he needed the solitude in which they could gather their contrary thoughts and hopefully come to some resolution.

O'Casey greeted them ecstatically the instant they set foot in the door. He seemed to sense that something momentous was in the air. Only with difficulty did they get him calmed down enough to let them catch their breath.

Padraic struck a match to the fire he had laid earlier and poured them each a generous measure of brandy. Mollie had sat down on the couch. He started to take a place beside her, then changed his mind and settled in a nearby chair, facing her.

At her quizzical look he shrugged. "I'm trying hard not to pressure you, but if I get within touching distance I won't be responsible for my good intentions."

Mollie's mood had lifted somewhat since they returned to the house. She managed a gentle smile. "That's very flattering."

"It's also quite serious. I've already told you that I want you back and that I'm not overly scrupulous about how I go about achieving that."

The note of self-disgust in his voice surprised and distressed her. "You didn't use to be so critical of yourself," she said. "I seem to remember that you were always quite ruthless but never thought twice about it."

"I've changed."

"Yes, I know."

"You believe me now?"

"I think I did from the beginning," she said.

"Then why...?"

"Am I still so uncertain?"

When he nodded, she sighed deeply. The words to explain herself did not come easily. At length she said, "You seem so happy here."

She was a little envious of that, even as she understood how hard won his contentment must have been. That he believed he would be happier still if she stayed with him, she did not doubt. But even without her, he had done quite well.

Could she say the same for herself?

Yes, Mollie decided after a moment, she could. And that was important, because her success without him lay at the heart of her difficulty in contemplating a reconciliation.

"Padraic... I have a good life in New York."

"I hadn't presumed otherwise."

"What I mean is, it's very satisfying in many ways. My work, for instance, is very important to me, but it also takes a great deal of time and effort."

"As does anything worthwhile," he said. "Besides, it's what you always wanted to do."

She remembered that he had somehow known that before she did herself, but it had not meant that he could truly accept it. "I can't give up any of that."

He leaned forward, elbows resting on his knees, his hands clasped together. "Of course not. Surely you don't think I'd expect you to?"

"I don't know what you'd expect. When we were married everything revolved around your work. I didn't blame you for that," she went on hastily, "or at least, if I did, I got over it. Your work is important, but so is mine."

"You don't hear me arguing, do you?"

It couldn't be that easy. Could it? "Just like that, you accept my career, all the demands of my business and my independence? You won't have any trouble with any of that?"

"Of course I will," he said. "From time to time. But the point is that I approve of what you're doing. To be blunt about it, I'm damn relieved that you're making your own life instead of trying to live in the reflection of mine."

Before she could comment he added, "And while we're on the subject of work, I ought to tell you that what I'm doing these days is no piece of cake and there may be times when you resent it."

"Just what are you doing?" she asked carefully. In the past he had never wanted to talk about his work until it was completed. While it was in process the mere attempt to uncover any information had been met with stony silence. That, too, had apparently changed.

"A novel," he said, and at her startled look, he laughed. "Remember when I used to make fun of novelists?"

"I seem to recall your saying something about them being self-indulgent because they wrote without the discipline of either actors or audience."

"I meant it, too," he said ruefully. "Which I suppose means it's only just that I should now be joining them."

"How's it coming along?"

"Better than I have any right to expect, considering my prejudices. But there's lots of hard work ahead, which is fine. Mind you, I'm not saying that I'm through writing for the stage. Someday I might go back to it. But in the meantime I have more than enough to keep me occupied."

She could well believe that. As comfortable as she was with the idea of sitting down and designing an entire new fashion line, that was how far she was from understanding how a play or a novel could be written. "You must need a great deal of peace and quiet."

"I can see where that train of thought is leading," he said lightly, "so let me head it off quickly. A writer makes his own concentration; surroundings can't create it for him. Sure I can write here, but I can also write in an apartment in New York, or anywhere else I choose to."

"How about on a roller coaster?" she asked deadpan. "Could you write there?"

"Well, now, I suppose my penmanship might leave something to be desired. Would you mind telling me how you came up with that one?"

"Because that's what my life often seems to be these days, and if we got back together you'd be caught right smack in the middle of it."

Ever a man to appreciate an inventive turn of mind, Padraic laughed. "It won't work, Mollie. If I have to take a roller coaster I will, but I'd be more interested in seeing if I couldn't help you get off it now and again."

"I've tried," she said, "and it doesn't seem to work out too well." The corners of her mouth lifted sardonically. "After all, this trip was supposed to be a rest cure."

"The best laid plans . . ."

"Yours seem to have worked out fine." She couldn't help but sound a little bitter. He had manipulated her very neatly.

He raised an eyebrow. "Have they?"

"I'm here, aren't I?"

"For the short term, which is not what I want."

"What's that line in *Winners and Losers*? 'Don't speak to me of tomorrow; the moment is all.'"

He flushed slightly. "A bit pretentious, don't you think?"

"No, I didn't mean it like that. The feeling that nothing is real except the present is perfectly understandable. Most of us have trouble either remembering the past or envisioning the future."

"But not us?"

She shook her head rather sadly. "Remembering the past as clearly as I do makes me afraid of any future we might try to have together."

His eyes narrowed, hiding the emerald glints. "You never impressed me as a woman who could be moved by fear."

"Touché."

"Have you become that?"

"No," she said, "of course not. But I have learned caution. I ask what you want, and you say 'you.' One word, not even two syllables. It's a bit scant for trying to plan a life."

He nodded slowly. "A valid criticism. The Bard may have thought all the world was a stage and we but players on it, but sometimes a good third act curtain line isn't enough."

She was silent, waiting for him to go on. He did so slowly and carefully. "I suppose what I really want— or more correctly, what I'm hoping for—is that we will find some way to combine our lives. They never really were, you know, not even when we were married. We existed in separate spheres that, if they touched at all, only did so around the outer edges."

The image was so apt that Mollie found herself nodding vigorously even as she changed it slightly. "Not spheres, though. Bubbles, that finally burst."

He grinned admiringly. "Ah, Mollie mine, which one of us is the storyteller, I'm wondering? You've got a fine eye for imagery."

"I should hope so, considering that's what I deal in. At any rate, I agree with you; we never did put our lives together. Do you really believe we could do so now?"

Padraic nodded firmly. "I've told you that I can work as well in New York as here. In fact, if you wanted to, we could keep this place for occasional weekends."

"Oh, no," Mollie said. "I wouldn't want that. The fact is, I've been trying to spend less time on managing my business and more on what I enjoy most, namely the designing itself. Little by little I'm finding people to work for me whom I can really trust, and I'm learning to delegate authority.''

His smile deepened with an eagerness that made her heart turn over. ''Then there's no problem,'' he said.

''Wait.'' He had started to rise. In another moment he would be touching her, and she would be lost. ''It's not that simple to me. This has all happened so fast. You've had months, maybe even longer, to grow accustomed to the idea of our getting back together. But it's completely new to me, and I need to think about it.'' Softly she added, ''Alone.''

He started to say something, then thought better of it. ''All right.''

Mollie walked a little distance away from the house. She was warmly bundled up against the cold, but suspected that she wouldn't have been aware of it anyway. Not when her mind was filled with such turbulent thoughts and her heart with such tumultuous emotions.

She stood at a crossroads in her life; the decision she made would shape not only her own future but Padraic's as well. The fact that she understood the source of her doubts and fears did not make them easy to dismiss. She had been hurt badly, and she had a natural reluctance to make herself vulnerable to such pain ever again.

Yet how could she live with herself if she turned her back on even the chance of love?

The night wind blew a swirl of snow from a nearby tree. She watched the flakes dance in intricate patterns of remarkable beauty that vanished in an instant. The elusive sense of sadness that had come over her after the service was returning. It was the melancholy of darkness and solitude, added to the weight of her own confusion.

She turned and looked back at the house. The curtains in the kitchen window were open. Through them she could see the Christmas tree, with its ornaments and twinkling lights. O'Casey was stretched out nearby, fast asleep in front of the fire. As she watched, Padraic rose from his chair and came to stand by the window, looking out.

She knew that he couldn't see her; the shadows of the trees near where she stood hid her from view. Yet she could almost feel his eyes touching her, filled with a yearning she could not ignore, if only because it was matched by her own.

Off in the distance the clear, high note of a church bell tolled the hour. It was Christmas morning. The single day of the year that had always meant more to her than any other had come again, as it had for almost two millenia as it would for countless time to come.

As a child she had delighted in the specialness of Christmas, all the beautiful objects and traditions kept apart from the rest of life and held intact for the celebration of that one day. Later she had come to see it in less material terms, deeply appreciating the sense of love that flowered in the cold of winter. Even if it was an idealized hope of what might be, it still spoke to the deepest human need for faith and caring.

She walked a short way into the woods and paused, looking up at the starlit sky. The greatest gift she had received from Christmas was that sense of love, which had sustained her even when she felt her own love for Padraic turning to ashes and blowing away on a bitter wind. But now she began to wonder if that was indeed what had happened.

The snowflakes she had watched dancing on the wind had seemed without substance, yet the essence of them had not vanished. It still existed in the piles of snow into which they had fallen. When they evaporated or melted it would still be present in the very fabric of the world, where nothing was ever destroyed.

Was love itself so ephemeral? She could not bring herself to believe that. Deep down inside was the knowledge that it, more than anything else, existed forever.

The child who had come into the world so long ago had carried that message. And, in the final moments of that earthly life, the message had been crystallized into a plea that weak and errant humanity be forgiven.

Forgiveness and love. They were intimately tied together; one could not exist without the other.

Mollie had known, and then rejected, her own capacity for love. Yet it remained strong within her. Forgiveness, however, was another matter. She had truly never thought much about it.

Now she did. The need was there, glowing within her with the white-hot intensity of truth. She had to forgive not only Padraic but also herself. The failure of their marriage had been a mutual defeat. But from it victory might yet be resurrected.

She turned back to the house. The door was open and through it light spilled. Padraic had waited long enough. He came toward her with firm, decisive strides that signaled his own determination.

She waited barely an instant before running to meet him.

* * * * *

A Note from Maura Seger

The fruitcake recipe I've sent along to you is a tradition in our family dating back several generations. My mother taught me to make it when I was a little girl, and I particularly remember her explaining that the water bath the cake is placed in is called "Queen Mary's bath" after Mary, Queen of Scots, who is said to have especially enjoyed cakes prepared in this manner.

That small, domestic connection helped whet my appetite for history and set me to exploring the personal details behind the great events that shape our world. Ultimately, I had to write about them, which is how I began to do historical and then contemporary romances.

The first bite of the fruitcake is the signal for me that the holiday has truly begun. Filled with eggs and butter, it melts on the tongue, but only at first. After an instant, the tang of the apricots and other fruits takes over and reminds me that this is a season to be relished for its unique beauty.

Amid the hubbub of presents, wrappings, ornaments—and fruitcake—we'll be taking time out to give thanks for the gift of our children and to renew our pledge to raise them in love and joy. We hope that you and your family will also enjoy the holiday, as well as a very happy New Year.

Best wishes,

Maura Seger

Under the Mistletoe

Tracy Sinclair

CHRISTMAS CONFETTI CAKE

1 3-oz pkg orange-flavored gelatin
1 3-oz pkg cherry-flavored gelatin
1 3-oz pkg lime-flavored gelatin
3 cups hot water
1½ cups cold water

Filling:
1 cup pineapple juice
¼ cup sugar
1 3-oz pkg lemon-flavored gelatin
½ cup cold water
2 cups heavy cream

Crumb Crust:
1 cup graham cracker crumbs
¼ cup butter or margarine, melted

Topping:
½ cup heavy cream (optional)

Prepare the first three packages of gelatin separately, using 1 cup hot water and ½ cup cold water for each. Pour into separate 8- × 8- × 2-inch pans and chill until firm. (For a hurry job, chill in ice trays, cube sections removed.)

Filling: Combine pineapple juice and sugar, and heat until sugar is dissolved. Remove from heat and dissolve lemon gelatin in hot liquid; add remaining ½ cup cold water. Chill just until syrupy.

Crumb Crust: Mix crumbs with melted butter. Press crumb mixture smoothly over bottom of a 9-inch springform pan.

Whip the 2 cups cream and fold into it the syrupy lemon-flavored gelatin.

Cut the firm orange, cherry and lime gelatin into cubes about ½ inch square. Do it this way: dip sharp knife into hot water and score gelatin, dipping knife after each cut. Run hot knife around edge of tray. Lift out gelatin with wide spatula, hot-water dipped. The pieces will fall apart easily, each a perfect cube.

Fold into whipped cream mixture, then pour into springform pan. Chill 8 hours in refrigerator. Before serving, remove sides of pan only. If desired, top sides of cake with ½ cup cream, whipped and sweetened.

Yield: 16 to 20 portions.

Chapter One

"I'm not sure we made enough sandwiches," Sarah Blake remarked to her niece as she surveyed the buffet table with a critical eye.

There seemed to be plenty of everything. In addition to large platters of sandwiches, there were bowls of nuts and potato chips, trays of cookies and several layer cakes.

Christy Blake looked fondly at the older woman. This annual open house had been a Christmas Eve tradition ever since she'd come to live at Sky Ranch with her aunt. Invitations were by word of mouth, so they never knew how many to expect. Anyone lonely or down on his luck was welcome, along with friends and neighbors.

There had been dire warnings about the dangers of two women alone taking strangers into the house, but Sarah Blake had been trusting her own instincts for fifty-eight years. So far, they hadn't failed her.

"We've never run out of sandwiches yet, but if we do I'll make some more," Christy promised.

"Half the party would follow you into the kitchen," Sarah answered dryly, gazing at her niece's flowerlike face.

Christy had been an adorable teenager when she had come to live with her father's only sister after being orphaned tragically. She was blessed with delicate features, silky blond hair and thickly lashed blue eyes. When her adolescent body matured into a curved figure and long slim legs, Christy was breathtaking. No one could understand why someone that outstanding remained in a little town like Pine Grove, which was only a village nestled in the northern California mountains.

"Here they come," Sarah announced as the doorbell rang.

People arrived regularly from then on. Christy divided her time between answering the door and circulating among the guests, making the ones who didn't know anybody feel at ease. The rooms were soon crowded with smiling people filled with the holiday spirit.

Matt Destry's handsome face didn't reflect the joyousness of the season. He was scowling at the twisting mountain road beyond the windshield of his sleek Jaguar sports coupe. The snow that was coming down like a lacy white curtain made visibility poor. The ski resort at Squaw Valley, where he was headed, was normally a four hour drive from San Francisco, but at this rate there was no telling how long it would take.

Matt's scowl could have been due to concentration, but it wasn't. He was feeling sorry for himself, all alone on Christmas Eve. The fact that he had turned down invitations to several parties didn't console him. And the knowledge that it would never occur to anyone else to feel sorry for him merely irritated Matt. He knew how the world perceived him—as the man who had it all.

The electronics company he'd started in a garage was now one of the largest in the industry. At thirty-three he was already a millionaire, with all the appropriate trappings of success: the penthouse apartment with a view that included the Golden Gate Bridge; lavish offices occupying a whole floor of the Transamerica Building; his suits were custom-made by an expensive tailor; he belonged to the best clubs and his girlfriends were always the most glamorous at any gathering.

So why did he feel subtly discontented lately? Perhaps because everyone he encountered seemed to want something from him, both men and women. Was it unrealistic to expect to be liked for himself alone? As soon as people found out he was president of CompuTrend, they had a whole wish list for Matt to fulfill.

Blinding headlights in the rearview mirror put an end to his somber thoughts temporarily. A pickup truck had appeared out of nowhere, traveling at a rate of speed that would be unsafe on a sunny summer day. Such speed was practically suicidal at night in a snowstorm.

Matt could scarcely believe it when the truck swung out to pass him as they were approaching a blind curve. When the truck drew abreast the radio was blaring loud enough for him to hear it through his closed window. After that, everything happened so swiftly that Matt acted out of instinct.

A car rounded the curve ahead, on a direct collision course with the truck. Matt swung sharply to the right to give the pickup room to get back in the proper lane. The Jaguar went into a skid, and he fought to keep it under control as he steered between giant pine trees laden with snow. There was a hideous grating sound as hidden rocks scraped the low undercarriage before the sports car came to a shuddering stop.

For a long moment Matt sat motionless behind the wheel. Then he started to swear savagely. That truck full of drunks could have killed everyone in all three vehicles! He got out of the car, flexing his tense muscles.

The intense cold immediately penetrated his light clothing. Since he hadn't expected to stop anywhere along the way, Matt had worn jeans, a T-shirt and a light denim jacket. It was too cold to stand by the roadside hoping someone would come along and give him a lift to the nearest town. No one would stop to investigate the wreck either, since the Jaguar was hidden from sight by a clump of trees. His only hope was finding a house out here in this godforsaken wilderness. Matt's generous mouth was compressed in a grim line as he wrapped his arms around his lean body and started slogging through the deep snow.

He was shivering so badly that his teeth were chattering by the time he finally found a lighted house. The sign over the arched front gate said Sky Ranch. Through the windows Matt could see that a party was in progress. Laughter mingled with the sweet sound of Christmas carols playing on a stereo set.

"Bah, humbug!" he muttered as he pressed the bell.

Christy opened the door with her usual welcoming smile. It changed to a startled awareness as she gazed at the newcomer. Her senses registered everything about him in one lightning instant: his powerful, lean-limbed body; his dark blue, intelligent eyes that seemed a little jaded; his straight nose and well-formed mouth. It even crossed her mind to wonder where he got such a deep tan in the middle of winter.

Matt was forming his own surprised impressions. He was used to beautiful women, but there was something about Christy that set her apart from the ones he knew. It wasn't only her beauty, although she was the most exquisite girl Matt had ever seen. Perhaps it was the air of innocence she radiated, he decided as he stared down into her wide, lovely eyes. She was like a slender, unawakened fawn, arousing a protectiveness Matt hadn't felt in years. It was neither required, nor desired by the women of his acquaintance.

Christy recovered first. She pinned her conventional smile back in place. "Please come in. We're so glad you could join us."

Matt looked surprised. "I don't want to interrupt your party, but—"

"There's plenty of food," she assured him before he could continue. "Just take a plate and help yourself."

"You don't understand. I was on my way to Squaw Valley, and—"

"Don't worry, we're very casual here," Christy interrupted again, acknowledging his jeans and T-shirt. She knew what was bothering him, and her soft heart melted. The poor man didn't have any decent clothes.

"Are you trying to freeze us out?" Sarah appeared at the door. "Come inside, young man, before we all catch pneumonia." She took his arm and led him to the buffet table. "I hope you like turkey, because we're all out of ham. My name's Sarah Blake, and I assume you met my niece, Christy."

Matt supplied his own name automatically before saying, "This is very kind of you, but I just came to use the telephone."

She looked at him shrewdly. So this was one of the ones who was ashamed of being hard up. "As long as you're here, why don't you have a sandwich first?" she asked casually. "Christy always makes too many, and if you don't help us out we'll be stuck with them. A big fellow like you doesn't have to be hungry to put away a little snack."

"Actually, I'm starving," Matt admitted. He had expected to have a late dinner at the hotel.

"Dig in then. And when you're finished, the telephone is in the hall," she added, to help him save face.

Matt felt a little better after he had eaten and thawed out. He was confused, though. What kind of people invited a perfect stranger into the house? When some of the other guests told him about Sarah's Christmas Eve tradition, he was even more baffled. Matt was used to the paranoia of the city. People there didn't even invite their neighbors in!

A frown creased his forehead as he watched Christy's graceful figure moving around the room. If the older woman didn't have sense enough to worry about her own safety, she ought to be concerned about her niece's. That beautiful girl shouldn't be exposed to danger.

Matt's own troubles occupied his full attention a short time later. When he finally got through to the auto club, a dispatcher told him they couldn't tow his car. There were calls stacked up that would take all night. To make matters worse, they were going to be closed on Christmas Day.

"What the hell is someone supposed to do if his car breaks down?" Matt's indignation crackled across the telephone wire.

"Don't ask me, Mac, I only work here." The line went dead with a note of finality.

So much for goodwill toward men, Matt thought grimly. Now what? Where was he going to find a hotel on the side of a mountain? Even if one existed it would have to be nearby, because he couldn't wander very far dressed as he was. Sleeping in the car was out, too. He'd freeze to death by morning.

Sarah paused on her way through the hall, looking disapprovingly at Matt's ferocious scowl. "Christmas is a time for rejoicing, young man. Instead of dwelling on your troubles, try counting your blessings."

Matt's mouth curved sardonically. "I'd be happy to if one of them was a hotel room."

"You don't have anyplace to sleep?"

"Not tonight, although I do have expectations for the future—if I have one," he added wryly.

Sarah stared at him speculatively as she made up her mind. "In that case, you can stay here tonight."

"You must be joking!" Incredulity was written all over Matt's face. "I could be a murderer or a rapist for all you know."

"Are you?"

"No, of course not!"

"Then there's no problem. I'll have Christy show you the guest room after the party." As Matt's expression changed unconsciously, Sarah said, "Make no mistake, young man, the invitation does not include my niece. If you have any ideas about wandering around during the night, you'll find neither of us is a helpless weakling."

"I would never make that mistake about you, at any rate." Matt looked at his hostess with respect.

"Don't underestimate Christy, either. There's more to that girl than a pretty face. Now go mingle with the guests. Enjoy yourself," Sarah ordered.

Matt followed her into the living room, but he found a corner where he could watch the festivities unobtrusively. He still had a dazed feeling of unreality about this whole night. Especially when Christy came over to join him. She was almost too perfect to be real.

Christy's smile expressed more confidence than she felt. There was something very daunting about this man. He looked as though he lived hard and played hard. His taut body had the power and grace of a jungle cat. If he wanted something badly enough, he would take it—including a woman.

With a flash of perception, Christy knew he would never have to use force. Women would share his bed willingly, and he would bring them pleasure beyond their wildest dreams. A tingling sensation raced through her veins as she imagined that lean, hawklike face poised over hers in the velvet darkness.

Christy's ivory skin warmed with color at the unbidden thought. It was so totally unlike her! "Aunt Sarah tells me you're staying here tonight," she said brightly.

"I hope you don't mind."

"Not at all."

Matt hesitated. "Does she do this sort of thing often? Ask strange men to stay the night, I mean."

Christy looked at him curiously. "Actually, you're the first one. You already know about these annual Christmas Eve parties, and there are all kinds of other causes she's interested in, but she's never taken anyone into the house before."

"Well, thank God for that!"

"Why?"

"*Why?* Because it could be dangerous. Take me, for instance. You don't know anything about me."

"I know you need a helping hand," Christy said simply.

Matt's eyes darkened to navy as he stared down at her upturned face. "You're very sweet, Christy, but I don't want to mislead you. I'm not broke and hungry as you suppose." When her eyes slid away from his, Matt remembered how he had wolfed down the sandwiches. "Well, I'll admit I was hungry when I arrived, but that was only because—"

"You don't have to explain," she interposed gently. "Anyone can have a run of bad luck."

He ruffled his thick dark hair in frustration. "How can I convince you?"

"Why does it matter?"

He examined her lovely features with a sense of wonderment. "I don't know, but it does. For the first time in my life, I want to brag about being at the top of the heap. I want to tell you everything I've done, and all the the things I hope to do in the future."

"You will, Matt." Her voice was very soft. "Aunt Sarah saw something special in you, and I do, too. I know you'll succeed eventually. We both have faith in you."

"It doesn't matter that I didn't even have a place to stay tonight?" he demanded.

Christy smiled. "You aren't the first person to look for lodgings on Christmas Eve." She saw her aunt beckoning. "I think Aunt Sarah wants us to mingle. If you know what's good for you, you'll do it."

Matt's intense expression changed to a broad grin. "I already got that impression. It was right after she told me you were off-limits."

Christy frowned. "That doesn't sound like Aunt Sarah. She's always trusted me to use my own judgment."

"Maybe I'm the one she doesn't trust." Matt's husky voice was very sensuous.

As their eyes met, something electric seemed to leap between them. He didn't touch her, but Christy got the impression that he was making love to her. It was almost as though she could feel his firm mouth moving over hers in an exquisite prelude. She wanted to move into his arms and let him mold her body to his hard contours.

Matt was the one who broke the spell. "Your aunt is a very wise woman," he said, smiling ruefully.

Christy was confused and troubled by her incomprehensible reaction to this man. It wasn't as though she hadn't had more than her share of male attention. She wasn't an impressionable teenager. Admittedly, Matt was an awesome specimen of masculinity, but she had met handsome men before.

What was this strange hold Matt Destry had over her? He was a homeless drifter who had appeared out of nowhere, and would disappear just as anonymously. She didn't know any more about him than that. He had even issued a subtle warning not to trust him. But strangely enough, Christy did. It was herself she was uncertain about.

The last guests didn't leave until almost midnight. When Matt looked at his watch, he was amazed to see how the time had flown. Usually he was restless at parties, bored by the empty chatter and ready to leave almost as soon as he arrived. But this evening he really enjoyed talking to the local residents. It delighted Matt to have people listen to him because he had something to say, not because he was Matt Destry, president of CompuTrend Industries.

Sarah surveyed the littered rooms after everyone had left. "Well, if debris means anything, I think everybody had a good time."

"That shouldn't come as any surprise." Christy began gathering used glasses and plates. "They always do."

"Just carry those things into the kitchen and leave them," her aunt instructed. "You'll be late for midnight service."

Christy slanted a glance at Matt. "Maybe I won't bother this year."

"You've been looking forward to it all day." Sarah correctly interpreted her reluctance. "Take Matt with you. A little sermon might do him good."

His eyes danced with laughter. "I always heard there was no free lunch."

"You don't have to go," Christy said hastily.

"I'd consider it an honor." There was a little catch in his voice as he gazed into her clear blue eyes. "It would be the perfect ending to a wonderful evening."

Christy looked suddenly doubtful. "You aren't dressed very warmly, and the heater in my car is broken."

"Take the pickup," Sarah suggested. She sized up Matt's tall, rangy frame. "And get Matt that old sheepskin coat Jake Dingle left behind when he quit. It'll keep him warm, even if it is a little skimpy."

They were ready to leave when Sarah noticed that Christy was still wearing the shoes that matched the silver belt on her white silk dress.

"You can't go out in this weather with those flimsy little sandals. Where are your boots?" she demanded.

"They won't fit over high heels," Christy explained.

"Then change to sensible shoes."

"There isn't time. I want Matt to hear the Christmas carols. Besides, the truck is in the garage. We'll go through the kitchen door."

"How about when you get to—" Sarah's protest was addressed to empty air. She listened to their hasty sounds of departure for a long moment. "I hope my instincts didn't pick this one time to be wrong," she muttered with a slight frown.

It had stopped snowing. The full moon shone down on a fairy-tale landscape painted in black and white. The tall pines were decorated with puffs of snow that reflected the sparkle of the glittering stars overhead. They formed a border around fields completely carpeted in white.

"I love it when it's quiet like this," Christy exclaimed. "Isn't it beautiful?"

Matt was gazing at the pure line of her profile as she watched the narrow road ahead. "I've never seen anything so lovely," he said in a muted voice.

"I hope you'll like the service," she remarked self-consciously. "I think it will be something different for you anyway, although I don't know what you're used to."

Matt never knew why he didn't tell her the truth right then. Afterward, he decided it was because he didn't want to shatter the dream. For this one night he wanted to be anonymous, free to be a man instead of a myth.

"I'm used to all sorts of things." He smiled. "I'm very adaptable."

"I suppose you've had to be."

She slanted a sideways glance at him. The faint light from the dashboard shaded Matt's high cheekbones and turned his eyes to inscrutable navy pools. The shifting shadows gave his face a predatory look.

"I can't complain." He shrugged off her sympathy.

"What kind of work do you usually do?" Christy asked delicately.

Matt chuckled. "You want to know what kind of work I'm out of?"

"I didn't mean to—"

"It's all right, honey." His big hand covered her slim fingers on the steering wheel. "I'm an engineer."

Christy was startled, although there was something about Matt that set him apart from the ordinary. "Surely you could get a job in your field."

"There isn't much hiring done at holiday time." That was true, he told himself.

"Well, don't worry, I'm sure things will get busy after the first of the year."

Matt sighed. "I suppose so."

"You mustn't get discouraged," she said earnestly. "A lot of people are in your predicament. You'll pull yourself out of it, though."

"Is that the standard pep talk you give to all of Aunt Sarah's lame ducks?" Matt asked dryly.

"Only when it's the truth," she assured him. "People can always tell when you're lying, and then they don't trust you. I really do believe you'll make a success of your life."

Matt was beginning to feel uncomfortable, but it would have been a little awkward to confess all at that particular moment. "The party's over and you've played the encouraging hostess long enough," he said lightly. "Tell me something about yourself. Have you lived here long?"

"Yes. I came to stay with Aunt Sarah when I was fifteen, after my parents were killed in a car crash. She's as dear to me as my own mother."

"I didn't meet her husband," Matt suddenly recalled. "Is your aunt a widow?"

Christy shook her head. "She never married. There was a fiancé once who was killed in the war. He was the great love of her life. It's sad that no one could ever take his place, but she's made a full life for herself in Pine Grove."

"It's rather a small town," Matt observed tentatively.

Christy sighed unconsciously. "Not to Aunt Sarah. She's completely happy right here."

"How about you?"

"I'm happy too." Christy's voice was slightly defensive. "She's been wonderful to me."

"What do you do? What kind of work, I mean."

"There aren't many jobs in Pine Grove, so I commute to Squaw Valley. It's about an hour's drive. I work for a realtor."

"You sell real estate?"

"No, I just work in the office—doing paper work mostly." She sounded vaguely discontented.

"One of life's necessary evils," Matt commented.

"I suppose so."

"What would you prefer doing?"

"All kinds of things! I got interested in the theater when I took drama in college. It's fascinating what you can do with a small stage. I'd love to get into set design, or maybe lighting." Her face sparkled with animation.

"Not acting?"

"I prefer the production end." The sparkle died. "It's just wishful thinking, though. There isn't even a little theater here."

"San Francisco isn't far away."

"I couldn't leave Aunt Sarah."

"She doesn't seem like the helpless sort." Matt chuckled. "Much less a clinging vine."

"Far from it! She's urged me to strike out on my own, but I'd worry about her terribly, all alone on the ranch."

"You intend to stay here the rest of your life?"

Christy's mouth curved in a lopsided smile. "It looks that way. I can't even get Aunt Sarah to take a trip with me."

Before Matt could reply, they arrived at the church, a small white building with a tall spire. Lights streaming out of the windows painted a golden circle in the snow. The voices of people greeting one another as they walked up the path mingled with Christmas carols coming from the church. It was the kind of charming, old-fashioned scene that Matt hadn't known still existed.

The early arrivals had taken the parking spaces near the entrance, so Christy was forced to park a short distance away. She looked dubiously from her open sandals to the deep snow on the ground. While she was bracing herself to take the plunge, Matt came around to the driver's side.

He scooped her into his arms, smiling down at her. "Now you know what Aunt Sarah was trying to tell you."

Christy was acutely conscious of the close contact with his lean body. The arm she put around his shoulders rested on solid muscle, and she could feel the tautness of his broad chest, even cushioned by her heavy coat and Matt's sheepskin jacket. He was rather dauntingly masculine.

"I suppose I should have listened to her," she said breathlessly.

His navy eyes had pinpoints of light as he gazed down at the golden hair spilling over his shoulder. "I'm glad you didn't," he murmured.

Christy's breath caught in her throat as she stared into the dark face so close to her own. The tiny laugh she managed sounded forced. "I'll bet you didn't know what you were letting yourself in for when you rang our bell tonight."

His teeth gleamed whitely. "Never in my wildest dreams."

"You didn't have to come with me," she said doubtfully.

Matt's laughter died. "I'll never forget this night as long as I live," he answered softly.

Christy was both relieved and reluctant when he put her down in the entry of the church. The emotions this enigmatic man aroused were very confusing. She didn't relax until the service began.

The pastor's sermon was on love and trust. It engrossed Christy so much that she wasn't aware of Matt's eyes resting often on her face. His expression would have surprised both of them.

At the end of the service, candles were passed out. The church lights were turned off and the whole congregation joined in singing "Silent Night." The lovely music sounded even more moving in the flickering candlelight. As the last pure notes died away, the lights came on and everyone turned to greet his neighbor and shake hands.

When Christy and Matt turned back to each other, he took both her hands. "Merry Christmas, little Christy," he said. "May all of your wishes come true."

"And yours, too," she whispered.

They stared into each other's eyes with a kind of wonder. It was as though something very special was about to happen. The magic moment slipped by when friends came over to say hello.

As they made their way toward the exit, Christy held out the car keys. "Would you mind bringing the truck around?"

Matt laughed. "Wasn't my door-to-door service satisfactory?"

"Well, uh, this way is easier."

"But not as much fun," he teased, his eyes glinting with mischief. "Okay, honey, if that's what you want."

Christy watched as he moved away lithely, remembering the feeling of being in his arms. It wouldn't be prudent to repeat the experience. Although Matt had been a perfect gentleman so far, she sensed that his expertise with women was awesome. Without even touching her, he had aroused emotions that made her heart beat like a tom-tom.

Christy liked the competent way Matt negotiated the icy roads. She had complete confidence in him as she studied his strong profile while they discussed the service.

"The candlelight ceremony was very moving," he remarked.

"It's a tradition that everyone looks forward to. People come from miles around to take part."

"I don't wonder. It was every bit as impressive in its way as the services at St. Paul's in London."

Christy's eyebrows rose. "Have you been there?"

A slight frown creased Matt's broad forehead. "Everybody's heard of them. Do I turn left here?" he asked before she could comment.

When they returned home the kitchen was neat, and Sarah had gone to bed.

"Would you like a cup of hot chocolate?" Christy asked. She was reluctant to see the evening end.

"Not really—unless you would," Matt said politely.

"No, I...I just thought it might help you get to sleep."

"I don't think I'll have any trouble." He laughed. "It's been quite a day."

"Yes, well, I'll show you to your room." She hesitated in the doorway. The quiet room seemed suddenly intimate, making her self-conscious.

Matt's expression changed as he looked at her slender figure. The white silk dress outlined Christy's high, firm breasts and clung to her tiny waist before falling in soft folds.

He moved toward her with the lithe grace of a panther. Before she knew what to expect, he put his arms around her waist.

"What are you doing?" she gasped.

Matt tilted his chin to look up at the mistletoe hanging overhead. "This is a Christmas tradition, too." He bent his head toward hers, but when Christy stiffened, he paused. "Just one kiss?"

Her panic subsided. Christy knew if she said no, he would let her go. Her rigid body relaxed, and she raised her face.

As Matt's firm lips touched hers, his arms tightened, drawing her slim body closer. His hands moved over her back in a sensuous rhythm that made tiny flames leap in Christy's veins. She felt herself turning liquid inside as his mouth devoured hers and his long fingers combed through her silky hair.

"Sweet, adorable Christy," he murmured. "You're like a beautiful dream. I've never met anyone so perfect."

His husky voice was smoky with desire, fanning the flames. Christy sensed that she was out of her depth. This man had experience beyond her knowledge. "You've known a lot of women, haven't you?" she whispered.

He touched the petal softness of her cheek almost reverently. "But none like you. I don't even understand the way I feel about you."

"Am I so different?" she asked uncertainly.

He cradled her head on his shoulder and buried his face in the shining brightness of her hair. "Partly because you don't even know why. Don't ever change, sweetheart."

Matt's hard body was awakening needs Christy hadn't been aware of. She moved unconsciously against him. His arms tightened for a moment before he put her firmly away.

"I think it's time you pointed the way to my room— *now!*" he stated.

Christy led the way down the hall silently. He was wise to call a halt. She should have done it herself, but when she was in Matt's arms it had seemed so right. She turned to leave with a murmured good-night, but he caught her hand.

"Thank you for the most memorable night of my life." He raised her hand and kissed the palm. "Merry Christmas, honey," Matt said gently.

Chapter Two

It was a long time before Christy got to sleep that night. She tried to put Matt out of her mind. He was a drifter. After tomorrow she would never see him again. He might even be gone before she got up. That thought made her even more tense.

Christy overslept the next morning after her brief, restless night. There were sounds coming from the kitchen, which meant Aunt Sarah was already making breakfast. When she didn't hear Matt's deep voice, Christy scrambled out of bed and ran down the hall without bothering to put on a robe. She stopped abruptly on seeing Matt alone in the kitchen.

"I thought maybe you'd gone," she said breathlessly.

"Without saying goodbye? That wouldn't be polite." He smiled as he gazed at her tousled hair and sleepy face. "Besides, your aunt asked me to stay for Christmas dinner."

Christy brightened considerably. That meant he would be there another whole day! "Where is Aunt Sarah?"

"She isn't back from church yet, so I started breakfast. How do you like your eggs?"

"You didn't have to do that," she protested. "I'll make breakfast."

"Don't you think you should put on some slippers first?" He looked appreciatively at her long bare legs exposed by the short flannel gown.

"Oh!" Until then Christy wasn't aware of how she was dressed. "I'll be right back."

"Take your time. Everything's under control."

After a quick shower, Christy put on jeans and a red-and-white checked shirt. The ranch hands had Christmas off, but the chores still had to be done. She tied her long hair back with a ribbon and hurried to the kitchen. Sarah had returned by then and breakfast was ready.

"You're a handy man to have around," Sarah said approvingly as she bit into a slice of perfectly browned bacon. "Have you had restaurant experience?"

Matt grinned. "No, but I've had to cook for myself, and I'm a harsh critic."

"You might give it some thought as a career," she remarked.

"Matt is an engineer," Christy said.

"A professional man! I knew there was something about you," Sarah exclaimed triumphantly. "I get so impatient with people who keep telling me not to trust strangers—as though I couldn't spot a phony when I saw one. My instincts haven't been wrong yet!"

"People may be right," Matt said quietly. "There's always a first time."

"Nonsense! Tell me about yourself. Are you hoping to build bridges and things?"

"No, I, uh, I'm interested in electronics."

Sarah nodded understandingly. "I hear there's been a recession in that field, but I'm sure things will ease up and you'll find a job."

Matt heartily cursed the whim that had made him go along with the charade of being unemployed. He couldn't continue to accept their hospitality under false pretenses. "I'm afraid I gave you the wrong impression last night. I'm not what you think I am."

"You don't have to explain to us," Sarah said firmly. "It isn't any disgrace to be down on your luck, Matt. We like you for what you are, not what you have. The important thing is that you're a genuine, honest human being."

"And when you're a big success you can write and tell us about it," Christy said softly.

He looked from one to the other, unable to say a word.

After breakfast Sarah said, "I'd better get the turkey in the oven before people begin stopping by. And you have to start on the chores," she told Christy.

"I'll help," Matt offered.

The snow had stopped, and the sun was a bright circle in the clear blue sky. Fresh snow glittered in the sunlight like miles of crushed diamonds. Only bird and rabbit tracks marred the smooth surface. It was clear, but very cold, and Christy was shivering before they even got to the hen house.

They had just finished feeding the chickens when there was a loud whinny outside. Christy frowned. "All the horses are supposed to be in the stable or the exercise yard."

They were greeted at the door by a magnificent palomino stallion. He tossed his head and swished his blond tail when he saw them, as though in triumph at his cleverness.

"Oh, no! It's Mischief," Christy groaned. "He's gotten out of the corral again."

"I gather by his name that he's done this before," Matt remarked.

"He should have been named Houdini," she grumbled. "Now I'll have to fix the fence."

"No problem. Show me where it is and I'll do it."

While Matt repaired the torn fencing, Christy chased Mischief back to the stable. It was no easy task. He was enjoying the romp, even if she wasn't. By the time she finally prevailed, and Matt finished with the fence, they were both thoroughly chilled.

"Let's go in the barn and warm up," Christy suggested.

It felt almost balmy inside after the sharp cold. They sat on a bed of sweet smelling hay while Christy removed her boots and shook out the snow.

"Blast that animal!" she said disgustedly. "He's always up to something. I wish there was a juvenile delinquent home for horses."

"He only wanted a little freedom." Matt's face was enigmatic. "Haven't you ever had that feeling?"

Christy slanted a startled look at him, then concentrated on her boots. "He has a good home, gentle treatment and plenty to eat. What more could a horse want?"

"That's enough for an animal," Matt agreed. "People are a different story. There's a whole world out there, Christy."

She didn't look up. "I thought we were talking about horses."

He stared at her bent head for a long moment. "That's true." He sighed. "I have no right to try to impose my values on you. They haven't even made me that happy."

She looked up then, troubled. "You will be, Matt. Someday all of your dreams will come true."

He made a sound of exasperation. "Why are you always concerned about other people? How about *your* dreams?"

"Maybe they'll come true too." A dimple appeared enchantingly at the corner of her mouth. "I'm working on it."

"How?"

"Promise you won't laugh?" When she received assurance, Christy said, "I've always wanted to travel to far-off places and do exciting things. You know, like snorkeling in Bermuda and skiing the Bavarian Alps." Her face was dreamy.

"Those places aren't so distant these days."

"They are for me." She sighed.

Matt frowned at the wistfulness in her eyes. "Are you waiting for your fairy godmother to make an airplane out of a pumpkin? *Do* something about it!"

"I told you, I am." She laughed self-consciously. "You've seen those contests where the grand prize is an all expense paid trip to somewhere glamorous? I enter every one I can find."

"You're kidding!"

"Well, someone has to win," she said defensively. "The only trouble is, I've sent in so many entry forms that if I ever do win, I won't remember which contest it was." Christy flopped back onto the hay with her arms crossed under her head. "But someday I'm going to get to all those places."

Matt stretched out next to her with his head propped on one hand. His eyes were tender as he gazed down at her delicate face. "I'd like to share the wonder when your dream is realized." He stroked her cheek gently. "If things were different I'd take you there myself."

She stared up into his darkened eyes, feeling a strange flutter in the pit of her stomach. "That would be nice," she whispered.

"It would be heaven! I want to see the world through your eyes. I'd like to climb the Eiffel Tower with you, and take a gondola ride on the Grand Canal. I wish I could buy you something in every shop on the Via Veneto."

Christy touched his high cheekbone tentatively. "You wouldn't need to do that. I'd just like to have you with me."

"Ah, Christy," he groaned. "Sweet, adorable, innocent Christy."

His mouth closed over hers with a restrained kind of hunger, but when she put her arms around his neck, the bonds snapped. Matt pulled her slender body against him and wrapped one leg around both of hers so she was joined to the full, hard length of him.

He parted her lips for a deep kiss that sent shock waves through Christy. She arched her body instinctively, tightening her arms around his neck. Without relinquishing possession of her mouth, Matt unzipped Christy's parka and pulled her inside his jacket.

The heat of his body turned smoldering embers to a torrid blaze. She twined shaking fingers through his thick dark hair as a primitive need engulfed her. Matt's rigid thighs responded automatically, pinning her even closer. Every taut muscle made its impression on her yielding legs. She was completely, willingly enveloped by him. Even their heartbeats merged in a wild thunder.

"You're unbelievable," he murmured, caressing her lingeringly. "My darling, passionate Christy."

She pulled his head down again, lifting her face for another drugging kiss. The glimpse of paradise he'd shown her made Christy eager to enter. Her lips parted in anticipation as his hands moved sensuously over her body.

Matt's kiss was even more urgent this time. He rolled her onto her back without letting her out of his arms. His tense body half covered hers. As his mouth continued its inflaming seduction, he slowly unfastened the top buttons of her shirt. Christy quivered when his hand slipped inside to stroke her intimately. She flamed in his arms, uttering tiny sounds of pleasure.

"I've never wanted anyone so much in my life," he muttered against her mouth.

"I want you too, Matt." Her palms moved over his chest, tracing the broad triangle down to his narrow waist.

He groaned. "You don't know what you're saying."

"Yes, I do," she whispered.

"Are you *sure*, Christy?" He anchored his hands in her bright hair, staring down at her intently.

"Can't you tell?" She looked up at him with wide, trusting eyes. "I've never felt like this before."

The excitement died from his expression. He lowered his head and closed his eyes. "Oh, God, what am I doing!"

"Matt?" She touched his hair tentatively. "What's wrong?"

He looked at her then, but all the passion was gone. "You're a virgin, aren't you, Christy?"

Her cheeks turned a bright, rosy pink. "I...does it matter?"

He stood up abruptly and turned his back to her, running a shaking hand through his hair. "Yes, it matters a great deal! I'm not usually in the habit of seducing virgins." His voice was almost savage.

"But you didn't," she faltered. "I wanted...I mean..."

"Forget everything I ever told you," he said bitingly. "Stay in Pine Grove for the rest of your life where you'll be safe from men like me."

Christy's long lashes swept down to veil her misery and embarrassment. She had offered herself and been turned down. The reason was just as insulting! Matt was appalled by her lack of experience. He didn't want to be bothered with such a naive innocent. When she'd responded so willingly, he'd gotten the wrong impression. But that wasn't her fault. He could make an angel turn in her wings!

"Thanks for the advice," Christy said bitterly, buttoning her shirt with trembling fingers. "Also, the hands-on demonstration. It was quite an object lesson."

He stared down morosely as she pulled on her boots. "Don't you see what—"

"You can go back to the house now," she interrupted. "I'll finish the chores alone."

"No, *I'll* do them. I feel the need for some exercise," he said grimly.

Christy didn't argue. All she wanted was to put distance between them. Her eyes were shadowed as she entered the kitchen a few minutes later. Fortunately, Sarah was busy at the stove and didn't notice.

"Done so soon? Where's Matt?" she asked.

"He's finishing up. I came back to help you."

"The turkey's already in the oven, and the vegetables are all cleaned." Sarah glanced at the clock. "You'd better change clothes. We'll open the presents when Matt gets back."

"Why don't we do that after he leaves?"

"I asked him to stay over tonight."

"You didn't!"

Sarah misunderstood her niece's concern. "It's all right. There's a present for him under the tree. I always have a few extra lying around, just in case."

"Don't you think you're carrying this hospitality thing too far?" Christy asked tautly.

"It's Christmas," the older woman chided. "You're supposed to love your fellow man."

"With some notable exceptions," Christy muttered, stalking out of the room.

Sarah stared after her thoughtfully. She was putting out potato chips and dip when Matt came into the kitchen a little later.

"What did you and Christy argue about?" she asked without preamble.

Matt stiffened in the act of taking off his jacket. "What makes you thing we argued?"

"She came in here madder than a bee that got locked out of the hive."

He recovered his poise. "I'm afraid that's my fault. I have a bad habit of giving unwanted advice."

Sarah raised her eyebrows in disbelief. "I may be old, but I'm not completely out of it. Did you make a pass at my niece?"

"It was inexcusable," Matt admitted with a sigh. "Do you want me to leave?"

"Not necessarily. Did anything come of it?"

"No." He looked her squarely in the eye.

"That's all right, then."

"I don't understand you!" Matt jammed his hands in his pockets, tightening the jeans over his strong thighs. "A complete stranger says he made a pass at your niece, and you say it's all right!"

"I didn't say I was delighted," she remarked dryly.

"If you had any sense, you'd throw me out on my ear!" he stormed.

"That wouldn't be easy." She smiled, looking at the long length of him. Her face became serious as she said, "You aren't the first man to be attracted to her, and you won't be the last. Christy's a big girl, Matt.

She has to learn to take care of herself. I won't be around to do it forever."

"You haven't done a very good job so far," he said grimly. "She's too trusting. Didn't you ever teach her the facts of life?"

"So that's the way it was," Sarah said softly.

His eyes became hooded. "I don't know what you're talking about."

"You're a good boy, Matt. I'm glad my faith in you wasn't misplaced."

He swore under his breath, stalking out of the room the way Christy had.

Christy changed to a cherry-colored wool dress, wondering how she was going to face Matt after that disgraceful incident in the barn. If only he'd have the decency to leave. She knew her aunt wouldn't hear of it though, unless she told her the truth. And Christy couldn't bring herself to do that. Let the older woman have her illusions. Why should both of theirs be shattered?

The afternoon Christy dreaded wasn't as bad as she had anticipated. Sarah's presence made the gift exchanging ceremony bearable, and after people began dropping by, it was easy to avoid Matt. The only difficulty came when some of Christy's friends wanted to meet him.

"He's gorgeous, Chris," her friend Irma gushed. "Who is he?"

Christy shrugged. "One of Aunt Sarah's stray dogs."

"I'll adopt him any day." Irma rolled her eyes expressively.

"How do you know he doesn't bite?" Christy asked distantly.

Irma grinned. "I hope he does."

After a brief introduction, Christy left them alone. She was annoyed to find her eyes returning often to the alcove where Irma had maneuvered Matt. Christy told herself that her inattention to old Mrs. Margolin's account of her arthritic knee was only because it was so boring. But there was no explanation for the pain she felt as she watched Matt smile down at her friend indulgently.

Christy was in the kitchen replenishing the punch bowl when he joined her unexpectedly. It was the first time they'd been alone all afternoon. She started to pick up the bowl and leave, but Matt took it from her.

"I want to apologize, Christy." His voice was very gentle.

"For what?" she asked tautly. "Not making love to me?"

When she tried to brush by him, Matt put his hands on her shoulders. "No, that's the one thing I've done right since I got here. You would have regretted it bitterly."

Would she? As Christy stared up at the strong planes of his hawklike face, she wasn't sure. Even now, after her humiliation, his touch was making her legs weak. Wouldn't it be worth anything to experience the ecstasy this man could bring?

As though he read her mind, Matt said, "You're too fine a person to indulge in . . . a brief encounter."

"I never—" Her eyelashes fluttered down. He already knew that!

"That's the reason I couldn't take advantage of you. I created a need in you because I was selfish and thoughtless." He brushed the soft hair off her forehead with caressing fingers. "You didn't really want me, honey."

"You needn't try to make me feel better," Christy said miserably. "We both know you were the one who lost interest."

He looked at her incredulously. "You can't honestly believe that?" He clasped her in his arms and rested his cheek on her temple. "Dear heart, it's taking all of my willpower not to carry you off to bed this minute!"

Did he really mean it? Christy looked up at him in confusion. She was so sure it was her inexperience that had turned him off.

Matt stared at her for a long moment, as though memorizing her lovely features. Then he released her. "Forget about me, honey. I'm not real. And neither are you," he muttered under his breath. "This is just a Christmas dream."

Sarah came in while they were gazing at each other wordlessly. She made a small sound of annoyance. "I sent you for that punch ages ago, Christy!"

"I'll carry it in," Matt said, lifting the heavy bowl.

"Come along, Christy," Sarah called over her shoulder. "We have guests."

Christy followed slowly, her thoughts in a turmoil. Matt's explanation of why he'd rejected her made Christy feel better, but telling her to forget him didn't.

No matter what he said, she would never forget this charismatic man, even though he'd touched her life only briefly.

After the guests left, they had dinner in the dining room. It was very festive, with candles and a centerpiece of poinsettias on the table. Matt was effortlessly charming, prompting Sarah to tell stories about her various activities. He also drew Christy out by asking questions about her job in Squaw Valley, and her friends in Pine Grove. He even seemed interested.

"If you're trying to find out if she has a steady boyfriend, why don't you come right out and ask her?" Sarah said bluntly.

"Can't you see he's just trying to be polite?" Christy scolded.

Matt smiled at the older woman. "I'm sure that's the first thing you would have told me."

She smiled back. "Well, maybe the second. Christy is very popular, though. She's just choosy."

Matt's enigmatic gaze rested on Christy's perturbed face. "Anyone that beautiful deserves to be."

"Will you two stop talking about me as though I weren't here?" she asked crossly. "I'd like to change the subject."

To her great relief, they complied. When the conversation became general once more, Christy relaxed and began to enjoy herself again. It was only much later that she realized Matt hadn't revealed anything about himself. Other than the fact that he was an engineer, they didn't know any more about him than they had when he rang the doorbell. Maybe he really *was* a dream, a Christmas gift that was only on loan.

The evening passed quickly, with much laughter and a warm feeling of companionship. The tension between herself and Matt had vanished. Christy had never spent a happier holiday. The only thing marring it was the knowledge that the next morning Matt would be gone, and she'd almost certainly never see him again.

Christy discovered that time was even more fleeting than she thought.

When it was time for bed, Matt said to Sarah, "How can I begin to thank you for your hospitality?"

"There's no need. We were happy to have you."

"I don't know what I would have done if you hadn't taken me in," he said simply.

"You would have survived." She looked appraisingly at the strong line of his jaw. "I have a feeling you always manage to land on your feet."

He smiled. "Not without a little help from my friends."

"We all need that. It's what Christmas is all about."

Matt's smile was replaced by deep emotion. "You're a remarkable woman, Sarah Blake. It's been a privilege to know you."

"No need to make a speech," Sarah said tartly, although it was clear that she was pleased. "You'll just have to do it all over again after breakfast."

He shook his head. "I'm leaving early."

Christy's face mirrored her dismay. She masked it quickly when Matt turned and took both her hands in a warm grip.

"Goodbye, Christy. It's been a privilege to know you, too." His voice was husky. "I hope you get all the good things you deserve out of life."

The auto club couldn't give Matt a definite time when they would show up to tow his car. They only promised it would be some time in the morning. Matt was there almost as soon as it was light, in order not to miss them.

The Jaguar had a generous icing of snow after a day and a half. Was that all it had been? He could hardly believe it. Surely he'd known Christy longer than that! She was more familiar to him than girls he'd taken out for months. The perfume of her skin lingered in his nostrils, and he could almost feel the silky texture of her glorious, pale blond hair.

Matt shook his head in disgust. That kind of thinking was for schoolboys, and he was far removed from that category. He took a tree branch and scraped away the snow so he could wait inside the car.

It was reasonably warm inside, but there was nothing to do. He had books in his luggage, but that meant scraping away more snow to get the trunk open. It didn't seem worth the effort since the tow truck might come at any moment. Only it didn't. As the time ticked away, Matt was alone with his thoughts, which kept returning to Christy.

She was a revelation to him. Matt hadn't known girls like her still existed. She was so sweet and pliant. He shifted restlessly as memories surfaced. The way she'd responded to him, the satin feel of her breasts, her shy delight as he awakened her.

Matt swore softly. It wasn't like him to lose control, especially when he knew how innocent she was. It would have been unforgivable if he'd taken her. At least that was something to be grateful for. It was bad enough that he'd lied to her and Sarah. Well, not lied actually. It was more a sin of omission. He'd *wanted* to tell them the truth about himself, but something always prevented it.

Matt sighed. Well, it was all over. He'd never see either of them again. It would be madness to stay in touch. He had used up all of his nobility when he'd resisted Christy the first time. Matt didn't trust himself to pass up another opportunity—and she deserved better.

His secretary was surprised when Matt showed up at the office early the next day. "I thought you went skiing." She followed him into the plush inner office that was furnished almost like an elegant den.

"I came back," he said curtly. He frowned at a pile of unopened envelopes on the big mahogany desk. "Have I been promoted to mail clerk around here?"

Her eyes widened at his bad temper. Matt was usually the soul of courtesy. "Those are personal. I thought you'd prefer to open your own Christmas cards."

He pushed the envelopes aside indifferently. "Get your book, Linda. I'd like you to do a couple of things for me."

When she was seated in front of his desk, Matt said, "I want to send a ten pound box of chocolates to Sarah and Christy Blake in Pine Grove. It's near

Squaw Valley. I don't know the address, but it's just a little town. I guess it will get to them.''

''No problem, I'll locate the address. What do you want me to say on the card?''

''I'll write it myself.'' He looked at her broodingly. ''On second thought, make that a five pound box instead.'' It wouldn't do to look too affluent.

She made a notation. ''Anything else?''

''Yes. Have some stationery printed with the name and address of one of the big cereal companies—Kellogg's or Post, any of the big ones will do.''

''A cereal company?'' Linda's brows climbed incredulously.

''Just do it!'' Matt said impatiently.

It was so unlike him that she was worried. He looked kind of drawn, too. ''Do you feel all right?''

As his eyes met her concerned ones, Matt sighed. ''I'm sorry, Linda. I didn't mean to be so abrupt. I guess I am rather out of sorts. My car got wrecked and I had to wait two hours for a tow truck. I never did get to Squaw Valley.''

''What a shame! You were all alone on Christmas?''

''No, some wonderful people took me in,'' he said softly.

''It wasn't like being with your friends, though.''

His mouth twisted in the semblance of a smile. ''No, it wasn't anything like that.''

''Well, you can make up for it New Year's Eve,'' she consoled him. ''Miss Warren phoned and left a message that you're invited to two cocktail parties before the dinner dance at the country club.''

Mimi Warren was a beautiful blonde. That was the only thing she and Christy had in common. Matt contemplated the coming festivities without enthusiasm. He hadn't escaped the Christmas parties, merely postponed them. It would be the same boring rounds. Even the conclusion of the evening was predictable. The only question was whether they would wind up in Mimi's bed or his own.

"How much stationery do you want printed?" Linda got back to business.

"Whatever's necessary. I only need one sheet." He turned his back on her surprised face. "Use it to write a letter to Miss Christy Blake in Pine Grove. The letter will read: 'Dear Miss Blake, we are pleased to inform you that you have won first prize in our grand sweepstakes contest, a two week, all expense paid cruise to the Caribbean aboard the *Sun Queen*.'" He paused to collect his thoughts. "'Please contact the local steamship office in San Francisco to arrange for the trip at your convenience.' Sign that, um, Jonathan Ridgely, President, Contest Division."

Linda managed a businesslike expression, although she was bursting with curiosity. "Will that be all?"

"I want it sent immediately."

"It's going to take a little time. Today's Friday."

"So?"

"The weekend's coming, and then New Year's. Not much gets done between the holidays."

"Pay extra for a rush job," he said impatiently. "I want that letter to go out as soon as possible. And arrange for a deluxe cabin in Miss Blake's name. Pay for it out of my personal account."

After Linda had gone, Matt walked to the window to stare out at the gray day that matched his mood. His debt was discharged. Would the trip make Christy as happy as she expected? He hoped so.

"God, I'd like to take it with her!" he muttered.

Chapter Three

Matt tried to control his temper that Friday, but everything irritated him. The people in the office walked softly, raising their eyebrows at one another in perplexity.

Friday night wasn't any more rewarding. In an effort to banish Christy from his thoughts, Matt called Mimi Warren.

"Darling, how wonderful!" she exclaimed. "I didn't expect you back so soon. You must have missed me."

"It wasn't the same without you," he answered dryly.

"You're a dear! I can't *wait* to see you. You're coming to the Debenham's tonight, aren't you? I was going with Tommy Armistead, but I'll make up some excuse."

"How would you like to go out for a quiet dinner instead?"

"Oh, lover, I'd adore it, but I couldn't possibly. Pat Stillman has already described my gown in tomorrow's column."

"I didn't realize," Matt said with exaggerated remorse. "We can't let the society editor down, can we?"

"Don't be cross, darling." Mimi's voice dropped to a suggestive purr. "The party won't last all night."

She couldn't believe it when Matt refused to accompany her. After coaxing was useless, she stifled her annoyance and said regretfully, "If there was any way I could get out of this thing you know I would, sweetie, but I'll make it up to you New Year's Eve."

Matt hung up feeling curiously relieved. He wondered what Christy was doing.

Christy wasn't in any better a mood.

"You've been moping around the house all day, child!" Sarah exclaimed in exasperation. "Why didn't you go to the movies with Craig Selby when he asked you?"

"I didn't feel like it." Christy's soft mouth drooped. "I have a headache."

Sarah suspected it was more like a heartache, but she didn't say so. "Well, take some aspirin and go to bed."

"It's only seven-thirty!"

"Then read a book, or watch television." Sarah went back to her crossword puzzle.

Christy picked up a magazine and sat down across from her aunt. She flipped through the pages disconsolately. "It's so depressing after Christmas." She sighed.

"There's always New Year's Eve to look forward to."

"I suppose so."

"I want you youngsters to be careful driving back from Squaw Valley. There are all kinds of nuts out on

New Year's Eve." Sarah hadn't been happy about Christy's plans to go to a dance at the lodge with a group of friends, but she made it a practice not to interfere.

"Craig is a safe driver." Christy stared moodily into the crackling fire. "He does everything safely. I don't think he's ever taken a chance in his life."

"You're hardly one to talk," Sarah said quietly.

Christy threw down the magazine and stood up. "Sometimes I think you want to get rid of me!"

"You know better than that," Sarah said calmly. "I only want what's best for you. Just because my life is here in Pine Grove doesn't mean you have to waste yours. There's a whole world out there, child!"

"You sound like Matt," Christy muttered.

"He's a very astute young man."

"You don't know anything about him!" Christy exclaimed in outrage. "He could be a criminal on the run for all we know. Did you notice the way he avoided talking about himself?"

"He probably had his reasons."

"You're too trusting," Christy scolded.

"Strange." Sarah penciled in a word. "He said the same thing about you."

Christy's cheeks flamed as she recalled her total surrender in Matt's arms. "Doesn't that give you some idea of the kind of women he's accustomed to?" she asked coldly.

"Satisfied ones, I imagine."

"Aunt Sarah!"

"There's no point in denying that he's a charming devil." The older woman looked thoughtful. "It will be interesting to see what he makes of himself."

"We'll never know," Christy said forlornly.

"I'm not so sure. I have a feeling we'll hear from Matt Destry again."

Matt was up early Saturday morning after a very dull evening of watching television. He felt keyed up and restless, so he called a friend and made a date for handball. That, at least, was satisfying. After a strenuous workout, he felt better, but the rest of the day and night stretched ahead like a vacuum.

About two in the afternoon, he faced his problem squarely. Christy had become an obsession. He was romanticizing one brief encounter. The unexpected circumstances, the storybook setting, everything had conspired to make their meeting something it wasn't. She was breathtakingly lovely, but he had known literally dozens of beautiful women. He and Christy had absolutely nothing in common. If he saw her again, he'd be disappointed.

Matt's eyes brightened as the idea took hold. That was what he needed—an exorcism! And while he was at it, he'd set the record straight about himself. The inadvertent deception continued to bother him.

Matt looked at his watch. He could be in Pine Grove before dinner. The Jaguar was in the repair shop, but that was only a minor hitch. He'd borrow one of the vans from CompuTrend's motor pool.

* * *

Christy was staring listlessly out at the snow. That was another depressing thing about winter. It was already dark, even though it was only five-thirty.

A strange van pulled into the driveway. She looked at it curiously, trying to make out the lettering on the side, but the light was too dim. A delivery at this hour? A man got out and walked toward the front door.

For a moment Christy thought he was a figment of her own wishful imagination, but there was no mistaking that broad-shouldered male frame, or the easy gliding walk. It was Matt!

She opened the door and raced out into the snow, throwing her arms around his neck. "You came back!"

His arms closed around her automatically, holding her so tightly that she could hear his heart pound. She clung to him, inhaling his familiar clean scent.

"I couldn't stay away." His mouth slid sensuously over her cheek. "Did you miss me?"

Christy drew back self-consciously. She was suddenly aware of her impulsive actions. "I...we wondered how you were doing."

"Not too great." The starlight was reflected in his navy eyes, making them glitter as he gazed at her lovely face.

It was all happening again, the mounting excitement, the inexpressible feeling that made her tremble.

"You're shivering. Come inside before you catch cold." Cradling her body against his for warmth, Matt led her to the house.

Christy moved to the fireplace while he took off his storm coat. She was startled to see that he was wearing a shirt and tie under a camel-hair jacket. The well-tailored slacks that completed the outfit were a far cry from his former blue jeans. He looked elegant and sophisticated, not at all like a man down on his luck.

"You look different," she said tentatively.

"You don't." He came to stand over her. "You're just as I remembered."

"It's only been two days."

"It has to be longer," he murmured huskily.

Christy tried valiantly to stem the rising tide of desire. She mustn't make a fool of herself again. "I'm sorry that things aren't going well for you, but it doesn't show. You're extremely dashing," she said lightly.

"I didn't say things weren't going well." He frowned slightly. "That's part of the reason I came back."

"You got a job!" Christy's face lit up. "Oh, Matt, I'm so happy for you."

"It isn't what you think," he began.

"I don't care what kind of job it is. You'll work your way up."

Matt couldn't go through with it when he looked at her glowing face. "Will you have dinner with me tonight? Aunt Sarah, too."

Maybe an opening would come up during the evening, he thought distractedly. Nothing was going according to plan. The minute Christy launched herself into his arms, he knew it had been a mistake to come.

The remembered feeling of her curved body mocked all his theories. She could never be a disappointment.

"Aunt Sarah's at a Ladies Aid meeting, but I'd love to go," Christy said. "Give me ten minutes to change clothes."

Christy left her sweater and jeans in an untidy pile, which she never usually did. After a brief deliberation, she chose the most sophisticated thing in her closet, a black knit dress with tiny pearls scattered over the bodice. It clung to her faultless figure like a second skin, and the matching high-heeled sling pumps flattered her long, slim legs. A few more moments were spent freshening her makeup and brushing her hair to a shining halo.

Something smoldered in Matt's eyes as he viewed the result. "That was fast."

Christy's laughter bubbled up spontaneously. "I didn't want you to change your mind."

"Is that your opinion of me, that I'm an Indian giver?" he teased.

"No, you've always been honorable with me." She meant it as a joke, but the memorable incident in the barn leaped to both their minds.

Matt's smile vanished. "In all the ways that count, anyway."

She bit her lip nervously. "Do you... Where would you like to eat? There isn't a wide choice in Pine Grove."

His urbanity returned. "I thought we'd drive to Squaw Valley. If you don't mind riding in a van, that is."

"It's fine with me, but we can take my car if you'd rather. I had the heater fixed."

"Maybe you'd be more comfortable. Do you mind if I drive?"

She handed him the keys, smiling. "Did my driving the other night scare you?"

"No, I was impressed with the way you handled the pickup on those icy roads. I'm just one of those insecure males who has to be in charge of a date."

"You don't strike me as being insecure," she commented as he opened the car door.

"It's a recent development," he answered dryly.

When they reached Squaw Valley, Matt pulled into the parking lot of the chalet. It had a coffee shop and a more formal dining room where there was dancing. He guided Christy toward the dining room.

She held back. "It's too expensive in there. Let's go to the coffee shop."

"This is a special occasion," Matt said easily. "I want to toast you with champagne."

"You can do that with apple cider. It's the same color, and a lot cheaper."

"Indulge me. I feel like celebrating."

"You don't know how expensive it is," she protested. "I had lunch here once and it was outrageous. I can just imagine what the dinner prices are like!"

He put his hands on her shoulders, gazing deeply into her eyes. "I want to do so much for you, Christy, and I can't. Let me have this evening."

It was at that moment that Christy realized she was in love with Matt. She had thought it was just a physical attraction, but it was so much more. He was everything she'd ever wanted in a man—tender, thoughtful, generous. It touched her that he wanted to give her things. If only he knew there was just one thing she wanted—him. Was it possible? He *had* come back, after a very final sounding goodbye. Christy was filled with hope as she followed Matt silently.

The maître d' led them to a choice table by the window where they could look out at the flaming torches that added a touch of color to the black-and-white landscape.

"Would you care for cocktails, sir?" The man's manner was respectful.

When Christy shook her head, Matt said, "I think we'll have wine instead. Will you send over the wine steward? Oh, and a guest menu too, if you have one."

"Certainly, sir."

Christy looked puzzled. "What's a guest menu?"

Matt smiled. "Something special for beautiful ladies."

He wouldn't tell her any more, but she discovered the difference for herself. "There aren't any prices!" she exclaimed.

"I want you to enjoy your dinner." He grinned.

"How can I when every bite is probably the equivalent of a dollar bill?"

"The dollar isn't worth what it used to be anyway. Just tell yourself you're providing a lot of people with jobs."

"It's a good thing *you* have one, although at the rate you're spending your advance, you're going to be poor for a long time yet."

A curtain dropped behind his dark eyes. "What if I told you I was rich?"

"I'd tell you money doesn't matter to me," she said gently. "I like you just the way you are."

"But what if it was really true?" he asked intently.

A slight frown marred Christy's smooth forehead as she considered the question. "I suppose I'd be very angry."

"Why?"

"Because it would mean you were making fun of us," she said slowly. "That you were secretly laughing at our small town ways."

"You couldn't possibly believe that!"

She looked at him uncertainly. "It would hurt a lot, but I don't really know anything about you. *Are* you rich, Matt?"

A muscle twitched at the point of his square jaw as he said, "I've never lied to you, Christy."

It was true, even if it was an evasion. How could he admit everything now? The web of deception was like a noose around his neck.

"You came from a wealthy family though, didn't you?" she asked. It would explain his assurance in what should have been foreign surroundings.

"They were comfortable," Matt admitted.

Christy hesitated. "You've never mentioned your family or friends. Is there a reason, Matt?"

His firm mouth twisted in a rueful smile. "I don't have a lurid past, if that's what you mean."

"But you don't want to talk about yourself." It was a cross between a question and a statement.

"Not tonight. I have a few problems to work out first." He reached over and took her hands. "This night is special. I don't want anything to ruin it."

Christy couldn't help wondering if Matt was hiding some dark secret, in spite of his reassurances. But when she looked into his steady eyes, it didn't seem possible. Even though she knew very little about him, Christy was sure he couldn't do anything dishonorable.

"Are you ready to order, sir?" The appearance of the waiter broke the tense atmosphere.

Matt knew that Christy was trying to figure out the least expensive thing on the menu, so he ordered for both of them. "We'll have oysters on the half shell, endive salad and steak Diane."

"Very good, sir," the man said. "And would you like a soufflé for dessert? It has to be ordered ahead of time."

"Excellent idea. We'll have a Grand Marnier soufflé. And you can pour the champagne now."

Christy watched wonderingly as Matt discussed vintages with the wine steward. His ease in the plush surroundings and the deference accorded to him were a revelation. Matt must have lived very well at one time.

"Tell me about your new job," she prompted when the waiter left. "Was that a company car you were driving? I saw some writing on the side, but I couldn't make out the name."

"CompuTrend," he answered briefly. "It's an electronics firm."

"That was exactly what you wanted! What do you do there?"

"A little bit of everything—like you." He shifted the focus of the conversation deftly. "Now that I think of it, this is something of a busman's holiday for you. You commute to Squaw Valley every day. Perhaps we should have had dinner in Pine Grove."

"You wouldn't have gotten anything like this."

Matt smiled. "It's the company, not the cuisine."

Christy laughed self-consciously. "I'd have to be very charming to make up for the food at the Elite Café."

"All you ever have to be is yourself." His voice dropped a note. "Don't ever change, Christy."

"Everyone changes," she said slowly. "It's part of maturing."

His gaze wandered over her delicate features. "You're perfect just as you are."

Christy dimly realized that for some reason, Matt had put her on a pedestal. "I'm a real person, Matt," she said urgently. "Not a princess in an ivory tower. I'm no different from the women you know."

Mimi Warren flashed into his mind, the games she played, her shallow values. "You couldn't be more wrong," he said.

"Tell me how I'm different—besides the fact that they have more experience." Christy's cheeks flushed, but her eyes held his.

Matt answered her question with one of his own. "What do you like to do in your free time?"

"Oh...ski in the winter, swim and play tennis in the summer."

"And in the evening?" he prompted.

"The same as anyone else I suppose—go to parties and movies with my friends. Not every night, though. Sometimes I just like to stay home and read."

"Have you ever gone to three parties in one night?"

She looked at him in surprise. "Why would anyone want to do that?"

The music started and Matt drew her to her feet. "I've just won my case," he said with satisfaction.

Christy accompanied him to the dance floor with a dozen unanswered questions churning around in her mind. Had she passed the test or flunked it? Did Matt enjoy an endless round of activities? Christy couldn't help knowing that he was attracted to her physically, but other than that, did he consider her boring?

When she slipped into his arms, the questions faded in importance. She relaxed against him, letting her senses take over. Matt didn't talk either. His hands trailed over her back, tracing its slender lines. They communicated wordlessly, moving as one person. Her body responded to every direction of his.

There was an awesome kind of chemistry between them that couldn't be denied. When Matt drew her closer and kissed her closed eyelids, Christy knew he was making love to her in the only way he would permit himself.

She sighed unconsciously, and he tilted her chin up. "What's wrong, sweetheart?"

She opened her eyes and gazed into his beloved face. "Nothing. I was just wishing..."

"What?" he asked when she stopped. "Tell me what it is, and I'll get it for you," he said urgently.

It wasn't that easy; you couldn't ask someone to fall in love with you. "Christmas is over." She managed a smile.

Matt smoothed a shining strand of hair behind her ear in a caressing gesture. "Maybe I can catch Santa Claus before he goes back to the North Pole."

"He gave me enough already," Christy said softly.

The music ended and they went back to their table.

It was a bittersweet evening. Every moment was precious because Christy didn't know if this was all there would be. Matt hadn't mentioned any future meetings. Would he disappear again and not return? She shook off the depression that caused. It was all the more reason to enjoy what time she had with him.

Christy had left a message for her aunt, telling where she'd gone. When they returned home, Sarah was in bed, but there was a note saying she'd made up the guest room for Matt.

"That was thoughtful of her, but I didn't expect to stay," he said.

"It's a three-hour drive," Christy protested. "You wouldn't get home until two-thirty."

"I've been up that late before." He smiled. "But I would like to see Aunt Sarah again. That's one wise lady."

"Who would be furious if I let you take that long drive at this hour. So it's all settled."

Matt grinned. "You talked me into it. Pretty soon I'll have to start paying rent."

"Or keep a spare pair of pajamas here."

"I don't use them."

An all too vivid picture of his naked male body sprang to Christy's mind. She had felt its hard contours often enough to provide all the details. Her cheeks warmed at the memory. "Well, uh, that's fortunate."

"I can't believe you're blushing! A lot of people sleep in the nude, honey."

"I know," she mumbled. Christy couldn't tell him that wasn't the reason for her high color.

"I should have expected it from a little puritan who wears a high-necked flannel gown to bed," he teased.

"I get cold," she muttered.

Matt's laughter died, and tiny pinpoints of light appeared in his navy eyes. "That's a pity," he said softly.

"It's my own fault. I should get an electric blanket," she murmured.

He didn't appear to hear her. Hooking a hand around her neck, he drew her closer. "I'd like to keep you warm, sweetheart. I'd like to hold your beautiful body in my arms all night. I want to kiss every inch of your satin skin and be the one to make you come alive."

Christy stared into his hypnotic eyes, feeling a throbbing in her midsection. Matt had made love to her in every way but the ultimate one. Was this the magic moment? Did she want it to be, knowing he'd be regretful afterward, even if she wouldn't?

He pulled her into his arms and kissed her almost savagely. "You're like a fever in my blood," he groaned. "I've never felt like this about a woman."

The minute his lips touched hers, all other consid-
erations became unimportant. Christy feathered tiny
kisses over the strong column of his throat. "Why
does it bother you, darling? We want each other. Isn't
that enough?" She loosened his tie and unfastened the
top buttons of his shirt.

"Oh, God, don't do that!" he exclaimed as her
fingers slipped inside to tangle in the thick mat of hair
on his chest.

"I've wanted to for such a long time." She sighed,
feeling sensual pleasure at the evidence of his masculinity.

"It's all wrong," he groaned, but his hand cupped
her breast and his thumb circled the hardened tip.

Christy quivered as an inexpressive feeling kindled
her body. "Tell me why," she whispered.

"I don't want to hurt you, don't you understand?"

"I know you'll be gentle," she murmured.

"That's not what I meant. Of course I'd be gentle!
But I can't take what you have to give."

She rubbed her cheek against the crisp hair on his
chest while she unbuttoned his shirt further. "I'm not
asking for anything in return."

"You should be!" He wrenched her chin up and
stared at her with blazing eyes. "Don't throw yourself away on someone like me. I'm not worth it!"

"Love me, Matt." Her angelic face was entreating.
"Just for tonight."

"How can I resist?" he muttered hoarsely.

He swung her into his arms and captured her mouth
for a deep, rousing kiss. Christy's fingers twined
through his thick hair as she strained against him. She

was on fire with love for this man, who was everything she had always dreamed of. It didn't matter at this moment that he didn't love her in return. She had to experience fulfillment in his arms, no matter what heartbreak came after.

Matt carried her slowly down the hall, as though prolonging the exquisite moment. His hands and mouth fed the excitement. While his lips wandered over her face and neck, his fingertips tantalized her body, arousing her with their intimate exploration. Christy moaned softly, digging her nails into the taut muscles of his back.

As they approached her room, a loud snore ripped through the stillness. It was a note of reality in an unreal world. They had both forgotten Christy's aunt. Their eyes met in consternation.

Matt lowered her to her feet. "This isn't the place," he murmured.

"No." Christy couldn't look at him.

She turned away, but he pulled her into his arms and kissed her briefly. "I'm sorry, sweetheart."

Christy undressed quickly and huddled under the covers, feeling waves of shame wash over her. Matt was certainly right—this *wasn't* the place! What if Aunt Sarah had awakened and come to ask if... Christy turned over and buried her face in the pillow.

It was unthinkable! She would be so disappointed. The older woman was very open-minded in most ways, but her generation was extremely rigid in its thinking about certain things. She wouldn't understand that Christy had fallen hopelessly in love with Matt, that she wanted to belong to him in every way.

Was he lying in bed across the hall in the darkness, aching with the same longing? Or was he relieved? Matt's conscience was formidable. It had failed him for a short time tonight, but that wasn't really his fault. He had tried to hold back, even though his need was as great as hers. Why? Why did he treat her so differently from other women?

Matt was sitting up in bed with his arms folded, asking himself the same question. What was there about Christy that tied him up in knots? She was driving him over the edge with wanting her, yet he couldn't take her. Why?

"She's so innocent!" Matt groaned aloud.

But at least he'd initiate her gently. Another man might not. The thought made him rake rigid fingers through his hair. Matt considered himself an honorable man. He had never seduced a woman. They had all been consenting adults. Christy certainly met the requirements. Why did he feel this urge to protect her at all costs? That was an emotion reserved for the woman you loved.

Matt got out of bed to pace the floor restlessly. The idea was too idiotic to consider! You didn't fall in love with someone you'd known exactly one day and two nights. The only thing involved here was basic sex. He had been attracted to Christy instantly, and the itch had grown stronger. It was sex that had brought him back to Pine Grove, but common sense would see to it that he never returned!

Only one person in the house got any sleep that night.

Chapter Four

Matt was in the kitchen with Sarah when Christy joined them the next morning. He was sprawled in a wooden chair with his long legs stretched out, laughing at something the older woman had said. Christy's breath caught in her throat at how handsome he was. His shirt was open at the collar, and his cuffs were rolled halfway up his well-developed forearms. He presented a strikingly virile picture.

"There you are, sleepyhead." Sarah turned and saw Christy in the doorway. "Did Matt keep you out too late last night?"

"No, he, uh, we got home before midnight." Christy's swift glance at him wasn't encouraging. Matt's easy laughter had fled, leaving his face almost austere.

"Did you two have a good time?" Sarah asked.

"Why didn't you ask Matt?" Christy went to the cupboard for silver and napkins to set the table.

"I was so busy going on about the argument at the Ladies Aid meeting that I didn't get around to it." She looked appraisingly at him. "You should be one of those interviewers on TV. You have a knack for getting people to talk about themselves."

"He's great on conversation." Christy's tone was biting. "As long as he doesn't have to take part."

Her nerves were wound to the breaking point. Matt's coldness after the night before was insulting. She hadn't thrown herself at him; he'd started it! If he couldn't make up his mind about how he felt, that was *his* problem. At least he could be civil. He hadn't even said good morning to her.

Sarah was looking at her in astonishment. "What's gotten into you this morning? You sound downright cranky."

"I'm afraid it's my fault, and I regret it." Matt's dark eyes were opaque. "I plied her with too much champagne last night, didn't I, Christy?"

He was always trying to give her an out, to pretend that her actions weren't voluntary, but his fault instead. Christy didn't appreciate his gallantry. They both knew the truth of the matter. What Matt didn't know was the reason she responded so readily—that she'd fallen in love with him. That was something he'd *never* know, she vowed.

Sarah glanced from one to the other, shrewdly sizing up the situation. It didn't take a genius to figure out how they felt about each other, but something had gone wrong. They were both suffering mightily. For the first time, Sarah was glad she wasn't young anymore.

Matt left right after breakfast. He politely refused Sarah's invitation to stay, pleading things to do in the city.

"All right, come back and see us soon," Sarah said, ignoring Christy's pointed silence.

"I expect the next few weeks to be rather hectic," he answered evasively.

"I don't doubt it, with the new job and all. Well, don't forget us."

"I'm not likely to." His face was expressionless as he turned to Christy. "Thank you for a delightful evening."

"I enjoyed it, too." She looked back at him with the same lack of emotion.

They were like two strangers, courteously going through the amenities. Sarah's heart went out to both of them.

After he'd gone, she was falsely cheerful. "Well, that was a nice surprise, having Matt drop by like that. Didn't I tell you we'd hear from him?"

Christy kept her head averted as she started to clear the table. "He won't be back."

"Would you like to tell me about it?" her aunt asked quietly, dropping the false gaiety.

"There's nothing to tell."

Sarah sighed. "You're in love with him, aren't you?"

"No!" When the older woman merely gazed at her steadily, Christy picked up some dishes and carried them to the sink. "I'll admit I find him attractive. He's very handsome. But we...we don't think alike. I don't want to see him again." She turned on the water, ending the discussion.

Matt concurred heartily: Christy was a closed incident in his life.

That Sunday night he took Diane Cooke to dinner. She was a brunette. On Monday night, after a long day at work, he took a stunning redhead to the opera.

Both women were surprised when he dropped each at her respective door afterward.

On Tuesday afternoon, he was the only one in the office.

"It's New Year's Eve," his secretary, Linda, informed him. "What are you still doing here?"

"I have some work to clear up."

"You ought to be home taking a nap." She grinned. "You have a big evening ahead."

"Yes, I suppose so," he said flatly.

"Everyone else has gone," Linda remarked hesitantly. "Do you want me to stick around?"

"No, go ahead. Have a good time tonight."

"You too, boss." Her eyes sparkled with anticipation as she left.

Matt envied her. His face was drawn as he tied his black tie into a precise bow some time later. He felt keyed up, but not with anticipation.

Mimi Warren looked breathtaking when Matt picked her up that evening. Her shining blond hair was swept up on top of her head in an intricate style that had taken the hairdresser hours to arrange. It was worthy of her elegant designer gown, a froth of black lace that showed off her excellent figure to perfection. The low-cut neckline exposed tantalizing glimpses of her full breasts.

"Do you like it?" She twirled for Matt's inspection.

"You're positively ravishing."

Matt looked at the beautiful woman who had shared his bed and felt absolutely nothing. A slender blond girl in jeans and a checkered shirt filled his mind instead.

"Thank you, darling. You look outstanding too." Mimi admired the black and white perfection of his broad-shouldered male form. She put her arms around his neck. "We make a perfect couple," she purred.

"Right." Matt reached for her fur jacket. "Come on, we don't want to be late for the Pomeroys' cocktail party."

It was at the country club, two cocktail parties later, that Matt capitulated. When someone asked Mimi to dance, he went to a pay phone and called Christy.

He let it ring endlessly, but there was no answer. Matt knew his disappointment was out of all proportion. It was New Year's Eve. Of course she wouldn't be sitting at home. He would even have settled for Sarah, though. At least she could have told him where Christy was, and when she'd be home. He called at intervals all evening, but there was never an answer. Matt found it difficult to mask his frustration as the festivities around him grew more frantic.

Christy's evening wasn't any more successful than Matt's.

Her new dress hadn't cost anywhere near what Mimi's had, but it was equally becoming. The peach-colored chiffon gown was both soft and flattering, bringing out golden highlights in her smooth skin. She had washed her hair and combed it into a simple style that floated around her shoulders like a silken curtain.

"You look lovely," Sarah said approvingly.

"Thanks," Christy answered without enthusiasm.

"Do you have your key? I won't be home tonight, remember."

Christy smiled. "I'd never hear the end of it if *I* stayed out all night."

"You wouldn't if you were playing bridge at Rhoda Turner's," Sarah said dryly.

"Just see that you ladies get along," Christy teased. "Those bridge games can get pretty competitive. You don't want to start the new year with a feud."

"Rhoda and I will massacre them," Sarah said calmly.

Christy laughed. "Remember to stop for a minute at twelve o'clock to say happy New Year."

"Don't worry about me. You just have a good time."

Christy's laughter faded. "I will."

"Craig's a nice boy, and he's crazy about you." Sarah hesitated. "It's something to think about. Sometimes it's better to settle for good, honest affection."

"*You* didn't," Christy said soberly.

"And I've been very lonely."

"I'm sorry, Aunt Sarah!"

"That's all right. I wouldn't do anything differently if I had it to do over again. Once you soar with an eagle, you can't settle for a homing pigeon. I think about Fred every day of my life," she said softly.

"Doesn't the memory ever fade?" Christy asked hopelessly.

Sarah regretted her self-indulgent lapse. "Of course it does! I'm just a stubborn old woman who likes living in the past. You're not a bit like me, thank goodness.''

The doorbell rang, announcing the arrival of Christy's date. Craig Selby was almost as blond as she, with a perennially boyish face. He seemed a little ill at ease in the unaccustomed formality of a tuxedo, but they made a handsome couple.

''You be careful driving now,'' Sarah instructed.

''I wouldn't take any chances with this little doll,'' Craig assured her. He put his arm around Christy's shoulders and drew her against his lanky body.

She couldn't help thinking how different it felt from Matt's powerful male frame. Christy pushed the thought firmly out of her mind. Eagles might soar, but they also destroyed weaker creatures. She didn't intend to become a victim.

All of Christy's friends were at the dance, including some she hadn't seen in a while. There was a lot of animated conversation as everyone exchanged news and gossip. The noise and laughter grew in volume as the hour got later.

At first, Christy enjoyed herself. The party atmosphere was infectious. But as the evening wore on, her pleasure dimmed, especially when Craig began holding her closer.

Christy honestly tried to respond. She like Craig. They had been going out together for a long time, and had a lot of shared interests. Rockets and pinwheels didn't explode when they were together, at least not for her, but it hadn't seemed important—until she met

Matt. He taught her what excitement there could be between a man and a woman.

Where was he tonight? Romancing some woman, undoubtedly. Was he telling her how beautiful she was, how exquisite and irresistible? Christy's heart started to pound at the memory of Matt's low, husky voice murmuring those rousing words. But he was whispering them to someone else now.

"Happy New Year, doll." Bells started to peal as Craig put his arms around her. "I'm hoping for big things to happen this year." His mouth covered hers urgently.

Matt would have left the country club after the midnight festivities, but Mimi thought he was joking. He convinced her to leave about two o'clock, after what amounted to a small scene at the dance. It turned uglier when he said good-night at her door without coming in. There had been a lot of recriminations, which Matt only half listened to. His full attention was centered on Christy.

He had called her twice more from the club, and now he was getting tense. Sure, it was New Year's Eve, but not everyone felt they had to stay out all night to prove they'd had a good time. He could hardly wait to get to the telephone again.

When there was no answer at three o'clock, Matt was almost paranoid. Had something happened to her? Had she done something foolish? Matt finally faced what was really bothering him. He knew Christy had felt rejected, in spite of his attempts to explain. Was she spending the night with some man just to prove she was desirable? The thought made a pulse throb at his temple.

When Christy finally answered the phone a little before four, Matt's relief translated into anger. "Where the hell have you been?" he flared.

"Matt?" For a moment she thought she was imagining things, that she had conjured him up out of her longing to hear his voice.

"I asked you a question. *Where were you?*"

"I went to a dance in Squaw Valley." His forcefulness drew the answer out of her.

"Don't you know it's dangerous to be on those mountain roads, tonight of all nights? There are a lot of drunks out there."

"We did see an accident," she admitted. "That's why it took so long to get home."

"What was Sarah thinking about, letting you go to Squaw on a night like this?" he raged.

Reaction was setting in and Christy was becoming annoyed. "Aunt Sarah doesn't tell me what to do, and it's certainly no concern of yours," she said coldly. "Why are you calling at this hour?"

Matt's anger evaporated suddenly. His voice dropped several notes. "I've been thinking of you all evening."

"I'll bet!"

"Did you think about me?" he asked softly.

"Not once," she lied.

"Tell me the truth, sweetheart." His throaty voice was caressing.

"Don't call me that!" she ordered. "I'm not your sweetheart, or anything else. There's nothing between us anymore. There never was," she corrected herself.

"You know that isn't true."

Christy was determined not to let him trap her into remembering. "What do you want, Matt?" she asked bluntly.

"For a long time I didn't know," he said slowly.

"Tell me something I *don't* know!"

"I can't blame you for being angry, honey. I gave you a rough time. But try to understand. I never met anyone like you."

"I guess they sacrificed all the virgins long ago," she answered sardonically. "We're a dying breed."

"That isn't what I meant!"

"Admit it! I scared the daylights out of you," she accused.

"But not for the reason you think. I didn't even understand it myself until tonight."

"Perhaps you'll share this revelation with me."

"I'm in love with you, Christy."

For a moment there was dead silence on the line. Christy couldn't believe he'd said what she'd longed to hear. Incredulous joy filled her—until caution set in. Matt had played games with her before.

"What gives you that idea?" she demanded.

"How do you explain love?" he asked simply. "I can't sleep. My temper's rotten. I can't concentrate. When you put it into words it sounds like flu symptoms."

"Maybe that's what you have," she said hesitantly.

"Darling Christy." He chuckled deeply. "If you were here, I'd show you how healthy I am."

She was filled with confusion. Christy didn't know whether to believe him or not. But why would he lie about something that important? It would be a cruel thing to do if it wasn't true, and that wasn't Matt's nature. Another solution occurred to her.

"How much have you had to drink?" she asked tentatively.

Matt's laughter had a joyous sound. "The only thing I'm drunk on is love. I'm coming up to see you, honey. Wait for me."

"It's almost morning. You'd better get some sleep first," she said anxiously.

"I suppose you're right," he answered reluctantly. "Okay, I'll be there this afternoon."

Christy managed only a few hours sleep herself. She was in the kitchen drinking coffee when Sarah came home late that morning.

"I didn't expect you to be up until noon," Sarah exclaimed. "Was the party a washout?"

"No, it was fun."

Sarah appraised the becoming color in her niece's cheeks, and the sparkle in her blue eyes. "Did you meet anybody new there?"

Christy gave her a brilliant smile. "Just the same old crowd."

Sarah gave it up as a bad job. Something was going on, but Christy would tell her in her own good time. "I intended to tiptoe around, but as long as you're up, I'll make breakfast."

"Not for me," Christy declined. "I have to get dressed."

"Are you going out?" Sarah expressed surprise. Christy usually watched the New Year's Day football games in her robe and slippers.

"No, Matt's coming up."

"How do you know that?"

"He called after I got home last night," Christy said self-consciously.

"I see." Sarah gazed at her for a long moment before making up her mind. Her voice was casual as she said, "I'm glad you'll have company. I just came home to change clothes. I promised Rhoda I'd come back to help her clean up."

Christy wasn't fooled. How much mess could four older ladies make? Did her aunt know what privacy meant to two people in love? Had she had her moment alone with Fred before he went off to war? Christy hoped so.

"Thank you, Aunt Sarah," she said gently.

The older woman stared at her somberly. "I very possibly should have my head examined," she muttered. When Christy's clear blue eyes met hers with confidence, Sarah said dryly, "I was referring to the way Rhoda takes advantage of me."

"I understood that." Christy couldn't suppress a smile.

"I won't be home until dinnertime. Not before five at the very earliest," Sarah warned.

Christy changed her mind three times before deciding what to wear. Her first impulse was to choose something soft and alluring, but pride wouldn't permit it. Matt could just take her the way she usually dressed at home. That meant jeans and a shirt, but Christy was reluctant to be *that* casual. She settled for a pair of white wool pants and a white sweater with a huge rose knitted on the front.

The color matched the becoming flush in her cheeks. That and the feverish glitter in her eyes were the only outward signs of inner turmoil. Although her nerves were stretched to the breaking point, Christy forced herself to appear calm as she heard a car pull into the driveway.

Matt was using the company van again, since his car was still in the repair shop. He pulled up to the front door with a feeling of coming home.

Christy didn't rush out into the snow to greet him this time. She waited until he rang the bell. She had been wild with impatience before, but now that he was here, she felt shy and uncertain. Did Matt really mean what he said in the early-morning hours, or had it been too much to drink, as she suspected? Still, he was here. She opened the door.

"Hello, Christy." His muted voice sent vibrations through her.

She stared at him, unable to think of anything to say. What occurred to her was ridiculous. "You should have worn a heavier coat." He had on a zippered leather jacket over charcoal slacks.

Matt threw back his head and laughed. "You sound just like your aunt."

Christy smiled nervously. "I suppose a lot of her has rubbed off on me through the years." When Matt came inside and closed the door, she backed away. "It snowed again this morning. Were the roads clear?"

"Reasonably so." Like a jungle cat stalking its prey, he followed her over to the fireplace. His glowing eyes added to the impression.

"Did...would you like something to eat?" she asked.

"No, thanks. I had something before I left."

"A cup of coffee then? Aunt Sarah made pecan rolls."

Matt shook his head, glancing around. "Where is Aunt Sarah? I want to say happy New Year."

"She stayed at her friend Rhoda's last night. They had a ladies' bridge party."

"So *that's* why nobody answered!" Matt exclaimed. "I was about to call the Pine Grove police."

"It was New Year's Eve," Christy pointed out. "I don't imagine *you* were sitting at home."

"No, I was having a lousy time worrying about you."

"I can't imagine why."

"Because I'm an idiot," he said somberly.

"You didn't know I went to Squaw Valley, so you couldn't have been worried about an accident," she said slowly.

"It doesn't matter now." He looked uncomfortable.

Christy frowned. She had never seen Matt's poise ruffled before. "What were you worried about?"

"I should have known better! But all kinds of crazy things pop into a man's mind when there's no answer all night long."

She looked at him incredulously. "You thought I wasn't coming home? That I was spending the night with someone?"

He caught her face between his palms, tangling his fingers fiercely in her hair. "I would have strangled him with my bare hands!"

As Christy stared up into his intent face, a sense of power flooded through her. Her smile had the wisdom of Mona Lisa's. "Oh, Matt, you really *are* an idiot."

"I know," he groaned, sweeping her into his arms. "I wouldn't blame you if you sent me packing after the way I've treated you."

She smoothed the lines in his forehead. "It hasn't been fun," she admitted. "Why did you act like it was goodbye every time you left?"

He swung her into his arms and carried her over to the couch. Pillowing her head against his shoulder, he gazed down at her tenderly. "I've never been in love before, so I didn't recognize the symptoms."

"It's rarely fatal," she teased.

"You sound like an authority. How often have *you* been in love?" His tone was joking, but there was an underlying intensity.

"Never before." She traced the line of his high cheekbone under the smooth skin.

"Does that mean . . ." He couldn't finish the question.

"I've been in love with you since I opened the door on Christmas Eve and found you shivering on the doorstep," she said simply. "Maybe I didn't know it at that exact moment, but I found out a lot sooner than you did."

"My darling angel!" His kiss held both passion and tenderness. It was a total commitment. "I didn't realize. I thought you—"

Christy's blue eyes sparkled with mischief as she finished the sentence for him. "Just wanted your fantastic body?"

Matt smile ruefully. "It crossed my mind."

"You weren't wrong," she said softly.

He looked at her searchingly. "Is that all, Christy?"

She put her arms around his neck and gazed at him fondly. "Don't you listen to anything I say?"

"You've been so sheltered." He continued to look troubled. "It would be so easy for you to confuse desire with love."

Christy's arms tightened. "Oh no you don't, Matt Destry! I'm not going to let you talk yourself into another disappearing act."

"Never again, sweetheart!" he declared fervently. "I couldn't leave you now if I tried." His long fingers combed through her hair as he looked at her with deep emotion.

"Promise?" There was a trace of fear in the query that was meant to sound playful. Christy still found it hard to believe.

"Does this answer your question?"

Matt's mouth closed over hers for a kiss that was sweetly gentle. It expressed all the love and longing he'd tried vainly to deny. It was a sweetheart's kiss, a pledge of love.

Christy's fingertips traced his features. She needed to touch him, to be sure she wasn't dreaming. Her feathery caresses ranged over his closed eyelids, the straight bridge of his nose. She stroked the strong column of his neck, and then slid her hand inside the opening of his sport shirt.

When her nails raked lightly through the mat of dark hair on his broad chest, Matt made a sound deep in his throat. His arms tightened and his mouth became more urgent against hers. A familiar ache began to build inside Christy as he parted her lips for an arousing kiss. She felt the same mounting excitement Matt always brought just by being near.

He was charged with the same emotion. His hands roamed restlessly over her back, down to her waist. He caressed the strip of soft skin exposed by her hiked-up sweater. Then one hand moved underneath the waistband, burning a path up Christy's midriff to her breast.

"I've dreamed about your beautiful body," he muttered against her parted lips. "You're absolute perfection."

When his fingertips slipped inside her bra to circle her taut nipple, Christy uttered a tiny sound.

"Do you like that, my darling?" he murmured. "I want to please you in every way."

"You always have," she whispered.

"Sweet, beautiful Christy!" He feathered her face with frantic kisses. "I'm going to fill you with such joy! You're going to belong to me completely."

Their eyes held as he stood up, holding her against his chest. She clasped her arms around his neck and buried her face in his broad shoulder. As he carried her down the hall to her bedroom, Matt's murmured words of love fueled the fire he had lit.

He stood her on her feet beside the bed then removed her sweater and bra. Christy trembled as he looked at her with blazing eyes. When he caressed her breasts lingeringly, she swayed toward him.

Matt took her in his arms and molded her body tightly against his hard frame. The awesome force of his desire dissolved all her inhibitions. She was the one who pulled his head down and parted his lips for a passionate kiss, demanding release from the sweet torture he was inflicting.

"Don't make me rush you, angel," he groaned. "I want it to be so good for you."

"It will be," she whispered as she tugged the shirt out of his slacks.

The feeling of his bare skin against her sensitized breasts made Christy's legs feel boneless. She clung to him as he unfastened her slacks. When they slipped to the floor, Matt lifted her onto the bed and knelt over her, sliding his fingertips inside the elastic of her lacy panties.

She twisted one leg over the other, feeling suddenly shy as he removed her last garment. She was completely nude under his burning eyes. Matt gently parted her legs, looking at her with such love that Christy's breath caught in her throat.

"Trust me, my darling." His husky voice was tender. "I'll be so very gentle with you." When he touched her, the last barrier toppled.

"Please, Matt," she begged. "I want you so!"

Her pleading words galvanized him. Matt left her for just a moment to fling off his clothes. He returned to clasp her against his hardened body. The sensation was electric. It was like nothing Christy could ever imagine. She strained against him, seeking the fulfillment she knew he could bring.

"You don't know what you're doing to me!" His hoarse voice held a note of desperation as he turned her on to her back and lowered his body to hers.

Christy was pierced by a molten sensation. When she tensed momentarily, Matt held her tightly.

"Let it happen, sweetheart," he murmured.

Her taut body relaxed in his arms. This was the man she loved. After a few moments, an aching throb filled her. Christy moved restlessly, surging against Matt in an attempt to put out the fire that was consuming her. When his own movements were restrained, she arched her body against his, forcing a response.

Matt answered her need with a driving force that was deeply satisfying. It carried her higher and higher. She was filled with ecstasy, trembling on the brink of an unknown, but glorious experience. Suddenly a molten wave engulfed her rigid body. Christy was catapulted into space, flooded with rapture so intense that she clung to Matt for protection.

He cradled her in his arms and guided her back to earth. The passion that had racked her dissipated slowly as she floated down safely in his embrace.

They remained intertwined for a long time. Finally Matt stirred. He kissed her closed eyelids tenderly. "Was it what you hoped for, sweetheart?" he murmured.

"It was so much more." She lifted her face for a kiss that was sweet with satisfied completion. "I didn't know it would be like this."

"It's going to be even better." His hand moved slowly over her body. "I'm going to make love to you every night. I'm going to satisfy you a hundred different ways."

Christy sighed happily at the delirious thought, even though she knew there were obstacles. "Are you planning to commute between here and San Francisco?" she teased.

He nibbled on her earlobe. "No, I'm planning on prying you out of Pine Grove."

She gave him a startled look. "What do you mean?"

"I want you in my bed every night." His eyes smoldered with awakening desire. "I want to hold you in my arms in the darkness, and see your beautiful face when I wake up every morning."

"Are you asking me to move in with you?" Christy asked slowly.

Matt smiled. "It sure beats commuting."

The idea was so foreign that she was speechless. Her conventional upbringing had always taught that girls didn't live with a man, even if they were planning on getting married. But times had changed. Matt's caressing hand on her bare body told Christy how much! Still, could she live with him openly?

Matt's expression was tender as he gazed at her sober face. "I know the idea is frightening, honey, but we'll be together. I'll see that you're happy."

Christy knew what her answer would be when his lips touched hers. A piece of paper wouldn't make their love any more sacred. She already belonged to this man totally. As the idea took hold, Christy was filled with rising excitement.

"I want to make you happy too." She smoothed his ruffled hair lovingly. "I'll get a fantastic job and help with the rent."

Matt's expression was suddenly guarded. "You won't have to do that, sweetheart."

"I want to help, Matt. I know you're just getting started. And besides, don't couples share everything equally in a modern relationship?" she asked earnestly.

He stared at her incredulously. "You think I want—" He stopped short, and then started again slowly. "I think you're confused about the sort of relationship I had in mind."

"No, I understand." Her clear blue eyes met his trustingly. "You've always been honest with me. It's the thing I respect most about you. We won't ever have to play games with each other."

Matt was appalled. He was so sure Christy knew he was asking her to marry him. Why hadn't he come right out with a proposal instead of letting her commit herself? Matt was touched that she had agreed to live with him, knowing what a difficult decision it must have been. But now she might think he'd been testing her, finding out if she loved him for himself instead of his money. Everything he'd done up to this point would seem to indicate as much. Would she understand how it had happened and forgive him?

Matt sighed. "We have to have a talk, angel." When Christy snuggled up against him, lifting her beautiful face, his body quickened. "It can wait," he muttered hoarsely.

Chapter Five

Matt never did get around to having a talk with Christy. Nothing was as important as holding her in his arms and repeating his vow of love endlessly. When their precious time together ran out and he had to leave, Matt eased his conscience by promising himself he'd straighten everything out on Saturday. It was only two days away.

On Friday Christy received the bogus letter informing her that she'd won a cruise. Her initial reaction was astounded joy. Then she thought about Matt and their new relationship. They hadn't had a chance to discuss when she'd be joining him in San Francisco, but it would be soon. Did she want to leave him for two weeks at the very beginning? It would be wonderful if Matt could go with her, but that was out of the question. He had just started a new job.

"This is what you've always dreamed of, child." Sarah couldn't understand Christy's curious reluctance to claim her prize. "It's lucky you don't have to be at work until Monday. You can use this time to drive to San Francisco and make the arrangements."

"There's no big hurry."

Christy had put off telling Sarah about Matt and their plans. It wasn't going to be easy. Although her aunt wouldn't try to stop her, Christy knew the older woman wouldn't be happy about the idea. It was probably cowardly, but Christy had decided to wait until Matt was with her before she broke the news.

"I don't understand you," Sarah scolded. "What are you waiting for?"

"Well, I have to get time off from my job, and . . . and buy some new clothes. I need a bathing suit," she finished lamely.

"You won't find any in Pine Grove at this time of year. You can go shopping when you're in San Francisco finding out when the next cruise is. For all you know, it might not be for a month yet. How are you going to ask for time off from work if you don't know when you want it?"

"That's true." Christy let herself be persuaded. "I guess it wouldn't hurt to pay a visit to the steamship line." The deciding factor was that she could also see Matt and start making plans.

Christy remembered the name of Matt's company from seeing it on the side of the van. She looked up the address in a phone book when she got to the city.

The Transamerica pyramid was one of the most prestigious office buildings in downtown San Francisco. Christy was suitably impressed when she discovered the corporate headquarters of Matt's new company occupied a whole floor near the top.

The reception room was furnished in tranquil beiges, with excellent prints on the cream-colored walls. Christy's footsteps were muffled by thick carpeting as she walked toward the receptionist's desk.

An attractive young woman greeted her with a smile. "Can I help you?"

"Yes, I'm looking for someone in the engineering department—a man named Matt Destry. He's a new employee here," Christy added helpfully.

The woman's smile faded. "Is this some kind of joke?"

Christy looked at her uncertainly. "I don't understand."

"Neither do I. Who did you want to see? Mr. Destry, or someone in engineering?"

Christy had a sense of foreboding. Had Matt lied to her about the job he held? Didn't he know it wouldn't matter to her if he were the janitor? She was tempted to leave before he found out she had discovered his secret. But Christy knew she mustn't let a lie develop between them.

"Matt said...that is... You *do* have a Mr. Destry working here?"

"Perhaps I'd better let you talk to his secretary," the receptionist said, looking at her cautiously. "It's the office at the end of the hall."

Christy followed the instructions automatically, although she felt slightly dazed. Hadn't she made herself clear? Surely Matt would have told her if he had a position grand enough for a secretary.

Another attractive woman greeted her in an office even more opulent that the waiting room. She also smiled and asked how she could help.

"I'm looking for Matt Destry," Christy said hesitantly.

"Do you have an appointment?"

"No, I . . . I just stopped by to talk to him."

"I'm sorry, but Mr. Destry only sees people by appointment."

Christy's feeling of unreality deepened. It was all very strange. Could there be two Matt Destrys? It wasn't very probable. Yet what other explanation was there? As she was staring at the other woman, wondering what to do, Matt came out of the inner office.

He was thumbing rapidly through the papers he held in one hand. "Linda, this report has to go to Newcombe as soon as—" The words broke off abruptly as he looked up and saw Christy. Matt's first expression was one of pleasure. "Christy! What are you doing here?"

"I came to see you, but no one would tell me where you worked."

Consternation replaced his joy. "Oh, God, I didn't want you to find out like this!"

"What is it, Matt? What are you keeping from me?"

"Come inside," he said gently, taking her arm and leading her toward the other room.

Christy looked around in disbelief at the comfortable leather couch and chairs, the paintings on the paneled walls. "What are we doing here? Whose office is this?"

"Sit down, darling. I have to talk to you."

Christy allowed Matt to guide her to the couch, although she had an overwhelming impulse to turn and run. Something was terribly wrong, and suddenly she didn't want to know what it was.

"Couldn't it wait until you come to Pine Grove tomorrow?" she asked haltingly.

"No, it's something I should have told you long ago. I did try several times, but it always ended in a misunderstanding. I never meant to deceive you, Christy." His face held deep regret.

The bottom was dropping out of Christy's world, and she had a glimmering of the reason. "What are you trying to say, Matt, that you're married?"

"Good Lord, no! Whatever gave you that idea?" He took both her hands. "I guess I'd better start at the beginning, which would be Christmas Eve."

"Don't drag it out, Matt! What does that have to do with all this?" Christy waved at the luxurious office.

"Hear me out, honey. It's all part of it. I was cold and hungry that night. You took me in a gave me the guest room. I couldn't believe it."

"You didn't have anyplace to stay," she said simply.

"Well, actually, I'd reserved a hotel room in Squaw Valley."

"You didn't tell us that!"

"I never had a chance. You and your aunt assumed I was a homeless drifter. Every time I tried to correct the misconception, you thought I was just saving face. At first it amused me. Then when you took me in without question, I was astonished. I'd never known such kind people."

Christy was having difficulty understanding any of it. "What were you doing in Pine Grove in the first place?"

"I was on my way to the ski lodge when my car was forced off the road and wrecked. I was looking for a phone, and yours was the closest house to the highway."

"But why did you stay?" she asked helplessly.

"Partly because the emergency service wouldn't tow me until the day after Christmas." His thumb moved slowly over the soft skin of her wrist. "But mostly because I met the most exquisite girl in the world, and I wanted to know her better."

Christy scarcely heard him. "You weren't out of a job either, were you?"

"No," he answered quietly.

She looked at him searchingly, noticing for the first time the elegantly tailored dark suit and handsome tie. He seemed like a complete stranger. "Who are you really, Matt?"

"I'm the same man I was before, honey. The rest is just window dressing."

Christy glanced around the spacious room. "This is your office, isn't it?"

Matt nodded.

"I don't suppose you're an engineer. What position do you hold here?"

"I really am an engineer, but I...also own CompuTrend."

She stared at him in shocked amazement. "The whole company?"

"Yes."

Christy felt as though she'd stumbled into a hall of crazed mirrors. Her whole world was distorted. The man she loved had made a fool of her! It was just starting to sink in.

"You lied to me!" She jerked her hands away and sprang to her feet.

"Be fair, Christy," Matt pleaded. "I never told you anything that was untrue."

"You knew exactly what you were doing," she stormed. "You accepted our hospitality under false pretenses. Our homespun Christmas must have made a hilarious story to tell your sophisticated friends. Is that why you came back, to get more material to amuse them with?" Her slim body was as taut as a violin string. "I hope you included that touching moment in the barn when I threw myself at you."

"Christy, darling, how can you even think—"

"It was too easy to take me then, wasn't it? I wasn't any challenge. The only way to make it fun was to build up to the big seduction act."

Matt's fingers bit into her rigid shoulders. "Stop it!" he commanded. "You know there isn't a word of truth in any of that."

"I suppose you really meant it when you said you loved me," she said scornfully.

"Didn't yesterday tell you anything?" he demanded.

"You have a knack for not answering awkward questions," she said sardonically. "But I finally get the message. You never intended to return on Saturday, did you? The charade was played out. If I hadn't come here today, I'd never have seen you again."

He looked at her incredulously. "How about the plans we made?"

"That must really have amused you—my offer to pay half the rent." Her laughter had a ragged sound. "If your apartment's anything like this office, you need a roommate with a better job than I could get."

"I never expected you to be my roommate, *or* pay for anything."

"That's what I just said." Christy swallowed hard to hold back the tears that clogged her throat. At least she wouldn't give him that satisfaction. "Goodbye, Matt. It's been—educational."

"You don't mean that, angel." He tried to draw her close, but she held him off with her hands on his forearms. "I'm sorry for not leveling with you in the beginning, but I never meant to hurt you. At least grant me that much."

"Conscience, Matt?" She managed a ghost of a smile. "Well, maybe there's hope for you yet." She twisted out of his grasp and started for the door, passing his secretary in the entrance.

"Your three o'clock appointment is in the waiting room, Mr. Destry," Linda said discreetly.

"Christy, wait!" Matt called over her shoulder. He put Linda aside, but the momentary delay enabled Christy to get away.

She ran down the hall, heedless of curious looks. Her one goal was to escape further humiliation. A waiting elevator was like a gift from heaven. Christy pushed the lobby button with a shaking finger.

At first she hurried down the block, dodging around slow-moving window-shoppers to gain distance in case Matt tried to follow her. Although it was scarcely likely, Christy thought bitterly. He'd had the grace to be ashamed of himself at the end. Misery washed over her in waves. How could she have misjudged Matt so? How could he have been so deliberately cruel?

She should have known he was hiding something when he avoided talking about himself. He had even told her she was too trusting. Well, never again! She'd learned a bitter lesson. Men would do anything to get what they wanted.

Matt had her staked out as prey from the moment she opened the door on Christmas Eve. Christy shivered, remembering the appreciative glimmer in his dark eyes when he saw her. He was like a hungry wolf sighting a helpless lamb.

Christy burned with indignation when she thought about how cunning he'd been, playing on her inexperience until *she* was the one who begged *him* to make love to her! But the truly unforgivable thing was letting her think he wanted to make it a permanent relationship.

After seeing Matt in his own environment, Christy knew he hadn't been serious. The idea that she would fit into his sophisticated life-style was laughable. She would be an embarrassment. Matt had practically admitted it in one unguarded moment. Christy suddenly remembered the strange look on his face when he said she'd misunderstood the kind of arrangement he had in mind. It was all pillow talk. She was supposed to go along with it, but not expect it to happen.

As Christy's footsteps dragged, she forced herself to stop dwelling on the past and face the future. What was she going to do now? All her plans had centered around Matt. He'd been the focal point of her life. It was folly to depend on another person to that extent, but the hurt was too new. She needed time to pull herself together, to get away alone until she was able to accept the fact that she'd made a terrible mistake.

Suddenly Christy recalled her sweepstakes prize, the reason she'd come to the city. It was at least a temporary answer. Her aimless steps quickened as she headed for the steamship office.

"When is your next cruise to the Caribbean on the *Sun Queen*?" she asked a reservation clerk a short time later.

"We have a sailing tomorrow," the young woman informed her.

"Great, I'll take it!" Christy exclaimed. It was the one ray of sunshine in a gray world.

"I'm afraid that isn't possible. We're sold out. I guess everyone wants to get away from the rain and fog this time of year, but we have another ship going out in six weeks."

"I can't wait that long! I won this contest, and they told me I could claim my prize whenever I wanted." Christy pulled the letter out of her purse.

The woman examined it with interest. "Well, lucky you, Miss Blake! The only problem is that we're filled to capacity, as I told you. I can book you on the next cruise, though."

"Don't you have anything at all?" Christy asked hopelessly.

"Let me double-check." After punching some keys on a computer, the reservation clerk viewed the small screen regretfully. "I'm really sorry. All we have is a tiny, inside cubbyhole that you wouldn't be interested in.'' She brightened momentarily. "We do have a cancellation on the Antigua suite. It's really elegant. You can have that if you pay the difference.''

"How much would it be?'' Christy asked. She blanched at the price quoted. It was completely out of the question. She couldn't wait six weeks, though. After a brief moment, Christy made up her mind. "I'll take the small cabin.''

"But you're entitled to a deluxe one,'' the woman objected. "I don't think we can refund the difference.''

"It doesn't matter. Just make out my ticket.''

Sarah was waiting expectantly when Christy got home. "Did you make the arrangements?''

"I leave tomorrow,'' Christy said grimly.

"Tomorrow! That's what I call fast work.'' The older woman frowned. "You don't seem too excited about it.''

"How can you say that?'' Christy tried to appear animated. "I'm positively ecstatic.''

"What's wrong, Christy?'' Sarah asked quietly.

"I don't know what you're talking about. Everything's just peachy.'' She gathered her things, averting her face. "I have a big day tomorrow, so I'd better get some sleep.''

"Matt has been calling every fifteen minutes. He wouldn't tell me what happened either. Did you two have an argument?''

Christy gathered her strength for a denial, but she couldn't go through with it. She had never lied to her aunt. "Oh, Aunt Sarah, what am I going to do?''

Sarah drew Christy into her arms and let her cry out all her grief. When the storm was over, Christy told her the whole story.

"None of this sounds like Matt," Sarah said slowly. "I'll admit it's a shock, but are you sure you didn't jump to conclusions about his motives?"

"His only excuse was that he never meant to hurt me," Christy said drearily.

"I can't believe I could be that wrong about a person." Sarah's face was troubled.

"We live in a different world. We haven't had any experience with men like Matt."

"Maybe." Sarah was unconvinced. "I'd still like to talk to him."

"Please don't," Christy begged. "Just chalk it up to experience. That's what I've done. By the time I get back from this cruise I'll have forgotten all about him."

Sarah's face was inscrutable. "That's the right idea, child. Go to bed and get some rest."

When the telephone rang, Christy looked panicky. "If that's for me, I don't want to talk to anyone!"

"Don't worry, I'll take care of it," Sarah soothed.

The phone call was evidently for her aunt, because Christy heard the murmur of her voice for a long time.

Sarah helped Christy pack the next morning, ignoring her lack of enthusiasm. Sarah was the one who insisted on including lacy underwear and evening clothes.

"I'm really going for a change of scenery," Christy protested. "The last thing I need is another romantic entanglement."

"It never hurts to be prepared," Sarah answered serenely. "Suppose you met a prince who was incognito?"

Christy smiled, one of her first natural reactions. "I'd probably tell him to buzz off, and get in trouble with the State Department for insulting a friendly nation."

"Well, try not to start World War Three," Sarah observed dryly. "You'd never forgive yourself."

Her aunt drove Christy to the ship but declined to go aboard. Christy clung to her for a long moment.

"I wish you were coming with me, Aunt Sarah."

"I imagine you'll have a better time without me. Don't dawdle, child. I have to get back to the ranch." The gentle expression on Sarah's face belied her imatient tone.

Christy walked slowly up the gangplank after her aunt had driven away, the only passenger without a smile of anticipation. She waited her turn listlessly at the purser's desk.

He greeted her with professional heartiness and located her name on a typewritten list. "Welcome aboard, Miss Blake. The steward will show you to your cabin."

Christy followed the uniformed steward into an elevator that rose several floors. She trailed after him down a long corridor to her designated cabin. But when he opened the door, Christy knew there had been a mistake. It was a luxurious suite.

The living room had a couch, several chairs and assorted tables. Opening off it was a bedroom with a king-size bed. Wide glass windows provided a stunning view of the ocean beyond a private lanai furnished with deck chairs.

"There's been a mistake," Christy said regretfully. "This isn't my cabin."

The steward referred to a slip of paper in his hand. "Miss Blake, Antigua suite."

"No, it was offered to me, but I couldn't afford it," she explained. "There must have been a mix-up."

"Why don't you wait here while I find out about it," the man advised.

Christy felt the engines start as she moved over to the window to look out at the Golden Gate Bridge. It would be lovely to occupy this luxurious cabin, but it was just one more thing she couldn't have. The ship gathered speed, and tiny ripples turned into white-capped waves.

"I took the small closet and left the large one for you," a deep, familiar voice remarked from behind her.

Christy was sure she was hearing things. She whirled to look disbelievingly at Matt. It couldn't be! She had to be imagining him, but he looked too vitally alive to be a mirage.

"What are you doing here?" she whispered.

Matt smiled, as though it was the most natural thing in the world. "Aunt Sarah thought you might be lonely, so she suggested I join you."

"She would never do a thing like that!"

Matt's smile turned into a grin that showed white teeth in his deeply tanned face. "Well she *does* expect me to marry you."

"How could you let her believe such a thing?" Christy's cheeks were pink with outrage. "This is even worse than all the other rotten tricks you've pulled! Haven't you done enough already? Did you have to destroy her faith completely? You are the most—"

Matt didn't seem the least bit disturbed by Christy's tirade. He closed the distance between them while she was ranting and took her in his arms. She struggled wildly, still sputtering angry words, but Matt's mouth effectively stopped them.

Christy was no match for his strength. His fingers anchored her long hair, holding her for a penetrating kiss that made shivers race up her spine, even in her outraged state. She was powerless to stop him when he molded her body so closely that she could feel every muscle in his hard thighs. Her struggles only made the contact more inflaming.

Gradually, a creeping warmth made her efforts less frantic. Christy's clutching fingers relaxed, and her hands moved tentatively over Matt's broad shoulders. Her mind protested that it was madness, but her body's response was more imperative. His mouth was irresistible, and his slow caresses overcame all objections.

When she stopped fighting him, Matt swung her into his arms and carried her into the bedroom. Christy burried her face in his neck, clinging to him tightly. It was insane to let him use her again, but she had no choice.

Matt joined her on the wide bed without letting her out of his arms. His dark head was poised over hers. "At least I've learned how to end an argument with you." He smiled mischievously.

She turned her head away, unable to look at him. "You don't fight fair," she muttered.

"You know that line about love and war."

His long fingers unfastened the top button of her blouse, and then the next one. Christy made a feeble motion to stop him, then dropped her hand. How could she deny her own longing when his mouth was leaving a trail of stinging little kisses on her sensitive skin? After her blouse was open to the waist, he unclasped her bra and smoothed it away from her breasts. Christy trembled as he bent his head to kiss each rosy peak.

"My beautiful love," he murmured. "Do you think I'd ever let you get away?"

A storm gathered inside Christy as he undressed her completely. It built in intensity as he caressed every secret part of her. When she was nude beneath his glowing eyes, Matt trailed his fingertips down the length of her body.

"How did I ever deserve such a gift?" His voice was husky. "You gave yourself to me, and now you're mine forever. I'll never let you go."

"Oh, Matt, Matt." Christy reached out for him blindly.

His face revealed naked emotion. "You don't know what it does to me when you call my name! I want to hear it on your lips when I bring you the greatest joy."

He left her briefly to fling off his clothes in a blur of movement, then returned to clasp her in his arms.

"Love me, darling," he murmured deeply.

"I do," she whispered in total surrender.

Matt moved her body tenderly under his. He kissed her gently at first, and then more urgently as she responded with unashamed passion. When Christy murmured in his ear, Matt's arms tightened convulsively.

Their need for each other was so great that the storm was brief, but totally satisfying. Afterward, Christy lay quietly with her cheek on Matt's bare chest, listening to his heart return to a slower beat. His caressing hand on her body was the final, perfect touch.

Neither stirred for a long time. Finally Matt said, "I arranged with the captain to marry us, but not until tomorrow. I hope you don't mind."

Christy drew back to look at him with incredulous hope. "You really mean it?"

Matt chuckled as he stared pointedly at her nude body. "Don't you think it's indicated? What would Aunt Sarah say if I didn't marry you?"

"You mean it's all a joke," she said dully.

Christy was filled with desolation. Once more she had let Matt raise her hopes. When would she ever learn?

Matt's expression changed as he saw the light go out of her eyes. He pulled her back in his arms and stroked her hair tenderly.

"Do you think after we're married for forty or fifty years you might start to trust me?" he asked gently. "I love you more than I ever thought it was possible for a man to love a woman. I want to marry you and live with you for the rest of our lives. Does that answer your question?''

Christy flung her arms around his neck and rained frantic kisses over his face. ''Oh, Matt, you don't know what I went through when I thought I'd never see you again!''

''Silly little Christy,'' he said fondly. ''You don't know much about men—and now you've lost your chance to learn.'' His eyes darkened with renewed passion. ''From now on, I'm the only man in your life.''

''I never wanted any other,'' she whispered.

He parted her lips for a kiss so blissful that Christy was sure this was what heaven must be like.

''I hear bells,'' she said dreamily.

Matt chuckled. ''That's the dinner gong.''

''I'm not hungry,'' she said softly.

''Neither am I,'' he murmured against her mouth. After a long moment he raised his head slightly. ''We're probably at the captain's table.''

Christy's lips slid along Matt's strong jawline. ''Do you think he'd mind if we were late?''

''I think he'd understand.'' Matt's voice held a special note as he gazed deeply into her eyes.

*   *   *   *   *

A Note from Tracy Sinclair

Making this dessert requires a little time, but I've always found the results worth it. On one occasion it was so well received that I had to make a second cake. Rather unexpectedly.

After completing preparations for a party the next night, I was working on the last chapter of a book—my romantic couple, Jessica and Todd, were about to consummate their love—when my eight-year-old son arrived home with two schoolmates.

"Can we have some milk and cookies, Mom?" he called.

"We're out of cookies." Before he began a grumbling comparison of me to mothers who didn't waste their shopping time on writing, I called out, "There's pudding in the refrigerator."

My conscience twinged only briefly. Chocolate pudding was certainly as nourishing as cookies. I went back to Jessica and Todd. His burning kisses on intimate parts of her anatomy were engrossing. My fingers flew over the typewriter keys.

" 'My dearest love,' " Todd breathed. " 'I'll never get enough of you.' "

I could almost hear his husky voice. Suddenly other male voices formed a background chorus, but these were high and boyish. They came from the kichen.

"This strawberry stuff is great!"

"I like the yellow chunks best. They're lemon."

"My favorite's the lime."

Strawberry? Lemon? Lime? What happened to chocolate? A horrible suspicion dawned on me. I raced into the kitchen—too late. Three small boys, happily scraping their bowls, had scooped out the middle of my elegant dessert. What I thought of as a cake, they considered pudding. An excellent one, they assured me, just as good as cookies.

To avoid a recurrence of this painful incident, I've adopted a strategy that I heartily recommend to anyone with children. If you want to ensure that something won't be eaten prematurely, put a sign on it: THIS IS VERY GOOD FOR YOU. It's foolproof. It wards off even husbands.

Tracy Sinclair

NORA ROBERTS

Love has a language all its own, and for centuries flowers have symbolized love's finest expression. Discover the language of flowers—and love—in this romantic collection of 48 favorite books by bestselling author Nora Roberts.

Two titles are available each month at your favorite retail outlet.

In December, look for:

Partners, **Volume #21**
Sullivan's Woman, **Volume #22**

In January, look for:

Summer Desserts, **Volume #23**
This Magic Moment, **Volume #24**

Collect all 48 titles
and become fluent in

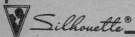

READY OR NOT . . . HERE THEY COME!

If you enjoyed the Silhouette Christmas Stories, get ready to ring in the New Year with your favorite Silhouette authors. Join us for four exciting love stories—guaranteed to enchant romance readers here, there and everywhere!

THE CAT THAT LIVED ON PARK AVENUE by Tracy Sinclair
Silhouette Special Edition, January 1993
Lawyer or catnapper—who was Jake Warning? That was the question detective Sabena Murphy had to answer. A million-dollar cat was missing, and the chief suspect was a man who was clearly a thief . . . of hearts.

HASTY WEDDING by Debbie Macomber
Silhouette Special Edition, February 1993
For years, *That Special Woman!* Claire Gilroy had thought she loved a man named Jack. But then she up and married renowned rebel Reed Tonasket. Could their hasty vows be one moment of temporary insanity, or was this true love?

MAN OF THE HOUR by Maura Seger
Silhouette Intimate Moments, April 1993
Years ago, fast cars and easy women had been bad-boy Mark Fletcher's style. Now all he wanted was a woman to share his life with—divorced young mother Lisa Morley. But someone else was out to get Lisa—and only Mark could save her.

FALLING FOR RACHEL by Nora Roberts
Silhouette Special Edition, April 1993
You met *Those Wild Ukrainians* in 1990 in TAMING NATASHA and LURING A LADY. Now public defender Rachel Stanislaski has to keep one juvenile delinquent out of jail—when it's really his older brother who's causing all the trouble!

They'll be coming your way . . . only from

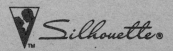

It takes a very special man to win

That
SPECIAL
Woman!

She's friend, wife, mother—she's you! And beside each Special Woman stands a wonderfully *special* man. It's a celebration of our heroines—and the men who become part of their lives.

Look for these exciting titles from Silhouette Special Edition:

January   BUILDING DREAMS by Ginna Gray
Heroine: Tess Benson—a woman faced with single motherhood who meets her better half.

February   HASTY WEDDING by Debbie Macomber
Heroine: Clare Gilroy—a woman whose one spontaneous act gives her more than she'd ever bargained for.

March   THE AWAKENING by Patricia Coughlin
Heroine: Sara McAllister—a woman of reserved nature who winds up in adventure with the man of her dreams.

April   FALLING FOR RACHEL by Nora Roberts
Heroine: Rachel Stanislaski—a woman dedicated to her career who finds that romance adds spice to life.

Don't miss THAT SPECIAL WOMAN! each month—from some of your special authors! Only from Silhouette Special Edition!

Silhouette Christmas Stories 1992

Experience the beauty of Yuletide romance with Silhouette Christmas Stories 1992—a collection of heartwarming stories by favorite Silhouette authors.

JONI'S MAGIC by Mary Lynn Baxter
HEARTS OF HOPE by Sondra Stanford
THE NIGHT SANTA CLAUS RETURNED by Marie Ferrarrella
BASKET OF LOVE by Jeanne Stephens

Also available this year are three popular early editions of Silhouette Christmas Stories—1986, 1987 and 1988. Look for these and you'll be well on your way to a complete collection of the best in holiday romance.

Plus, as an added bonus, you can receive a FREE keepsake Christmas ornament. Just collect four proofs of purchase from any November or December 1992 Harlequin or Silhouette series novels, or from any Harlequin or Silhouette Christmas collection, and receive a beautiful dated brass Christmas candle ornament.

Mail this certificate along with four (4) proof-of-purchase coupons, plus $1.50 postage and handling (check or money order—do not send cash), payable to Silhouette Books, to: **In the U.S.:** P.O. Box 9057, Buffalo, NY 14269-9057; **In Canada:** P.O. Box 622, Fort Erie, Ontario, L2A 5X3.